HORS D'OEUVRES II

Hors d'oeuvres II

Bugs And Other Short Stories

Ronnie Remonda

iUniverse, Inc.
Bloomington

HORS D'OEUVRES II
BUGS and other short stories

iUniverse books may be ordered through booksellers or by contacting:

iUniverse
1663 Liberty Drive
Bloomington, IN 47403
www.iuniverse.com
1-800-Authors (1-800-288-4677)

ISBN: 978-1-4759-6474-5 (sc)
ISBN: 978-1-4759-6475-2 (ebk)

Printed in the United States of America

iUniverse rev. date: 12/06/2012

CONTENTS

DEDICATION

To Carol, whose support and encouragement has given
me the courage to take myself seriously.

BUGS

A bright fireball streaked across the early morning sky, lighting up the surrounding desert. It struck the earth with great force, forming a crater six-feet deep. As the refrigerator sized meteorite cooled it began to split, and from the widening crack emerged a small creature about an inch long. It was insect-like, with a body consisting of five segments; a pair of three-jointed legs was attached to each segment. Two gill-like appendages suddenly appeared behind a pair of large mandibles, providing the only distinction between front and back. It scurried off across the desert.

Shortly, another appeared, and then another, until in all, twenty-five had emerged, opened their gill-like appendages, and scurried off in different directions as if each one had been given a different assignment.

The sun began to rise just as another meteorite crashed into the desert floor. This one, about a mile away, sheared the top from a large saguaro cactus. In the distance others followed, leaving smoky trails in the cloudless sky, until the sky was full of streaks and the air choked with dust and debris.

A six-inch Desert Hairy Scorpion, returning home after a night of hunting, made its way back to its burrow beneath a large rock. It was suddenly confronted by a creature less than a third of its bulk. Not one to pass up an opportunity, she corralled the creature with her claws, and began to feel for a chink between its plates to administer the coup de grace. *Just a quick snack before the morning siesta.* She was quickly seized between the mighty mandibles and devoured, head first, even as her stinger plunged repeatedly against the impenetrable plating.

The creature only paused for a moment before rushing off, quickly growing to nearly half again its original size. Across the desert the black wave moved on, as this scene was repeated each time any living thing was encountered. Nor did snake, nor mice, nor even coyotes fend any better. All things were cut down as they ran and consumed while their hearts still beat and their cries fell silent. No quick kill, nor mercy here.

By nightfall the black mass had moved on, unrelenting even as other creatures paused to rest. They needed no rest. They drew their energy from their victims and grew larger after every feeding. They left behind a landscape stripped of life and sound. By dawn's light man would soon have his first encounter with this moving horde.

Tom Blanchard awoke early for his morning milking, just as he had done every day for nearly fifty years. His wife scraped some bacon and scrambled eggs onto his plate. The only thing that broke their silence was the sudden pop of the toaster. It was then that he heard it. His wife heard it, too; the sound of an animal in pain.

"Coyotes" Tom shouted, and went to get his shotgun. The sun wasn't fully up yet, so he grabbed his flashlight and headed out the door.

Sarah could only follow his dark form as far as the gate that separated farm from lawn. From there it was only the swaying movement of the flashlight. "*Damn coyotes*," she thought. They had taken two of their calves the year before. Their small farm couldn't afford to lose another cow.

Just as Tom Blanchard reached the north pasture the sun began to illuminate the landscape. He could see the silhouette of a cow on its side and could hear it blatting, but there were no coyotes. Nevertheless, he leveled his shotgun as he moved forward. The sun hadn't yet peeked over the hill, and Tom's eyes were playing tricks on him. The ground seemed to be moving. He removed his glasses and wiped his eyes.

The cow had ceased to move, and now lay quite. There was a black blanket covering most of its body. When he was fifty feet away, he could see that it was moving. As the sun's rays popped over the distant hillside, he could make out what looked like huge cockroaches, but they were the size of cats. He took aim and fired. The double-aught cleared a spot on the cow's carcass, but it filled in again almost instantly.

Tom hadn't run for nearly twenty years, but this seemed like a good time to break precedence. He hit the gate latch on the run and never broke stride until he reached the back door to the kitchen.

Sarah held the door while he stumbled inside. "What?" she asked.

"911!" Tom shouted between breaths. "Call 911."

"What hap . . . ?" Sarah began.

"Call the damn number, woman!" Tom yelled, as he slumped into one of the kitchen chairs. "No time for talking. We need help, and fast."

Sarah dialed the number and handed the phone to Tom.

"911," said a woman's voice. "What is your emergency?"

"Bugs! Big bugs." Tom was holding his chest trying to stop the pain that was welling up there.

"Sir, you want an exterminator. I'm sure if you check your local yellow pages you can find someone who can help you. This line is for real emergencies only."

Tom took a deep breath. "You don't understand. These are huge bugs, the size of cats. There are thousands of them. I just watched them take down one of my cows. I need help. Send in the Army, or something."

"Sir, have you been drinking?"

"This is Tom Blanchard, from Coffyville. I haven't touched a drop in thirty years. Everybody knows me. They know that I'm a good, honest person."

"I'm sorry, sir. This is 911, out of Baker City. I don't know you from Adam. If this is supposed to be some kind of joke, let me remind you that there are severe penalties for this sort of thing."

"Lady, please just listen to me. I don't know what these things are, or where they came from, but if I don't get some help pretty soon there won't be an animal left alive on my farm. Couldn't you send someone out? If I'm lying, like you think, then just throw me in jail."

"Very well, sir. Help is on the way. An emergency unit out of Coffyville should be there within fifteen minutes."

Tom and Sarah watched in horror as the cows stampeding around the north pasture. One by one the cows were dragged down, as the black hoard swarmed over them. They watched as they stripped a carcass to the bone and moved on to the next. Now, they were as large as dogs and moving ever closer to the fence.

Tom reloaded his shotgun, and then went upstairs to the bedroom to retrieve his 38-caliber revolver from under his pillow. When he returned to the kitchen with it in his hand, Sarah shot him a funny look.

"This is for us," he said, "just in case. Grab what you can; checkbook, credit cards, cash, whatever we have lying around. We need to get the hell out of here."

They exited the front door. Sarah threw a hastily packed suitcase in the back of the old pickup; then she jumped into the passenger's side.

"Jesus! Tom yelled. I forgot the damn keys!" He jumped from the truck and ran for the house, just as the back fence gave way.

This was the third or fourth time, today, that Sarah had heard Tom cuss. He wasn't a man who took to cussing, and never used the Lord's name in vain. "*Silly old fool,*" she thought. "*We could die any minute and all you can think about is Tom saying a few bad words? Still in all, it was not a good time to be using the Lord's name in vain*".

It seemed like forever before Tom returned with the keys.

"They were in my jacket pocket," he explained. "I forgot to put them back on the hook."

He started the truck just as something slammed into the side. Sarah screamed as this huge insect-like face appeared in the window, its mandibles scraping the glass as it tried to grasp her head. Another appeared, this time near the rear post. Its mandibles pierced the window and barely missed her head by inches as the glass exploded.

Tom slammed the gas pedal to the floor. The tires spun as he tried, without much luck, to pull away from the gathering horde. The truck flipped onto its side, the engine still racing and the tires spinning wildly; until the engine, choked with oil, finally died. Sarah lay on top of Tom, struggling to gain the seat again. She wedged herself against the dash.

Tom had managed to free the shotgun from the rack and blasted the head from the first creature as it tried to enter through the broken passenger side window. He knew that he couldn't fight them all off. This was merely to gain time.

Sarah clamped his face in her hand and kissed him softly as her tears streamed down onto him. "I love you," she said.

"I love you, too," he said. He placed the gun against her temple and pulled the trigger.

The driver of the first fire truck arriving at the scene heard the second shot. He looked on in horror as huge, cockroach-looking bugs pulled two lifeless bodies from an overturned pickup, tore them apart, and devoured them, bones and all. They were the size of full-grown pigs. He barely got the door open before he lost it. It was then that he realized that opening the door wasn't such a good idea. They were moving his way, hundreds of them.

He jammed the truck into reverse; the gears ground and the engine raced. His mind definitely wasn't on his driving. He backed up and started forward just as the rescue vehicle was coming over the hill. It stopped and blocked his way. As one of the guys jumped out, he tried to wave him off. It was too late. The black horde was upon them, clambering over the trucks like a tidal wave.

Deputy Sheriff Marlow had been delayed a few minutes. He needed his morning coffee, and he was sure that the nut case he was sent to arrest would still be there when he got there. The sight that met him, when he came over the hill, caused him to dump his coffee into his lap. He never even felt the pain until he had backed off three miles down the road and called for backup.

Colonel Briggs had set up a perimeter of nearly twenty miles to contain the "menace". This included eight farms and nearly twelve hundred head of cattle, plus hundreds of pigs, goats, chickens, and even a few llamas. This was just one "pocket". There were twenty others, covering some twenty-five hundred square miles. In between, mop up operations had begun, but not without casualties and much difficulty.

In the open areas incendiaries were found to be effective, but only to a small extent. It had to be a direct hit as many of these creatures were as large as cows and had a hard shell that seemed resistant to patches of flaming napalm. Nothing less than a direct hit from a missile, artillery shell, or tank round could take them out and they could move so fast, they were nearly impossible to hit. They could outrun and out maneuver an Abrams tank, and on one occasion had even surrounded one and upended it.

Earlier that day a farmer had killed one with a shotgun. Now, their armor had become thick enough to withstand heavy machine gun fire. It was almost as if they were evolving and adapting as the need arose.

The Army had begun the evacuation of the entire area. There was some discussion about using Sarin, or some other type of gas, but there was the fear that a freak wind might take it into populated areas. Besides, studies of this strange creature had just begun. There was no confirmation that Sarin or anything else would adversely affect these life forms. The only consensus was that this is an alien life form, and since their arrival the carbon dioxide levels have gone up nearly one tenth of one percent.

"This may not seem significant to most people," informed Dr. McGanan, a leading Biologist and Entomologist brought in by the Army to study these new creatures. "Our atmosphere normally contains four tenths of a percent of carbon dioxide. Most animals cannot withstand much more than five percent carbon dioxide in the atmosphere without suffocating. If these creatures can raise the level of carbon dioxide one tenth of one percent in a few days, imagine what they can do in a month, or a year. If we don't destroy them, gentlemen, they will destroy us, one way or another."

From the surrounding hillside suppressing fire was laid down and two platoons were sent in to humanly put down the remaining livestock. One man was lost when he was overtaken in an ambush. He begged to be shot, and Sergeant Wilson obliged him. Wilson refused to talk about it at his subsequent court marshal. Two days later, he commandeered a gun and shot himself.

The closest estimate is that there were 20,000 "Clackers", as the troops were now calling them . . . for the sound they made when the clacked their mandibles together . . . within the perimeter. They were kept at bay by a ring of fire kept going by the Army with the help of many civilian volunteers. Firewood was brought in to keep small bomb fires going and tanks and flamethrowers were kept at the ready. One thing they had learned early on was that these creatures didn't like fire. Still, no one was willing to bet that the line of fire would contain them once the last of their food supply was devoured. There was talk of bringing in more cattle, but that was dismissed as a stopgap solution.

"We are going to have to fight them, eventually," said General Raintree, and reverting back to his Indian heritage, added, "Today is a good day to die."

In the days that followed, the troops watched as the Clackers grew even larger on their large cache of food: soon, as big as rhinos, now, challenging the ancient dinosaurs. Their armor grew thicker as their bodies grew larger. Eventually a direct hit from a 105 mm Abrams tank gun could roll one over, but within seconds it was on its feet again. The only advantage, now, was that they could no longer sneak up on you. You could hear those huge feet hit the ground several yards away. Of course, they could still outrun you, so it was a good idea not to stray too far from a tank or someone with a flamethrower. Bazookas and hand-held missiles were useful. It didn't kill them, but did seem to inflict damage.

At first, there were only a few stragglers challenging the perimeter, but as the numbers grew, it was decided to fall back to more easily defendable terrain: the mountains to the east, the river to the west, a gully to the south and the open desert to the north. Barricades were erected: huge concrete walls twenty feet high, with razor wire and barbed wire to slow their progress, and minefields to exploit their soft underbellies, if they existed. This opened the perimeter up to over one thousand square miles and another two hundred and fifty thousand troops were brought in to fill the voids.

Colonel Briggs was replaced by General Schertz, a hard-nosed no-nonsense, battle hardened, neo-nazi, with true killer instincts. He, quickly, looked over the situation and shook his head.

"Gentlemen, this corral is for cowboys. We are soldiers, not cowboys. I don't want to herd these things. I wish to destroy them. In two days I want our troops ready for an all out assault. We will annihilate them, or we will die in the attempt."

I won't fill you in on the details, but during the wholesale slaughter we lost over fifty-two thousand men. Even the planes were ineffective; something about acid vapor, a product of their excrement, taking out the electronics. Planes were going down everywhere, pilots unable to control them; tanks were being overwhelmed, and the occupants unable to escape. It was total chaos. Radio components dissolved and communications broke down as General Schertz tried to recall his men.

It has since been compared to Custer's last stand; and the General has been referred to as "General Schertz, 'The general who lost his shirt'."

As a result, the perimeters were breached, and as each of the twenty "pockets" was breached, they became one huge pocket that encompassed over sixty-two hundred square miles. Troops were called home from overseas as a huge military machine moved west. General Fleckenstein, who relied more on history and astrology for his guidance, replaced General Schertz.

Since the concrete barricades did little to halt the advance of creatures that could easily climb such things, it was decided to dig a huge ditch. The debate among the generals was what to fill it with: water, incendiaries, oil, napalm, or insecticide. Deciding to use all of them, the napalm and insecticide to be added at the last, possible moment, settled the debate. Every available backhoe, earthmover, and dozer was brought in. The earth was piled in front to form a second barrier. Multiple liners were added to prevent the water from soaking into the ground while thousands of tankers plugged the highways for miles.

The black horde moved forward, fighting over the last scraps of some unfortunate coyote, or mule deer that might have blundered into their path. Still hungry, they had become a formidable menace.

At twenty miles, General Fleckenstein ordered open fire, and thousands of guns barked with a thunderous roar. Some went down, hit by numerous hits, but as a whole, the black blanket moved forward rapidly. Valves were opened, and the last of the chemicals were added to the concoction. The trench was torched just as the first of the clackers came over the wall of dirt.

Losses were estimated at one hundred and fifty-three thousand men. Two survivors said that they watched General Fleckenstein being torn apart by a couple of clackers. Apparently, they have no respect for rank. A couple of his gold stars were found a few of days later. No one volunteered to dig through the clacker poop to find the rest of him.

Canada and Mexico were now involved, and the next line of defense was set at the Great Divide. There was talk about nuclear weapons, but the environmentalists fought it tooth and nail. A line of defense was established with conventional weapons and barriers built, even though we knew that they were excellent climbers.

Mexico City fell in three days and everything that could float was descending upon the beaches of Texas, Louisiana, Mississippi, Alabama, Florida and Cuba. One large boat that drifted into New Orleans contained no survivors, but one, well-fed, clacker. The police hit it with mace and teargas, while a local crane operator squished it by dropping a cement truck on it. The resulting stench overwhelmed half of the city.

Few clackers ventured north, into Canada, having no love for the colder climate; nevertheless, Canada sent twenty thousand troops to help contain them, here. Cold weather doesn't last forever. There would be no help from Europe, Asia or Africa, as the rest of the world was having its own problems with the menace. General Belington was now in charge, under direct orders of the President, a brilliant strategist who was mostly noted for being able to outflank the enemy. Unfortunately, outflanking this enemy might not have been the best approach, here.

Despite the heavy losses, it was determined that over five hundred clackers met their demise at the pits, with the napalm and the insecticide probably taking the heaviest toll. Perhaps they sacrificed themselves so that their comrades could clamber over their bodies to get to the other sides. Ants sometimes do this by forming bridges over bodies of water. With all of the pockets merged, now, there were still estimated to be nearly half a million surviving clackers. Half of these were moving south into Mexico and Central, and South America. That was their problem. For now, we had over 250 thousand of these monsters making their way toward the east coast.

The only creatures who were safe, now, where the insects, tiny mice, scorpions and hairy spiders that now scurried about to avoid being crushed by their thundering feet. After all, they were simply too small to bother with. Not for long, though, as the eggs left behind began to hatch.

The skies opened up and there were heavy rains over the Rockies. This hampered operations, but it didn't slow down the advancing horde. They moved forward, day and night, devouring everything from rabbits to buffalo, to any fool human stupid enough to stay behind.

High altitude bombers hit them with everything they had, from missiles to cluster bombs. The concussion would knock them over, but nothing could penetrate their thick shells. Their armor had grown to nearly a foot thick; an armor that was light, flexible, and yet harder than steel. Armor piercing shells would bounce right off of it. The shell would flex and the round would be diverted in another direction.

After several days of pounding away at the clackers, the General Staff determined that nothing short of nuclear weapons were going to stop this wave of destruction. With half the country in exile and the other half aghast at what was materializing on their television screens, the moral outcry of the environmentalists and the other naysayers came through as a mere whimper. The lessons of Hiroshima and Nagasaki long forgotten, a nuclear arsenal emerged from places that most never even knew existed.

Ironically, on Friday the thirteenth, the first assault with nuclear weapons was unleashed on the advancing horde. Envisioning the movie, "War of the Worlds" a stealth bomber, a progeny of the Flying Wing, dealt the first blow. We all watched, anxiously, as the familiar mushroom cloud formed over the drop zone. As the dust cleared, we waited for the forward observers to give us a body count. The results were far less than were originally determined: six. We needed a bigger bomb.

The next candidate was an H-bomb. At thirteen hundred hours it was dropped in the midst of the advancing throng. The ground shook, trees were uprooted and thousands of manmade structures were instantly vaporized.

The advance had stopped. The entire hoard lay on the ground, shaking and quivering. The cheers could be heard streaming in through the TV, the windows, and even the air conditioners. We had won! The day of reckoning had come and we had persevered. We as a country, and as a species had shown, again, that we were unbeatable.

It was as if someone had flicked a switch. The cheering had suddenly stopped as millions of people watch the clackers, one by one, get to their feet. The bomb hadn't defeated them. It only made them stronger. Somehow, after the first bomb, they had developed a resistance.

I'm sure that if we had had time, we would have defeated them, but once the carbon dioxide levels reached over five percent, people started dropping like flies. So here I sit, talking into this recorder, perhaps one of the few remaining humans. Ironically, the clackers weren't much more tolerant than we were. They, eventually, killed themselves off; dying from asphyxiation, intolerant to the carbon dioxide their own bodies produced. Perhaps where they had come from the atmosphere was much thinner and it was more easily dispersed, or they might not have gotten a large there. Who knows?

You may wonder why I'm still alive. The building I live in is full of bottles of breathable oxygen. I've been here for four month and I am down to the last two bottles. Maybe there is a whiff or two in some of the bottles waiting to be refilled, but even so, what is that going to gain me? I can't really call this living. I'm sure that there are other people, much smarter than I am, somewhere, perhaps in the North, who are making their own oxygen, but since I'm not that clever, my time on this earth is limited to two bottles worth. Eventually, I'm sure, the carbon dioxide levels will drop, unless the new tenants decide to keep it at this level.

I've seen them, the aliens. They look strange, like nothing I'd ever expect. The ships started to arrive two months ago. They've seen me. I hold their interest no more than a kangaroo or a bird spider would mine, something to observe and then walk away from, if you can call what they do walking. I must look pathetic, half naked, unclean, having to drag a bottle wherever I go. To them I must look very small and insignificant.

They have already leveled nearly half of the city. They are building their own city from the rubble, shining, glass-like structures that seem to go up overnight. They will be here, where I am, in a week or so. It doesn't really matter; I'll be long gone by then. How easy it was for them. The bugs did it all. They never had to fire a shot. They took advantage of a lesser species to do their bidding for them. I guess, in that way, we have something in common.

AIN'T LIFE HELL

The following article was originally published in the April issue of "*Biotec*" magazine, in 2033:

SENSATO:

*Fifteen years into this century, **Kantona Corporation**, the well-known manufacturer of software and video games, released what they considered to be the ultimate video game. It was called Sensato. What made this video game so unique was the fact that it incorporated all the senses. Instead of manipulating a character on a video screen, or headset, as you would with a computer-animated game, you could actually become part of the program. Your mind became the screen and all the objects comprising the program could be touched, smelled and tasted, as well as seen and heard, in what was known as SUVR, or "Super ultra-virtual reality". Although actual conversations were limited, reactions to touch and verbal commands could be programmed into the system with unlimited possibilities. Since the program did not rely on a dot matrix or liquid crystal media, the images were clear and extremely realistic.*

*The only drawback with the Sensato system was the fact that it had to be wired directly into the cerebral cortex of the brain. Many doctors refused to perform the "simple" operation and, at first, there were few takers. However, as with anything else, there were always those willing to take the risk, and those who did said it was the most gratifying experience of their lives. It wasn't long before there were clinics opening all over the country; despite the high cost of the operation. Probes were wired into the brain and a small gold receptacle was placed at the base of the skull. In the privacy of one's own living room, an individual could hook up to a **Sensato** unit and, by placing* *small disk into a slot, they could be sent to the world of his or her choice.*

At first there were adventure disks, Disney disks, and disks that could send you off to exotic lands and far away planets. As popularity increased, costs came down and the operation itself was soon considered commonplace. "Chop shops" opened up all over the country, offering "in and out service" and easy payment plans. Many mothers eventually allowed their children to become "wired", rather than listen to that familiar rumpus, "But Johnny has one!"

*Unfortunately, it wasn't long before the "girly" or "sex" disks came onto the market. This led to even more radical perversions. Eventually, **Sensato** was outlawed in most states, especially after several people died from strokes, brought on by "bad" disks. It was discovered that a deep scratch or bad programming, could send the viewer into something resembling a fit or at least a severe, horrible nightmare. **Cantona Corporation** finally eliminated the scratch problem by sealing the disks into an airtight plastic sheath and limiting the life to eight to ten viewings. Some of the "bad disks" that where created in the aftermarket, were so horrific, they could cause failure of the heart and nervous systems. Eventually, the viewers were left to weed out these disks for themselves.*

*People, while hooked up to the **Sensato** system, would be placed into a kind of trance, but only while a disk was in play. They would be virtually unaware of anything going on around them, as if they were in a deep sleep. One man, wearing the new "back pack" system, had his house burn down around him, and although he was burned over ninety-five percent of his body, he survived until the very second his disk ran out. Many operations were performed on people under the "**Sensato** trance" along with many robberies, rapes and murders.*

*It was also discovered that people would respond to voice commands while in a "**Sensato** trance" and could actually be taught to do certain, "low keyed" jobs while under its influence. Employers offered to pay for the operation and supply **Sensato** systems to their employees if they would sign up, for a year or more, to do jobs usually considered too boring or too "nasty"*

13

for the general public. This practice was banned after it was discovered that people, thinking they were being hired for legitimate employment, were unwittingly used in robberies, prostitution, and illegal drug operations.

*Before the **Sensato** system was finally outlawed in 2029 a large number of people, mostly southern poor, had signed up for this system. A few of the southern states were the last to ban **Sensato**. Today the **Sensato** system has been banned by every state, and the sale or exchange of **Sensato** disks is considered, in most states, to be a felony offense. Yet the disks are still being pirated and sold on the black-market. "Packies", so called because of the compact, **Sensato** backpack they wear, still roam the south in small bands, many working just for food and disks*

"Damn it! I think I lost one!" Brandon Fisk was a large, fat, dumpy man, who was already showing signs of baldness at the age of twenty-nine. He was sitting beneath a large oak tree poking through a small black box.

"Ya gotta be more careful, Brandon," Pogue said, "We ain't got but a dozen left!" Pogue Brahman was sitting next to him, plucking sandspurs from his socks. He was short, thin, small-boned, and definitely the runt of the litter.

"What do you mean 'we', Pogue?" Brandon's voice was angry. Y'ain't got nothin' more'n the shirt on yer back. Nobody said nothin' 'bout no community property. Y'heah?"

"Ya shared em with me before, Brandon. Hell, we've been kickin' around together fer more'n two years, now. I thought we was best friends."

"We is friends, Pogue, but that don't mean we's partners. Besides, I always thought I could get more. Now, I ain't so damn sure."

"I'll help ya get some more, Brandon. Come on, now, don't be such an ass."

"OK, Pogue, ya can have this one." Brandon handed him a small disc about the size of a quarter.

Pugue took it from him, eagerly, and held it up to the light so he could read the tiny label. "Disney?" he shouted. "Don't ya got nothin' with girls?"

"Y'all don't want it? Ain't nobody gonna force ya ta take it, boy. Ya just give it on back heah."

"No man! I like Disney just fine," Pogue said, clutching the disc to his chest, "but when I help ya get some more, let's get lots of em, with girls."

Brandon watched, as Pogue slip the disc into his backpack, his face suddenly becoming blank and expressionless, and his eyes rolling back into his head.

"Jump on one foot," Brandon ordered. He watched, as Pogue, obeying his orders, got to his feet and began bouncing on one foot, his face still void of any emotion. Brandon laughed to himself as he slipped a disk into his own backpack.

This time he was on a tropical island, sitting on a sunlit beach, the sound of the raging surf nearly drowning out the cry of the squawking sea birds. Tall, coconut palms, they're lofty summits burdened with fruit, bathed him in cool shade, while a fair, young, island beauty wiped his brow with a damp, scented, cloth. He reached up and grabbed her by her long, dark hair and brought her face to his. She came eagerly, her lips parting. He crushed her lips to his, soft, warm, stained, and with the taste of sweet, succulent berries.

"Did ya tell me tah jump on one leg?" Pogue was sitting under the tree, rubbing his right leg with both hands. "Ya did! Didn't ya? Ya asshole! Ya son-of-a-bitch! My leg's gonna be sore fer a week, now! Why'd ya want ta go an do that, fer?"

Brandon laughed, "What's the matter, Pogue, ain't y'all got no stamina, no more?"

"Well, I don't think it's funny, Brandon. If I done it ta you, y'd a kilt me!"

"You bet yer sweet ass, boy," Brandon said, laughing all the harder.

"I'll tell yah somethin' else, Brandon. I ain't gonna do no Disney, no more. At first them little chipmunks was cute, but after a time they like ta got on my nerves. I swear if I could a caught em, I would a rung their scrawny, little necks! An y'all, ya big asshole! I bet you got a sweet piece a ass, didn't ya? Which one did ya do?"

"That island one," Brandon said, now on his feet and stretching.

"The one with that little, dark-haired girl, with the nice ass and them sweet, berry lips?"

"That would be the one," Brandon replied, smugly.

"Man! I could do that one every day, ten times a day, an wouldn't much care if I didn't never do nothin' else. How many times ya do er, Brandon?"

"Five or six; can't remember. She's OK, but I'd get sick of the same one all the time. I must have two or three of those discs with that same girl. I'll sure be glad when we get some more."

"Ya ever get bored again, Brandon, ya just hand em over ta me. Ya got any more good ones in there, Brandon?" Pogue asked, looking at the steel box now setting next to Brandon's leg.

"Got the one with the Eskimo woman," Brandon said, rubbing the top of the box, affectionately, "an the one with the stripper; the one with them big tits." He gestured with his hands.

"Oh, yeah, man, I ain't seen that one in a long time. I remember once, I rapped them big things right around my head. Ya wouldn't let me do that one, would ya?"

"Nah, I don't think so, Pogue. Ain't got more'n half a dozen left. I ain't gonna use no more today. Right now I want ta get some'n ta eat. We ain't had nothin' ta eat since Tuesday. I can't go no two days without food, like you can."

"You ain't gonna trade no disc fer food, is ya?" Pogue looked worried.

"If I need ta, I will. I'm damn, powerful hungry."

"Well, don't ya trade that 'Stripper' disc, man. I'll give ya two fer that one when I get em!"

"I ain't gonna trade no 'Stripper' fer food, ya dumb ass, I got other ones I can trade. Let's go down ta the crossroads. I heah there's a store there. I heah that sometimes guys come in lookin' fer 'packys' when they got some'n no one else'll do. I heared they even have discs, good ones that they trade or let ya use."

They picked up their bedrolls and packs and headed down the dusty graded road. There was little traffic. They were glad of that. When a car did go by, it filled the air with clouds of choking dust that seemed to hang in the air forever. The sun was high; it was beginning to warm up. Brandon was beginning to sweat profusely, dabbing at his head with a dirty bandanna. It took them about an hour to reach the crossroads. Pogue noted that there wasn't much there. On one corner was an old barn. Actually, a skeleton of what had once been a barn.

One section of the roof had collapsed and many of the siding boards were missing exposing its hand-hewed framework. Pigeons still nested in what was left of the loft, and they took off in mass confusion when Pogue walked inside.

"Don't go pokin' around in there, Pogue," Brandon said, softly, as if he were afraid someone would hear. "Ya want ta get our heads blowed off?"

"Don't get all worked up," said Pogue, coming back through a hole in the wall. "Ain't nothin' in there but a bunch a junk an lots a pigeon shit."

Across the street was an abandoned gas station and on the adjacent corner was the store. It was old, weather-beaten; it's facing void of any trace of paint, its cedar roof green with moss and covered with needles from the towering, long-needle pines beside it. It sagged in the center, like some swayback horse, the front porch leaning precariously toward the dusty, graded road. Its wooden steps were well worn, grooved by countless footfalls; its warped and weathered boards bleached white in the summer sun. Inside was no better. The floor dropped dangerously toward the center, while the sparsely filled shelves, some shimmed to provide some degree of vertical attitude, wandered this way and that. At the counter sat an old woman, cracked and weathered, and blending in well with the rest of the decor.

"What do you 'packys' want?" she asked. "If you're not here to buy somethin', get your asses out!"

"We was hope'n ta find some work," said Brandon, removing his hat and striking his most subservient pose.

"You boys are late. It's half-past noon. If you boys want work, you get your tails here in the mornin'."

"We had a long walk, Ma'am," Brandon lied. "We had ta come clear from Stonerville."

"Well, get what you want and get out. You can park your carcasses out there by the big oak till mornin', but if you don't find no work, I want you out a here before noon. You hear me?"

"Thank ya, Ma'am," said Pogue, stepping forward. We sure do heah ya good."

"You're pretty puny for a 'packy', ain't you?"

"No Ma'am," he said, setting down his pack and making a muscle with his right arm, "I'm as potent as a wild cat."

"We'd like some food Ma'am," interrupted, Brandon, "if it wouldn't be too much trouble."

The old woman shook her head. "I take it you boys ain't got no money. Otherwise you wouldn't be so damn polite."

"That's right; Ma'am, but I do got some discs." Brandon came forward and set his pack down next to the counter. He removed the black box and set it in front of her. From around his neck, he took a key and unlocked it. "I got this Disney one," he offered.

"I don't want no Disney. Only kids like them, an they ain't got no money. What else you got?"

"Got one a them race car ones, Ma'am." Brandon removed the disc from the box, and held it between his thumb and forefinger, so she could see.

"Ain't that the one that killed that 'packy' over in Brookfield, about a year ago?"

"T'weren't the disc, Ma'am; just had a bad heart," offered Pogue.

"How about one of those girly ones? I see you've got 'The Stripper'. I'll give you food and ten dollars cash for that one."

"No, Ma'am! I ain't a swappin' that one, but I got this Eskimo woman." Brandon carefully plucked a green disk from the box.

"Damn! Damn, Brandon!" Pogue had dropped his packs and was jumping around, waving his arms. "Ya said ya weren't gonna trade no girlies fer food. I would a gived ya something fer that!"

"Y'all ain't got nothin' ta give, Pogue! Now, shut up if ya wanna eat!"

"I'll give you two bags of chips, half a dozen, day-old sandwiches, a bag a hard donuts, a six-pack a beer and five dollars, cash," the old woman offered.

"Damn, Ma'am! That ain't diddly-squat," Brandon pleaded, "Can't ya do no better'n that?"

"I'll give you another six-pack, and I'll make it eight dollars, but that's the best I can do."

"That's a girly disk," said Pogue, "it's worth more than that."

"Look sonny," the old woman began, "I got to have about fifty of these discs, now. If you don't like my offer, you can take it on down to the next store, it's about eight, nine miles that-a-way. There's no guarantee that he's gonna want it, neither, seein' as it is against the law ta buy or sell them, in this state."

Brandon saw the way she was pointing and he would have none of it. "Shut up Pogue!" he yelled. "I'm hungry an I ain't walkin' no eight or nine miles. Can we pick out the kind a beer we want?"

"Help yourself, boys," she said, "The cooler's on the left."

Their arms full of food; they left and found the picnic table. It set under a big oak tree to the left of the building.

"She dicked us good, Brandon!" Pogue complained. "She got into us hard'n heavy!"

"Shut up, Pogue! It's too late ta worry about that, now. Let's just concentrate on drinkin' this beer before it all gets warm an eatin' these sandwiches, before these flies do." He was waving his hands over the food.

They ate and drank in silence. The more Pogue drank, the more he thought. The more he thought, the madder he got.

"How about lettin' me have a girly disc, Brandon?" Pogue asked.

"In yer wildest dreams, Pogue! I ain't got but a couple left."

"That ole bag's got lots a em, Brandon. Ya heard 'er say she had fifty girly discs, alone."

"We got us eight dollars, Pogue. That ain't a gonna buy us no girly discs. I'll bet that old bag gets thirty, forty dollars apiece fer em, at least; maybe even more."

"I got some'n here'll buy us all she's got." Pogue fumbled around in his bag and produced a snub-nosed .22 pistol.

"Where the hell'd ya get that, Pogue?"

"From that last employer we worked fer. Took it from his desk when he weren't lookin'."

"Damn Pogue! Something like that could a got us both kilt. Ain't ya got no sense at all? Besides, she ain't gonna give ya more than twenty dollars fer that gun"

"I ain't gonna sell it ta her. I'm gonna stuff it under her damn fool nose an tell 'er I want all the discs she's got!"

"Yer talkin' crazy, Pogue. She'd have the law on us before we got a mile away. Shit, they'd hunt us down like dogs an shoot us sure as shit!"

"She ain't got no phone, she ain't got no car, an she ain't got no customers. We could cut cross-fields an be long gone by sundown. What she gonna do? Walk ta the nearest store? She said it was eight, nine miles. It'd take that ole bag a week ta walk that far."

"I still say it's crazy, Pogue, but if'n ya think we can pull it off, well we ain't got a whole lot else goin' fer us, lately."

Pogue opened the gun and looked into the chamber. Ain't got but two bullets left, but that don't make no never-mind. She ain't gonna argue with no pistol. Would you?"

As they entered the store, the old woman looked up from her television. "What do you boys want now?" she asked, annoyed by they're interruption. "You can't still be hungry."

"We want them discs, old woman," said Pogue, his voice shaky. He was holding the gun in both hands, trying to keep it steady. "Now!" he said, trying to sound more forceful.

"Sure, boys," said the old woman, holding her hands in front of her. "They're right here, under the counter. Now, you be careful with that gun, boy."

She bent to reach under the counter and Pogue looked over at Brandon and smiled. She came up with a sawed-off shotgun in her hand, leveling it at Pogue. Pogue reacted by pulling the trigger, but the hammer came down on an empty chamber. Realizing that the safety was on, the old woman fumbled for the lever. Pogue pulled the trigger, again. This time the gun fired! The bullet caught her between the eyes. She stood there for the longest time, her eyes funny. Pogue pulled the trigger again, but again it hit an empty chamber. The old woman suddenly collapsed like a deflating balloon!

"Damn, Pogue! Ya kilt her! Ya damn fool! Ya kilt her!" Brandon was holding his head between his hands and jumping around. "What the hell we gonna do now? They'll hunt us down like dogs fer sure!"

Pogue stood there motionless, his body frozen with fear.

"Snap out of it, Pogue! What, the hell, we gonna do now? We're gonna die, boy! We're gonna die, fer sure, an it's all yer fault!"

Pogue looked at the gun in his hand. The barrel was still smoking. "We got ta think about this," he said, softly. "Lock the door."

"What?"

"Lock the door, man," Pogue repeated. "Turn that sign around an lock the door."

Brandon obeyed. Pogue was obviously in charge now. He walked to the cooler and got out a cold beer. "Want one?" he asked.

"We got better'n a six-pack outside." Brandon said, nervously.

"We got all we want right here," Pogue's voice was cold. "Let's look fer them discs. That's what we came fer."

"I ain't a goin' back there with no dead body," Brandon's face was flushed.

Pogue went behind the counter. He grabbed the old woman's legs and pulled her out of the way. Under the counter, he discovered an old shoebox, and inside an abundance of discs. He studied the contents of the box. "The old bitch lied to us," he shouted, over the counter, "ain't more'n about ten er twelve girly discs in here, the rest er Disney an stuff. Here's a couple of them car race ones she said she didn't take. I'll bet that ole bag'd take anything she could get, if the price was right."

"Let's get the hell out a here, Pogue. I'm real scart!"

"Hold yer shirt, Brandon." Pogue's demeanor was now cool and calculating. He opened the cash register and removed all the cash. There was only thirty-six dollars. "We can't go off half-cocked. We got ta make us some plans. I say, we pack up some food an all the beer an ice we can carry an take off cross-fields fer the woods, like I said. We could make the deep woods by nightfall. They ain't gonna track us tonight. With the door locked, they might think she's closed. It may be a week before they find her body."

"Well, let's get then, Pogue. I don't want ta be here no longer'n I have ta. I sure don't like bein' around no dead bodies."

They open their blanket rolls and filled them with food. Brandon found a large, picnic cooler in the back storeroom and they filled it full of beer, ice, and cold cuts. They left the store, locking the door behind them, and crossed the open fields toward the deep woods. By nightfall, they had reached the woods, and by sheer luck, found a cool, dry cave large enough for them and their gear. They gathered some wood and built a small fire. Then they emptied their blanket rolls, storing the food on a ledge in the back of the cave. The cooler was set between them on the ground. They ate their fill and each had a couple of beers. Pogue set the shoebox in front of him and began sorting through the discs.

'Pick out any one ya want, Brandon, but I want 'The Stripper'.'

"Ain't we gonna divide em up, Pogue?"

"I'm the one that kilt the bitch with my own gun. The way I see it, these discs is mine." He waved the gun in front of Brandon's face. "I got me one bullet left," he continued, "Is ya feelin' lucky?"

"No, Pogue! Sounds good ta me," he handed Pogue the 'Stripper' disc, "I'll just pick out a good one."

"Good. Now you go first, this time," Pogue said an evil smirk on his face.

Brandon slipped the disc into his backpack. Pogue watched as his face took on the familiar blank expression. "Get up, Brandon." Brandon obeyed, mindlessly. "Now, jump on one foot."

A familiar face and an exquisite body greeted Pogue. She stood before him, her huge breasts heaving with every sigh. He stepped forward, and taking one magnificent breast in his hand, he peeled back the pasty and began to suckle.

"Well, boys, you're back."

Two men stood before them, they're shoulder patches clearly displaying the familiar Morgan County, Sheriff's emblems. The heavy-set, older man in the front held a flashlight, while a tall, young man behind him held a sewed-off shotgun leveled at they're heads.

"Let me introduce myself, boys. I'm Sheriff Hogan and this young man behind me is Deputy Rollins. It appears you boys have been naughty. I stopped at Felma's store, like I do every after-noon, to get me a soda pop, and I found the door locked. Now, I thought that was pretty unusual behavior for Felma. In twenty years, I've never known her to lock the door once during the day. Well, I knew there was something wrong, especially when she didn't answer, so we broke it open. What do ya think I found? There was poor, old Felma with a hole right between her eyes. I could see that the cash-drawer was empty and the box was missing she kept them 'Packy' discs in. Well, I go outside and I look around. There, on the picnic table, is a warm six-pack of beer, some empty beer cans, and some food wrappers. I see these tracks headin' out across the field, toward the woods. You boys were carryin' so much gear you left tracks so deep it was all I could do ta keep from trippin' over them. Well, we just followed the tracks, and they led us right here to this here cave. Here you were, 'packied' out in 'Never-Never Land.' The big guy was jumping up and down on one leg, stoned out of his mind. Me, and the Deputy here, well, we just sat here an watched. We had us a couple cold beers an waited for y'all ta come on back."

Pogue looked down at his belt.

"If yer lookin' for yer gun, boy, I already got it," the Sheriff waved it in his free hand, and then put it back in his belt.

"Now what am I gonna do with you boys?" the Sheriff asked.

"Ain't ya gonna take us in, Sheriff?"

"I don't know, boys," the Sheriff said, rubbing his chin. "We seem ta have a predicament. It's gettin' dark out there, an it's gotta be three, four miles back ta were we parked our car. We got all those fences ta climb. One, or both of you boys might try ta get away and we'd have ta go an shoot ya. Do you know what a twelve gage with buckshot will do ta a body? It ain't pretty, boys. Is it, Rollins?"

"No Sheriff," said Rollins, "it ain't pretty, atall."

"We might be better off just ta shoot ya here and save all that bother."

"Y'all ain't gonna shoot us in cold blood, is ya Sheriff?" Pogue was visibly shaken.

"Now son," the Sheriff said, laughing. "I was just trying ta get your goat. I am a law officer. I have sworn to uphold the law. I am hurt, you would doubt my integrity. Besides, I don't much like all that blood an guts."

"What are ya gonna do with us, then, Sheriff?" asked Brandon.

The Sheriff reached into his pocket. "I got me a couple of discs here, boys; compliments of the county. Now, what we can do is have you slip in these discs. Now, these discs are about one hour long. While you boys are in a stupor, me an Rollins, here, will go back, get the car, and bring it back to this road that's about a quarter mile north a here. That'd be an easy walk from here, even in the dark. How does that sound ta y'all?"

"Sounds better than havin' my brains blowed out," said Pogue, "but can't I just use one of these?" He pointed to the shoebox.

"Now you know ya can't do that, boy. That's evidence."

Pogue came forward, and took one of the discs. Brandon followed suit, and they slipped the discs into their backpacks.

Brandon was in a room full of beautiful, naked women. They rubbed their bodies against his, stripping him, caressing him, wanting him. Soft, moist lips were kissing every part of his body. He looked up to see the most beautiful creature he had ever seen walking toward him. She was tall, long-legged, and blond, with a wasp-like waist you could easily put your hands around. The other girls stepped aside as she came closer. She took his head in her hands and brought his lips to hers. Her breath was hot and her lips soft and full. Her lips traced a path across his chest and then down his hairy belly. As she passed his waist, he cupped her firm breasts and closed his eyes in anticipation. Suddenly, Brandon found himself screaming in pain! As he looked down in disbelief, he could see that the creature before him was no longer the beautiful blonde, but a hideous, hairy, creature with fiery, red eyes and long needle-sharp teeth. A fire rose quickly around him, searing his flesh from his bones! He cried out for Pogue! Pogue couldn't help him. In mortal pain, he too was calling out, for Brandon!

"What is that disc called, Sheriff?" asked Rollins, opening a fresh bag of chips.

"It's a little something I had made up special, son," said the Sheriff, popping the top on another beer and setting back to watch the show. "I call it *Living Hell*. Ain't no 'packy' ever lived through one of these discs. They cost the County about one hundred bucks apiece, but they sure save a heap a bother."

The deputy looked up, "Damn, Sheriff, look at them boys squirm!"

"They tell me a bad disc, like that, is kinda like getting your brains ripped out. Well I'll be damned," he said, getting to his feet, "looks like them boys just ran out of disc." The Sheriff removed the discs from the backpacks and put it into his pocket. He closed the lid on the cooler. "Give me a hand with this, will ya son? Ain't no sense in wastin' all this good beer."

CAR-NIVORE

"Your fuel is low," announced the familiar, soft, feminine voice emitting from the car's surround sound system.

"I know when the fuel's low, you God damn, stupid, freakin' car! I've still got a little less than a quarter of a tank!"

Buddy Boyle whipped the big Lincoln into the parking lot of Boyle Steel and Salvage. He slammed his hands down menacingly on the plastic steering handles. He pressed the "off" button and waited for the whiny, non-polluting, diesel/electric engine to shut down. He impatiently flicked the door button several times; knowing full well it would not open until the engine had completely shut down and the two side-mounted emission tubes had cooled sufficiently.

"Progress," he thought.

He was a small, portly man barely five feet tall, with squinty eyes and bushy eyebrows that had earned him the name of "Mr. McGoo" among his employees, although never to his face; for you see, Buddy Boyle has never possessed a sense of humor.

"The door is ajar," said the voice.

"I know it's ajar, you useless, G-damned piece of shit! I'm getting out!" He kicked the door open with his foot and flicked the ashes from his big cigar onto the seat. "One of these days I'm gonna scramble your brain and rip out your freakin' speakers, you big mouthed, mother of a Ford! No, I can't call you that can I? You were more like a Chevy, after the two companies merged and before the Chinese finally took over. Now you're just another piece of Chinese crap!"

It was the same threat Buddy had made for the last two months, ever since he had purchased the car. It wasn't an idle threat. Buddy Boyle didn't make idle threats. He just had other more important things on his mind, money being the most important.

His feet hit the ground as the sound of the "open door" buzzer sounded in his ears. He reached his hand under the dash until he felt the vibration. He closed his hand around the plastic box and the sound deadened. Two hard yanks and the noise stopped. He smiled as he tossed the buzzer onto the back seat.

His office was an old, rusty Amtrak car. His secretary's office was in the front half and his office was in the back, only his half was twice as big. Julie complained once about her cramped space within that rusty old hulk. Buddy informed her that he dealt in junk and that junk was what he had. He told her she should be glad he didn't deal in used shit! She never bothered to complain again. What would be the use?

She had come to work at Boyle Steel and Salvage just a little over six years ago. It was right after Buddy's father and founder of the company had passed away. The former secretary, a Miss Greene, had quit without notice, stating the she could not work for a "foal mouthed degenerate" like Buddy Boyle. Julie was sixty-seven at the time, and not yet old enough to receive her meager Social Security. She was in desperate need of a job, and the pay was good. How she had managed to stick it out all these years, she still didn't know. Here she was, seventy-three and wondering why she hadn't retired when she was eligible, nearly a year ago.

"There is a man in your office to see you," she informed Buddy as he came through the door. "He said he was from the APACC."

Buddy didn't believe in casual greetings, such as "Hello" or "Good morning" during working hours. The office was for business, not socializing.

"What the shit has APACC got to do with me?" he asked. "Isn't that the outfit that deals with stray dogs and cats?"

"I've asked you not to use that kind of language, Buddy!" Julie said, angrily.

"I'm so sorry," Buddy said, in a condescending voice.

Julie pretended she didn't notice, "You're thinking of the SPCA."

"So what the shit is APACC?"

Julie shook her head in disgust. "According to his card his name is Harold Bradfield and he's the president of 'Americans for the Preservation of Antique and Classic Cars'." She held up the card.

"Another frickin', goddamn, bleeding heart! Give me the damn card!" He snatched the card from her hand and stuffed it into his the top pocket of his shirt. He poured himself a cup of coffee, took a sip, and then poured the coffee into the sink. "Make a fresh pot," he ordered, "this mud must be two hours old. It tastes like crap!"

The man in Buddy's office was tall, thin and thirtyish. He was hiding behind a large, handlebar mustache and reeked of English Leather. He wore a blue suit, a maroon tie, and thick, brass rimmed glasses that made his eyes look three times as big. Buddy pegged him, immediately, as a geek. He jumped to his feet, as Buddy entered the room, and extended his hand.

"So you're Bradford?" Buddy asked, sliding behind his desk without shaking hands.

"Bradfield, Mr. Boyle," the man corrected, returning to his seat, "have you heard of me?"

"No," said Buddy, taking a deep drag on his cigar and blowing the smoke in the man's direction, "should I have?"

"APACC is a large organization," the man replied, fanning the smoke from his face. "We have a lot of member clubs all across the country."

"I have never heard of A-PRICK, or whatever you call yourselves, so what the shit does this have to do with me?"

"We at APACC are concerned with what you intend to do with your latest acquisition."

"I assume you mean the twenty-four acres of junk cars I recently purchased, at auction, near Heilmansville." Buddy leaned forward on his desk. "Well duh! I'm in the junk business. Apparently you failed to notice the sign out front. This is a salvage yard. I buy junk. I sell junk. It's a dirty business, but it's a good business. I just bought twenty-four acres of junk cars, which I will crush into little square blocks and sell to the Chinese; hopefully at a profit. This puts money in my pocket, and food on my table."

"Please hear me out, Mr. Boyle," Bradfield pleaded. "I heard your secretary call you Buddy. May I call you Buddy?"

"My friends call me Buddy. I don't have too many friends. You see, Mr. Broadfield," Buddy leaned back in his chair, "friends always want something, and most of the time they want it for nothing. You may call me Mr. Boyle."

"Yes, I see, Mr. Boyle." Harold Bradfield shifted uncomfortably in the chair. "You see," he continued, "the Heilmansville junk yard was owned by a man named Ben Graham. Mr. Graham believed in the same things that we at APACC believe in: the preservation of the

American car. Once these cars are gone they will be gone forever. Each one is a piece of our American heritage; the American dream."

"Oh, bull shit!" shouted Buddy. "You buy a car, you enjoy the new car smell, the new upholstery, the fresh paint job, the shiny chrome, or in the case of the modern car, the shiny, new plastic. In a few years the smell goes away, the upholstery wears out, the paint fades, the shiny chrome rusts, and the plastic cracks. You bring it to me, I crush it into a little cube, and the Chinese will make you a shiny new car. I recycle."

"Please, Mr. Boyle, maybe we can make a deal. Some of these cars are, as you say, junk, but some of them are restorable, while others are useful for parts. Let us buy some of the cars from you. We're not a rich organization, but we'll pay you a fair price for them."

"My father started this business in '73." Buddy got to his feet, circled the room and stopped to look at a large picture hanging on the wall. The stern looking elderly man staring back at him seemed cruel and pompous. The brass plate across the bottom read, "Thomas Hardy Boyle . . . 1950-2016." Harold Bradfield assumed it was Buddy's father as he could see a strong family resemblance. "That was sixty-nine years ago," Buddy continued. "Back then my father went were the money was. He sold parts: transmissions, tires, hubcaps, you name it. Back then a crushed car would maybe bring in a hundred, maybe one hundred and fifty dollars, no more. Back then they were worth more for the good parts you could pull off of them. That was sixty-nine years ago. That was long before United Europe, United Africa, United Asia, United this, and United that. Back then they talked of third world countries. Today, there are no third world countries. The world has grown up, Broadford, and like a big baby, it's hungry. What's it hungry for? Raw materials, like steel. Even twenty years ago, if you were to offer two hundred for one of these cars, the old man would have been happy to sell it to you. It would have saved the trouble of having to strip it and crush it. Things have changed a lot in twenty years."

"OK Mr. Boyle, if we gave you five hundred or even one thousand for some of the better ones, surely that would be a fair price."

"Look, Bradstein, it was an open auction. It was well publicized. It's too bad old Ben bit the bullet. Unfortunately, it looks like his daughter didn't share the old man's dreams. I understand she came out from New York, put the old man in the ground, put his house in the hands of a realtor, turned the junk yard over to an auction house, and went back to New York. She was a smart girl. Now she's a smart, rich girl. Your people had the chance to bid like everybody else."

"Excuse me," Julie interrupted as she handed Buddy a cup of coffee.

Buddy took a sip. "OK, this is much better," he said. This was the closest he got to saying "thank you".

"Would you like a cup, Mr. Bradfield?" she asked.

"That won't be necessary," Buddy interrupted, "he's not going to be here that long." He waved her away with his hand.

Julie shook her head and left.

"The bid went too high," Bradfield offered, now with an angry tone, "we didn't have enough money."

"Why do you think the bid went so high?" Buddy asked, rhetorically. "Let me tell you, Bradford. There are twenty-four acres of cars, some of them old cars from the fifties and sixties. Let's say each one would yield maybe two thousand pounds of good steel. That's nearly two times the amount you can get from a modern car. Now say the market is running one-ninety, two dollars a pound. I crush just enough to make my investment, say about four hundred, maybe five hundred cars. Figure it out for yourself. Once I make my investment, I might crush a few to pay the taxes on the land, but the rest is like money in the bank. In a few years, let's say, the market goes up to two-fifty or even three dollars a pound. That would make these cars worth about six grand apiece. Has your organization got that kind of money? I think not. Like I say, the world is hungry and it's only going to get hungrier. Now I'm a busy man, and since your organization has no business with me, why don't you take your lost cause and get the hell out of my office!"

"We're trying to get legislation to stop people like you! Mark my word, Mr. Boyle, we will stop you!"

"Wake up and smell the coffee, Breadfart! Nobody cares about your stupid little club, especially the politicians. They're like me; they go wherever the money is. If you like old cars so much, get yourself an old 2016 Osprey. Now there's a car I wouldn't fight you for. It ain't worth much to me crushed, too much plastic. The environmentalists won't let me burn them off anymore, so we have to strip them by hand. That's getting too costly. The ironic thing is, someday there'll be junk yards full of cars like that, and no one will want them!"

Bradfield picked up his briefcase and stepped toward the door. He paused for a moment, removed his brass-rimmed glasses, and looked back. "We will, Mr. Boyle. We will!" He reached into his briefcase and retrieved a small box. "I was to offer this to you as a token of our good faith. It's a flask of vintage brandy with our logo engraved on the front. 'Gradu diverso, via una' stands for 'the same road by different steps'. If you should change your mind, I wish you would keep us in mind."

Buddy removed the flask from the box, unscrewed the cap and sniffed the contents. "Yeah, well, fat chance of that, huh," he said. "Thanks for the brandy though. He poured a little into his coffee and took a sip. I'm more of a whiskey man myself, but what the shit; it's the thought that counts, right?"

Bradfield passed by Julie as he left. She was sure she caught a smile on his face as he mumbled something under his breath. She stuck her head through the doorway of Buddy's office. "The first load is here, Mr. Boyle," she said.

"Well, it's about damn time," he said getting up from his desk. He paused for a moment to pour some more brandy into his coffee, and then he left the office to meet the driver. *Good shit,* he thought to himself, as he took another sip. *It's got a pretty good kick for brandy.*

He left the office and walked across the compound to where the truck was parked. For a moment, his thoughts drifted to his daughter, Mandy. How much she and Bradfield were alike; both of them wasting their time fighting lost causes. He hadn't seen her in six years. She was just out of college, at the time. It was just before she went off to try to save the whales, or was it sharks? She had dedicated her whole life to one useless cause or another. He would have liked to have brought her into the business. With his ex-wife gone, Mandy was the only family he had left. If it were up to her, she would have sold the cars to Bradfield. Fortunately, Buddy was here to see that this would never happen. He would sit on the cars for another ten years. By then the market would be up and he would then dump them at a huge profit. He would set up a trust fund for his daughter, and she would be free to chase her whales and never have to want for anything again.

He looked first at the truck and then at the driver. "Two? That's all you could get on that freakin' truck, is two? I've got twenty-four acres of junk cars and all you can bring me is two lousy, cars?"

The driver removed his hat and wiped sweat from his brow with his sleeve. "That's all that would fit on the truck, Mr. Boyle. As you can see, the last one is hanging off the back quite a piece."

"Why the hell couldn't you have put them on sideways?" Buddy asked.

"Too wide, Boss, they'd take up the whole lane. It would be too dangerous to haul them like that."

Buddy shook his head. "This is unacceptable. At this rate it would take forever to get those freakin' cars down here. Go tell Julie to call Phil over at Milton Salvage. Tell him I need his portable crusher, another truck and a couple of drivers. Can you remember that?"

"Yeah, sure, Boss."

"Then move!" Buddy motioned to one of the yard hands, "Johnny, get your ass over here."

"Yeah, Boss. What do you need?"

"What the hell does it look like, Dummy? Get this truck unloaded and get these cars over to the crusher."

"Wow Boss, ain't that a fifty-seven Chevy? I ain't seen one of them since I was a little kid. Look at it, Boss, it ain't in too bad a shape. You ain't gonna crush that, too, are ya?"

"Into a little freakin' cube. Now get the fork truck and get this shit over to the crusher."

The thirty-mile stint from the interstate to Heilmansville was full of potholes, narrow country roads, and farm machinery. The flatbed had to swing wide to make the last turn out of Heilmansville, but the two semi trucks had to back up and jockey around the tight turn.

Buddy had pulled to the side of the road and was now out of his car. He was jumping up and down, ranting and raving. "Screw the stop sign," he shouted. "Let them bastards put it back. They shouldn't have made the freakin' road so damn narrow in the first place. Leave it in the ditch, Johnny, we'll run over it on the way out anyway. Let's get this shit moving guys! Phil charges by the hour. Let's go people, let's go!"

The last two hundred feet was a bumpy, well-worn, dirt road, but Buddy didn't seem to notice. He was too busy looking at the cars. There were thousands of them, their windshield glistening in the sunlight. To his eyes it was a beautiful sight, a junkman's paradise. They may have been old hulks with broken windows and rusty chrome, but to Buddy they looked like uncut gems; gems that were waiting for him to mold them into little cubes; little cubes destined to feed a hungry world.

Buddy unlocked the gate and guided the trucks inside. "Pull the crusher over here," he ordered. "We'll start with this row and work that way." He was waving his arms much like a conductor directing a great symphony. "Johnny, go get the fork truck and bring it over here. Carlos, bring the flatbed up here. We'll load that first. Let's go people! Time is money!"

The fork truck was old and was belching smoke, but it seemed to run well. Johnny guided it to the first car in the row. It was a 2003 Buick.

"Hey!" Buddy yelled, over the roar of the engine. "I used to own one of these, but mine was maroon."

"Did you want to keep it, Boss?" asked Carlos, shielding his ears from the noise.

"Hell no, Carlos!" Buddy replied, stepping closer. "What do I look like, some sentimental fool? Just crush it. I want them crushed two at a time and I want them stacked, six high. The flatbed ought to handle about twelve and the semi . . . what, eighteen, twenty-four?"

"Gee, I don't know, Boss," Carlos said, shrugging his shoulders.

"Well ask the driver, Dummy. He ought to know."

As Carlos went to talk to the semi driver, Buddy looked around at his newest acquisition, perhaps in much the same way that Genghis Khan must have surveyed his latest conquest, just before he raped and plundered.

Carlos returned shortly and informed Buddy that the driver agreed to haul eighteen.

"OK," Buddy said, "whatever. You do know what to do, don't you?"

"Sure, Boss. We need to get all these cars loaded."

"Yeah, that's good, Carlos. You do that. I'm gonna look around a bit. I'll be right back. Don't screw around now. Remember, time is money!"

"OK," assured Carlos, "we won't."

Buddy walked between the rows of junk cars. There were many from the fifties and sixties. Way in the back, there were some that were even older. They were square looking cars: forties, thirties, or older. He could see why Bradfield had been so interested in this junkyard. There had to be at least two thousand old cars here that were still intact. Not to mention all the ones that would still be good for parts. What Buddy couldn't understand was why anyone would want these old cars. After all, most of these old junkers had been hard to steer, had poor braking systems, rode like lumber wagons, and had huge, gas guzzling engines. Technology had long passed them by. With the price of gas being what it is today, who could afford to drive one? "I should get a metal for taking them out of the foolish assholes' temptation!"

With the roar of the machinery he knew he was out of earshot. He had struck up a conversation with the one person he knew he could communicate with intelligently, Buddy Boyle. "You've got it made, Buddy," he said to himself, smiling smugly. "You're gonna clean up on this deal. You freakin' cars are gonna make me so filthy rich I'll never have to work again." He waved his arms, encompassing the whole junkyard.

He stopped in front of an old pickup. "Hey, this looks just like the first thing I ever owned. It was 1987 El Camino. I bought and paid for it myself; with money I earned working for my old man in the junkyard, after school. The old man never bought me anything. The son-of-a-bitch never gave me nothing. 'If you want money you're going to have to earn it,' the bastard would say, 'I had to earn every dime I ever made'. That old fart never gave me shit, except the junk business and I had to practically pry that from his cold, dead, fucking fingers. May you rest in peace, you piece of shit!"

"Hell, it's the same color and everything," he said, as he looked the car over. "I wonder if it's got an eight-track". The door opened with a clunk; and Buddy slid in behind the wheel. "It sure does. Man, I can remember how I got my first piece of ass on a vinyl seat just like this one." He rubbed his hand over the cracked, well-worn upholstery.

"Nicole Poloski," he said, smiling. "She was eighteen and I had just turned twenty. I remember after I screwed her, how she had to practically peel her bare ass of the seat like a wet postage stamp. Nicole Poloski. What a hot bitch she was. I picked up some burgers, fries, and a bottle of cheap hooch, and hauled her up to Holland's Hill to look at the lights of the city. I didn't have much money at the time, since I had to pay for my own plates and insurance, as well as room and board to my old man. We sure didn't look at the lights for long. Hell, after the first ten minutes, we couldn't even see out the windows, they were so steamed up."

"God, she had a nice body: full lips, nice ass, great face and those big, freakin' tits!" He closed his eyes and tried to visualize her again. "She was hot. I remember how I couldn't undo her bra, it was so damn tight. I was practically a virgin, and hadn't quite developed the proper skills. She had to undo it for me. I did have a great time, even though the old man did tear into me when I got home. He said that I shouldn't be drinking and cavorting with whores when I was two weeks behind on my room and board. I blew the engine a week later. By the time I got my truck back on the road, Nicole was already going with some guy named Billy, from Kormanville. He had a late model Mustang with a back seat that I'm sure they got to use a lot. I only saw her once after that. She was with some new guy named Roy."

He reached over and turned the knob on the radio and it started to play. "I don't believe it. The battery is still good. Hell, I didn't know there were any stations that still played these old songs. I remember how my old man had a bunch of really old, cassette tapes, in a box in the garage. I used to carry a bunch of them around in the glove compartment. Let me see if I can still remember. There was the Beetles, the Stones, Led Zeppelins and, let's see, Meatloaf was another." He reached over and pushed the button on the glove compartment. The door dropped down and inside he found a bunch of old cassette tapes. "Holy shit! This is really spooky! If I didn't know better I say this was my old truck! It couldn't be. I totaled that son-of-a-bitch in '01 coming home drunk from a party." He rubbed a large scar on his forehead. "It took six stitches to close this up. The old man tore into me that night, too. The compassionate bastard!" He pulled out one of the tapes and was about to cram it into the radio, when he heard a voice.

"Are you going to give me a ride, Buddy?"

Buddy's heart nearly stopped beating. There framed in the passenger's side door was a young girl. She had Nicole Poloski's face, her lips, her hair, her body, and her big tits. She was wearing the same fuzzy sweater and the same short skirt that Nicole Poloski had worn on their first date.

"Sure, Honey, hop in," he heard himself saying.

She slid in close to him and closed the door. He could feel the warmth of her leg against his. As she slid over, her skirt hiked up and he could see the bottoms of her pink panties. She rubbed his leg with her hand. His heart was racing, he was breathing hard, and beads of sweat were forming on his forehead.

"Oh! The Beatles," she said, pushing in the tape. The Beetles were now singing "Michelle". "I just love these old songs. I love your truck, too, Buddy. We don't have to go anywhere if you don't want to. I'm cool for staying right here and listening to your tapes."

She put her arms around his neck and pulled him toward her. Her full, warm lips were on his, her tongue probing the depths of his mouth. He tried to suck in his big gut, but when he looked it was gone. He pulled down the rear-view mirror and looked at himself. He was sixteen again! He reached his hands under her sweater and felt for the snaps on her bra. This time they yielded easily to his touch. Her young, firm breasts sprang forth, and as he pulled up her sweater, they surrendered eagerly to his hot, hungry mouth. With her help, her pink panties slid easily down past her knees, while she, having already mastered his belt and zipper, helped to rid him of his pants and underwear.

"Oh, Buddy, Buddy," her soft lips whispered against his ear.

Carlos wiped the sweat from his face with a dirty rag. "That's the last one," he said. "Tie them down, Johnny and I'll go see if I can find Buddy."

"Hey! Carlos!" Johnny yelled. "What the hell is that? It's coming out of that old El Camino! Hey, man! It looks like blood!"

"Cars don't bleed, Johnny. It's probably just transmission fluid. We just cracked the transmission case when we crushed it."

"Yeah, I guess you're right, Carlos, but it sure does look like blood."

Julie didn't even bother to lock up when she left. After all, what was left in that old Amtrak car that was worth stealing? She knew the answer to that, nothing. Just last week she had made this wonderful discovery. She had discovered the combination to the safe in Buddy's office.

Part of her duties as Buddy's secretary, were to mop the floors and dust the offices. This is something she did reluctantly. After all, she was hired to be a secretary and not a maid. Nonetheless, it was something she had done every Wednesday for the last six years. The big safe in

Buddy's office had always been a fascination to her. She knew that he was skimming the business and how he kept two sets of books. Most of the cash that he took in never found its way back into the business, and it didn't get deposited in the bank. She knew this for sure, because she was the one that did all the banking. The only money that got deposited into the Boyle Steel and Salvage account was in the form of checks. Buddy was one for dealing in cash, and most of the time he insisted on it.

There was a lot of cash going out each day, also. This was the nature of the salvage business. Bill Denver was the man who worked the scales. Each evening he would bring in the cash box and Buddy would go over the weigh tickets and compare them with the amount of cash still left in the box. Each morning, Bill would pick the box up again at Buddy's office. Julie never knew how much money was in that box, but she assumed it was at least forty or fifty thousand, judging from the amount of scrap taken in.

Every Wednesday, Buddy would make the rounds of the various companies he dealt with and pick up a check and an undetermined amount of cash. Julie knew he was collecting cash. Why else would he carry a brief case with him if all he had to pick up were a half a dozen checks? Besides, why not just have them mail the checks? He would come back and lock himself in his office for an hour or more. When he came out again he would always have a smile on his face. It didn't take a genius to figure out that he most have had a good week. He would hand her the checks so she could deposit them before she had to make out the payroll on Thursday. You sure couldn't tell by the checks Julie was given that he had a good week. There would barely be enough money to keep up with the bills and the payroll. Buddy had to have been skimming the business. From what Julie could see, he was skimming it big time!

There had only been one cash deposit made in the last six years. This was just after Buddy had acquired the Heilmansville property at auction. Buddy had her make out the deposit slip and mail a check to a Miss Monica Graham, in New York City. The check was for over one and a half million dollars. Her hands were shaking all the time she wrote it. Buddy had made that deposit himself, and when he opened his brief case to put in the deposit slip, she saw the money. There was row after row of neatly stacked bills, bound in little paper ties that read

$10,000 each. It made "goose bumps" pop out on the back of her neck. The money, she knew, had come out of his office; out of that big safe.

There was a reason that she picked Wednesdays to do the cleaning. Buddy was out of the office and she didn't have to clean around him. However, the real reason was because, when Buddy was away, she could search his office. For six years she had been looking for the combination to the big safe. She knew it had to be somewhere handy, either in the office or in that little black book that Buddy carried around in his pocket. Buddy had a hard time remembering even the simplest things. He wrote everything down and chanced nothing to memory. Julie knew that something as important as the combination to the safe would be written down and close at hand, but where?

It wasn't until this last Wednesday that it had dawned on her. The combination was right there in plain sight all the time! She had been dusting the picture of Buddy's father for the three or four hundredth time. She could never understand why Buddy would have this picture hanging in his office when he had told her, on many occasions, how much he hated the old man. For the first time she got a really good look at the brass plaque at the bottom of the picture. Oh, she had read the inscription many times. "Thomas Hardy Boyle . . . 1950-2016". A little simple math would have told her that he would have been 66 years old. Buddy had told her, on several occasions, that his father has been 78 when he died and that he had died only two weeks before she had come to work for him, six years ago. That would mean that the old man had died in August of 2026. Taking the calculator from Buddy's desk she concluded that, if his father was really 78 when he died, he would have been born in 1948, not 1950 and would have died in 2026, not 2016. If the plaque was wrong it had to be wrong on purpose. Buddy would have never let anything like that slide. This just had to be the combination. Buddy was a lot more clever that she had thought.

Even armed with this information, it still took her a while to get the safe to open. 19-50-20-16 didn't work, even when she reversed the "lefts" and the "rights". She tried 19-16-20-50. That didn't work either. She turned it around and tried to work it backward, 61-02-05-91. Still she had no luck. Finally, she tried turning just the second number around. Bingo! She had hit the jackpot. 19-50-02-61 was the right combination. Her heart was pounding as she swung the big door open.

There, stacked neatly on the shelves, were row upon row of bills, each stack tied neatly with a paper band that read $10,000. She counted them slowly and meticulously several times. There were exactly eight hundred and six. It took so long to count them that she constantly worried that Buddy might come back and catch her in the act. That added up to over eight million dollars.

This all took place last Wednesday. Now, on Monday, she was on her way. She had started planning four days ago, working most of the details out over the weekend. Her plan was to slip something into Buddy's coffee, and while he was out, she would clean out the safe and make good her escape. It was a stroke of luck that Buddy had taken off with the crew early this morning. It would have been awkward cleaning out his safe with him passed out at his desk.

She loaded a large, overnight bag onto the front seat of her car and slid in next to it. She placed her hand over the top as if to assure her that none of the money would escape. She started the little two-cylinder engine and pulled the 2026 Manx 200 onto the street. She had bought the little car four years ago and hated it ever since. It was gutless, ugly and cramped, but it was all she could afford. She opened her pocket book and removed the Airlines tickets. Paris, France . . . she would leave in four hours and be there before supper. This would give her enough time to sew the money into the lining of her luggage so that the airline security wouldn't be able to spot it. She would leave her little Manx in the parking lot and buy something sleek and sporty, when she got there. She even planned to leave the keys in it. Maybe some poor fool would steal it. "But then who would want it?" she wondered.

She thought briefly of Buddy and wondered if he had enjoyed his morning coffee. "The drugs should have taken effect by now," she thought. "I wonder what kinds of dreams you're having now, Buddy? The man assured me you would be all right in a few hours. The drug would just make him hallucinate and dream happy dreams. I'm sorry to have messed with your brain, Buddy, but I needed to buy some time. If I had known you were leaving, it wouldn't have been necessary. Oh well. Don't you just love those new designer drugs?"

Harold Bradfield rocked back in his chair and waited for someone on the other end to pick up the phone.

"Yes," he said, "is this the Bureau of Drug Enforcement? My name is Harold Bradfield. I'm a concerned citizen. I have some information about a man named Buddy Boyle. He's the owner of Boyle Steel and Salvage at one hundred and twelve, East Eighth Street, just off of the mid-town causeway. Yes, that's right, one hundred and twelve. Well today I was in his office and I noticed he had a flask with 'Gradu diverso, via una' engraved on the front. Yes, that's right, the motto of the 'Libertas'. The group that believes drugs should be accessible to anyone who wants them. Yes, I realize that just having a 'Libertas' flash doesn't make him a member, but believe me the man really looked like he was into some heavy stuff. I only called because I'm concerned for the safety of our children. With drug pushers and users like him at large, is anyone really safe? You'll look into it then? Thank you, I really appreciate it."

He hung up and dialed another number. The phone rang several times before someone picked up.

"Milton Salvage."

"Phil? It's me, Harold. It's all taken care of. When they find that flask on him, there's enough illegal shit in it to put him away for the next twenty years. He'll be in so much hot water; he'll be begging you to take that property off his hands, for any price. Who the hell else is gonna buy it? Yeah, he bought that APACC crap, hook, line, and sinker. I wore those thick glasses I bought at the joke shop. That and a fake mustache gave me just the look I wanted. Shit, Partner, I watched him put enough stuff in his coffee to knock out a horse. He ought to be easy to find. About an hour or so after he took it, it would have knocked him out for at least four hours. No man, it ain't going to kill him. Don't worry, there's no way his daughter is going to get any part of his holdings. We sure as hell don't want to have to deal with that "Save the Whale", liberal minded, bitch. Shit, Phil, Buddy would rather see you get it than her. Wherever he is, he'll be sleeping like a baby. The Feds shouldn't have any trouble finding him. His secretary will tell them that he's up in Heilmansville. They'll probably pick him up there. Hell, Phil, It's the perfect plan. Quit your worrying. What the hell could possibly go wrong?"

A LIFE WORTH DYING FOR

I still look back on the sixties with fond reverence even though, at one point, it could have marked the end of my twenty-year existence. Back then I was simply known as "Snake" and belonged to a little bike club that called themselves the *Road Devils*. I didn't have a place of my own, so I crashed with friends who did. I usually stayed until I felt that my presents was no longer appreciated, or until they started to ask me to contribute toward the rent, help clean up the place, or take turns with the laundry; things that no self-respecting biker would be caught dead doing.

I finally ended up staying with a fellow biker we called "Ski". I didn't know what his real name was; I just figure that he had one of those long Polish, or Russian names that no one could pronounce. He was big; about six foot three and weighed in at something like two hundred and twenty pounds. With his blond hair, blue eyes, good looks, and short ponytail, he could have been the poster boy for *Bikers Monthly*. And, if he was the poster boy, his house was a shoe-in for House of the Month, in *Ghetto Magazine*.

His late aunt, Mildred, left the house to him, presumably because there was simply no one else to leave it to. It had once nestled amid a neighborhood of middle class, one-family dwellings, whose manicured lawns, trimmed hedges, and well maintained out buildings were the pride of the community. This was until Ski moved in. Ski had little use for things like lawn mowers, hedge trimmers, or paint.

The neighbors complained, partitioned, and finally moved. A far less disapproving group of individuals filtered into the neighborhood, many of them squatters who came and went more often than Ski changed his socks. Lawns became littered with abandoned cars and washing machines, and Ski's house again took on the distinction of being one of the neatest in the neighborhood.

He was; however, meticulous about his bike. When he wasn't polishing the chrome, or tuning the carbs, he was changing the oil, or lubing the chain. All of this activity took place in the middle of the living room, where he would sit on the oil-stained rug, drink beer, and watch the soaps. He always seemed to have a few coins when he needed them, even though he never had a steady job. I don't know how he managed, but that was none of my business, and my policy was: if it ain't none of your business, don't ask.

The house was usually a mess. Pizza boxes were stacked high on the kitchen counter, along with fast-food wrappers, dishes, and opened and un-opened condiments. There were beer cans and empty gallon wine bottles stacked on everything in the house, except Ski's precious toolbox, and overflowing ash trays that were never emptied until they were gleaned for every, non-living, non-six-legged roach that could possibly be salvaged.

Fortunately, there was a parade of chicks willing to come in, at least once a month, and clean up the mess. After, Ski would take them into his bedroom and show them his appreciation, sometimes two at a time. They must have liked it; they always came back for more.

Ski was never serious about any one chick. Me, I had me an old lady, named Molly. I don't know why, maybe it was just the way her lip curled, or the way she would look at me out of the corner of her eye, but I liked having her around, if you know what I mean. We weren't engaged or nothing. I was not really into that stuff. I mean, what the hell, I wasn't ready to settle down with a job, kids, and that entire domestic shit. I had my bike, and I needed my freedom. Hey, it ain't like I was cheating if I were to happen to have a get-together with some sweet thing I met at the amusement park, or the mall or something, which is pretty much what happened that night.

This new chick I met, Nancy, wasn't at the park or the mall that night, so I went up to her house. It turned out that this wasn't one of the smartest things I'd ever done. It was about midnight when I got there. She was barely eighteen, and lived with her folks in a large ranch style house about a mile up this back, country road. It was the only house on the road and there weren't any streetlights, so the only light was from the glow of the full moon. I parked my bike across the road and went up to the house. I snuck up to her window . . . I'd been there before . . . and tapped on it. She didn't hear me, so it tapped a little harder. When she still didn't answer, I picked up a rock and tapped so hard I thought I was going to break the glass. Just when I was about to give up, I saw her face in the window.

"Snake?"

"Yeah, Baby," I said, "open the window."

With a little effort, she managed to jerk it open. "This is crazy, Snake, coming here. If my father sees you, he'll kill you."

"Your old man knows about me?"

"One of my girlfriends told her mother I was dating a biker, and her mother told my mother, and she told my Dad. That's why I can't go to the park or hang at the mall anymore."

"Move over, Baby, I'm coming in." I climbed in through the window.

"But Snake," she started to protest.

I grabbed her up and started kissing her all over. She was wearing one of those flannel nightgowns; and she felt like a bagful of warm goodies. As I eased her toward the bed her lips were on mine, soft and tasty. I picked her up and deposited her on the bed. There was nothin' to her. After kicking off my boots, I worked on the large buckle of my black leather belt. My jeans went down around my knees and I was about to kick them off, when something went wrong with the bed and it came crashing down onto the floor. Now, at any other time this would have been funny, but not late at night with this girl's parents in the other room.

"Lena," I heard a booming voice shout. "What the hell was that?"

"I don't know, dear," I heard a woman's voice say. "I think it came from Nancy's room."

"Jesus!" Nancy shouted, a little louder than I would have liked. "Go, Snake! Go!"

Before the second "go" was out of her mouth, I was already at the window. I was at somewhat of a disadvantage, as my pants were still around my knees and I was holding my boots in my hand. I somehow managed to hobble across the lawn to the driveway. This was when the garage door flew open and her old man appeared holding a shotgun. He and the old lady were wrestling with it.

"John! Give me the gun!" she was shouting.

"Let go, Lena!" he shouted. "No God-damn biker is molesting my daughter and getting away with it!"

"Please, Daddy," Nancy was pleading, "don't shoot him. I love him!"

In my mind, I was thinking, *why, the hell, did she have to say that?*

I heard the gun go off, and as I turned, briefly, I could see that he had just blown the front window out of his brand new pickup. I knew that this wasn't going to make him any happier, so I threw my leg over my bike and came down hard on the kick-starter. Up until this time, I had managed to put on my pants, but only one boot. Unfortunately, it was the wrong boot. When my stocking foot hit the peg, I knew that I had broken my foot seconds before the pain, pulsing through my brain, confirmed it. For another $100 I could have opted for an electric starter, but a real biker wouldn't be caught dead with an electric starter; ironically, this biker was about to be caught dead without one.

They say that you never hear the one that gets you. They lie like hell. I saw the flash, I heard the blast, I felt myself being knocked off of my bike as if hit by some colossal fist. Then things got dark.

The next thing I remember, I was standing in this room. Well, I can't really say it was a room, as everything was white and I really don't remember seeing any walls. It was bright, I do remember that, and in front of me was this desk with a guy dressed in white seated behind it. I got the idea that he was tall, although he was sitting down. He was wearing what looked like a robe or toga of some kind. He had a white beard, long white hair, and looked to be about thirty, in spite of all the white hair. His pink cheeks and lips were about the only things in the room that weren't white . . . besides me.

"You must be Matthew Briggs," he said, not bothering to look up.

"Snake," I replied.

"What?"

"My friends call me, Snake," I said. I don't know why I said that. Who the hell was this jerk, anyway? He certainly wasn't one of my friends.

"Snake," he repeated. He looked up and softly stroked his white beard. "Isn't that term usually associated with a serpent?"

"Yeah, and your point is?" (This may not be exactly what I said then, but it sounds cooler to say that now)

"It's just that you don't look like a serpent. You look more like a young human. Besides, if you were, indeed, a serpent, you would have been sent to level five."

"Down with the dumb animals, huh?"

"Actually, in many ways, snakes are considered to be more intelligent than humans," he informed me. "Humans rank about eight points below tubeworms."

"Are you trying to tell me that humans are one of the most stupidest creatures on earth?

"I Believe," he continued, "that one of your most intelligent expressions is, "Stupid is, as stupid does. "When was the last time you saw a tubeworm doing anything stupid?"

"What makes you think that humans are so stupid?" I asked, angrily.

"Let me see," he said, looking down at the papers on his desk. "This young girl was living with her parents. You went to her home in the middle of the night. You ran from the house, half-dressed, and climbed onto an inferior contrivance. You eventually succumbed to injuries sustained from pellets emitted by an explosive device contained in a tube. Little analysis was needed to determine that the situation was eminent."

"Jesus!" you don't mean I'm . . . dead!" I suddenly felt very weak in the knees.

"If you are referring to the circumstances relating to the termination of your physical being, then I would have to say that you have ceased to exist physically. You conscience mind remains active for a few minutes longer and your sub-science for a bit longer, yet."

"Jesus!" I suddenly realized that it might not be a good idea to keep saying

'Jesus.' "Is this Heaven?"

"Heaven? Oh yes, that hypothetical place where all good people go after death." He began to chuckle.

"Then this must be Hell!"

"Rest assured, my friend, that you are neither in Heaven nor Hell. You are in *Substation X-4, Division of Human Understanding and Developmental Research.* Here is where we determine what went wrong with your life."

"What do you mean, 'what went wrong'?"

"You are only twenty. I realize that among various species of your planet, twenty may be considered a long life, but for a human it is a bit short. Don't you agree?"

"Yeah," I had to admit. "There are still a lot of places I wanted to see and things I wanted to do." I looked down at the boot I still had in my hand. "Is it all right if I put my other boot on?"

"Of course; and please," he motioned to a chair in front of his desk, "take a seat". He got to his feet and took my hand. "Processing might take a while; you might as well be comfortable. By the way, my name is Maximilian."

I shifted my boot to my left hand so I could shake his hand. I could see, now, that he was a big man, well over six-feet, with shoulders like a football player. His grip was firm and I got the impression that he could have crushed my hand, easily. I slid into the chair and finished putting on my other boot. "Processing? What do you mean?"

"Well," he said, "it is actually more of a debriefing. Looking over your records, this may take longer than I thought."

"My records?"

"Your accomplishments; actually, your lack of accomplishments. Not much here. You seem to have spent much of your time drinking, having sexual encounters, and doing something called 'biking'."

I was more than a little upset. "You don't know what a bike is?"

"I seem to recall a contrivance with two wheels, two petals and a chain."

"That's a bicycle. I'm talking about a scooter, a chopper, a hog, a friggin' motorcycle, man! Jesus, don't they teach ya anything, here?"

"Ah!" he said. "You mean like a Honda." He really looked proud of himself.

"Jesus!" I said, again. I wanted to bite my lip, because I was still sure that this was Heaven and I certainly didn't want to piss off the guy "upstairs" in the remote possibility that I still might have a chance to get in. I figured that this jerk was here to make me slip up. Well, it was working. "No self-respecting biker would be caught on a 'rice burner'. We all ride Harleys: Pan heads, Knuckleheads, and Shovelheads. Hogs! Choppers, man! How many Honda ringy-ding choppers have you ever seen?"

"What's a chopper?" he asked.

45

"What kind of angel are ya? Why a chopper is as close to Heaven as you're ever gonna get. Ya take a bike, ya put on an extended front-end, ya add a "T" bar, or a high-rise handlebar, some nice pipes, a custom tank, maybe, hard-tail it, add a fantastic paint-job, and ya got your own, personal ride. More than that; ya got a piece of art."

"I'm not an angel. I am merely a researcher, this is not Heaven, and you are not, technically, dead; at least not yet."

"Now I'm really confused. If I ain't dead, what am I doing here?"

He stroked his white beard and looked away. "Hum. How can I explain this? There are many layers involved, here. There is the aspect of your life. You have various choices you must make. There are crossroads in life, and at each crossroad you must decide which way you will go. When you were in grade school, the choices were few: should I do my homework, or should I not. You chose not to. When you dropped out of school, you had to choose whether you were going to get a good, steady job, or not. Again, you chose not to."

"What has this to do with whether I'm dead or not?" I asked.

"Well," he began, "look upon this as a kind of debriefing. We need to know what went wrong with your life. By determining this, we might be able to make some adjustments to keep it from happening again. Do you understand?"

"No."

"Let's say, for argument sake, that you are a piece of machinery that keeps breaking down because of a defective computer chip which causes the machine to do things that constantly create short circuits in the system. What do you think we should do to correct the problem?"

"Replace the chip?"

"Precisely."

It felt good to know, for once in my life, I actually got the right answer. My feeling of elatedness was short lived; however, when it dawned on me that my life had ended when that shotgun went off.

"Yeah, well that's all well and good," I said, "but I'm not a machine and you can't just replace a chip."

"Au contraire, my friend. Although, most of the time, we find it inappropriate to interpose our will in situations of natural course, we do reserve certain expedients for the purpose of emendating things that we adjudge to be a bit malapropos even for a ne'er-do-well, such as you."

"I don't know what language you're speakin', Max," I informed him, "but it wasn't nothing that I understand."

"I am so sorry. Sometimes I have trouble articulating . . . communicating my thoughts. What I meant to say was that sometimes we do intervene, if the outcome of a certain violent act might not be justified by the circumstances of the event. In this case, a young man dies because of a stupid decision, and a husband and a father of two could spend the rest of his life in prison for his one moment of irrationality. Now do you understand?"

"Sorta. You mean that you can wave some magic wand and bring me back to life?"

"No. It doesn't work that way. We do, however, have certain 'guardians' in place, who have the essential skills to correct the situation. In your case, there is a certain surgeon with great skills."

I put my hands behind my neck and leaned back in the chair. "Great! Send me back."

"It's not that easy. First we must determine that you both don't deserve to be permanently removed from society. How do we know if, because of your reckless nature, you won't cause injury or death to someone down the road? As for the father . . . ," he fumbled around in the files on his desk and pulled up a wad of papers, ". . . George Gregory; how do we know that he isn't a psychopathic killer?"

"Hey, that guy, George, he was pretty pissed. He just blew the windshield out of his pickup and the way he and the old lady were wrestling with the gun, who's ta say it wasn't an accident? He might of just wanted ta scare me, and the gun was just pointed in the wrong direction. Besides, I can hardly blame the guy, after all, I was tryin' ta do his daughter in her own bedroom. If it were me, I might have done the same thing."

Maximilian was making notes. "Quite admirable," he said, "forgiving someone who blasted you at close range with buckshot. How astute to be able to see another's point of view, especially, in doing so, it puts you in a bad light. It proves that you do have cunning and intelligence that you have heretofore failed to display."

At this point I got to my feet. "Hey! I don't suck up to nobody!" I shouted. "I'd rather be dead than kiss anybody's friggin' ass!"

"Ah, now the pendulum swings the other way, from one moment of rationalism to a bout of irrational anger. You are willing to throw your life and future away for the sake of pride. What about your children and your grandchildren?"

"What are you talking about? I'm not even married. I don't have any kids, at least not that I know of."

"I'm talking about your future. How long do you think this fascination with motorcycles is going to last? Someday you will grow tired of them and go on with your life."

"You're wrong, Max. Bikes are my life. I can't imagine a life without them. I would rather be dead."

Maximilian ran his hand through his long, white hair. "Interesting," he said, "explain this fascination to me. Make me feel the passion that you feel for this life of motorcycles."

"How can I?" I asked. "It's something you have to experience. There's that feeling you get when you're straddling a big machine, your feet setting on the highway pegs, your old lady sitting behind you, her arms around you, and her breasts pressed hard against your back. You're in a pack, two abreast, and the combined sounds of each engine creates a rumbling that is more music than all of the symphonies and rock-n-roll combined. The wind is in your hair, the sun is reflecting off the chrome, and the vibrations are feeding back through the handlebars and coursing through your whole body. There is that feeling of power you get every time you twist the throttle, and that overwhelming sense of freedom. As you pass by the citizens, you see them looking back, admiring your bike, and secretly wishing that they where you. Tell me; is there anything in Heaven better than that?"

Maximilian had stopped writing. The, now, pink glow of his face was dramatically outlined by the whiteness of his hair. He sat back in his chair, his hands across his stomach, looking much like a man who had just finished the last crumb of pumpkin pie at the end of a large Thanksgiving dinner. I could almost see him rolling my words over in his head, digesting each phrase with succulent relish. He got to his feet, leaned over the desk and reached out his hand.

"Goodbye, Matth . . ." He stopped, "I mean, goodbye Snake."

I never got to shake his hand. I awoke in a strange bed. Molly was seated in a chair beside me, her head tilted sideways in deep sleep.

"Hello!" I yelled, "Where the hell am I?"

Molly jumped from the chair and threw herself onto me, "You're awake!" she shouted, as if I didn't know.

"Ouch!" I cried, "You're hurting my side."

"I'm sorry, Hon, but you've been out of it for three days. Some specialist came in from Cincinnati. Everyone thought you were a goner, but he pulled you through. Nobody knows who hired him . . . some anonymous benefactor. Maybe it was the Gregory's. I mean, if you died, he was looking at some serious shit. Everybody's been here, including that little bitch that got you shot in the first place. I put her in her place. I told her that if she ever came near you again I would cut her up so bad, there'd be no one who'd look at her."

"Shut up," I said, "you talk too much. You know I never loved anybody but you."

Tears were running from her eyes and soaking my hospital gown. "You . . . never . . . said . . . you . . . loved . . . me," she said between sobs, "before!"

"Well, I'm telling you now." I said it and I meant it. No one was more surprised than I was.

The guys went and picked up my bike. Old George even lent them some ramps and helped them load it. They told me that he said that he was sorry about the whole mess and wished me a quick recovery. He still had some charges to face; something about disturbing the peace and discharging a firearm in a residential area, but when I told the cops that it was all an unfortunate accident, the judge let him out on his own recognizance.

The tank was in bad shape, having caught the blunt of the shot. Ski took the bike to his place and replaced the tank for me. He did one of his famous costume paint jobs. The guys started calling me "Fearless Fostic" after the cop in some old comic strip who keeps getting shot full of holes, but it doesn't seem to bother him, much.

I ended up at Molly's apartment because she felt that Ski's place was too much of a "germ haven" to be a good place for me to recover. Even though she had to work, she set it up so I didn't have to be alone for any length of time. One of her friends or one of the club members would always be there if I needed something. Brenda Grat, who had a face that could curdle milk, was one of her friends who came a lot. I never saw Mary Jane Bomgard, or Pamela Josski, though. I did both of them at one time or another, and I think Molly knew it.

Not that I would have been interested in rolling around in the sack with either one of them, even if I could. As it was, I was in pretty good pain, and it was nearly three months before I was really up and about. I mean there were painful pilgrimages to the bathroom, scuffing along in bedroom slippers, like an old man, wrapped in Molly's pink bathrobe, looking quite undignified, I'm sure. Somehow, I didn't care. I was just glad to be alive.

I finally made it over to Ski's and got a look at my bike. I rode over in Molly's VW bug. Ski had put a new muffler on it the year before and it sounded a lot like a bike. Ski had also taken good care of my bike. The chrome was polished and the tank looked great. It was purple, but changed colors as the sun hit it from different directions. It had a red flame-job that was pinstriped in gold. On the side cover was a picture of Fearless Fostic shooting it out with several bad guys, one of them was wearing a ski mask and holding a shotgun.

Being back on my bike was like being reunited with an old friend. I was still a little sore, so Ski kicked it over for me. It fired on the second kick. Molly snuggled in behind me and grabbed both sides of my belt. Ski wheeled his bike out of the house and down the ramp. The roar of his pipes added to mine as we pulled out onto the street. It felt a little awkward, at first, but by the time we got to the light on the second block it was as if I had never been off of the bike.

When we pulled up at the Chain Drive Bar there were already ten or twelve bikes there. The *Road Devils* met there every Friday night. There was no set time, and we had no real meeting like the kind where you take dues or keep minutes. We were just a bunch of guys with the same interests. Sure, we got rowdy sometimes, but never out of hand. Bill, who owned the Chain Drive Bar, was an old biker himself. He had a boss Harley that he kept in a room behind the bar.

This night I was in for a surprise. It seems that while I was gone, we got a new member. The guy was from Chicago; he had long, white hair and a scraggly white beard and looked a lot like the guy in my dream. I never believed that my encounter with Maximilian was anything more than that, but here he was, sitting at the long table, sipping suds with my buddies.

He got to his feet as we walked toward the table. "Hi," he said, extending his hand to me. "We've never met," he said, but I swore I saw him wink, "my name is Max. I heard you almost bought the farm. Glad to see that you're doing better. Let me buy you a beer. Hell, I'll buy everyone a beer. This is cause to celebrate."

The guys got to their feet and started to sing, "For He's a Jolly Good Fellow" only they substituted the word "biker" for "fellow", and "fuckin'" for jolly, and everybody started laughing. Max told me that he was opening a bike shop. He asked if I needed a job. He told me that Ski had already contracted to do all of his custom painting.

"I'm going to have my own line of custom choppers. We build our own frames, our own tanks, and we do our own custom paint jobs. What do you think; are you interested?"

"What do I do?" I asked.

"Why you will run the place," he said. "You'll answer the phone, run the showroom, order the parts, and dazzle the customers."

"How do you know I can do all of that?"

"I don't. But, hey man, you're Fearless Fostic, the man that can't be killed. You're more of a celebrity in the bike world than you realize. Hell, we've heard about you in Chicago. They will come in droves just to see if you are real. What do you say? Want the job?"

"Sure," I said, although I don't know why. The last thing on my mind was looking for a job.

Ski leaned over, "You've got ta see Max's bike, man. It's the nicest bike I've ever seen,"

We all went out back to see Max's bike. I guess the other guys just wanted to see the look on my face. They weren't disappointed. It was the nicest bike I had ever seen. First, there was no chrome. I swear that most of the metal on the bike was plated with real gold; except for the tank, that is. This was done in a kind of satiny material that wasn't really fabric. The seats were made out of some kind of exotic leather and the taillight looked like one gigantic ruby. The sissy bar was two-feet high, and on top was a large "M" studded with diamonds and emeralds. The exhaust system wasn't gold, either; it looked more like platinum. He claimed that it was all imitation, but somehow I didn't believe him. When he started the engine my heart almost stopped. If an engine can play music, this one was producing a serenade.

That was twenty-five years ago. The bike shop is doing great. I have two of the best partners in the world. Yeah, that's right; we're all partners, now. Ski is married, has two kids in college and has put on about sixty pounds. Molly and I got married. We have five great kids. I'm losing my hair, but you know what? I don't give a shit. Max hasn't changed much at all; maybe a little heavier. He still puts together some of the most amazing bikes I've ever seen, and he does it without putting pen to paper. He says the plans are in his head.

Every year, for one week, we shut the business down, wheel out our bikes, and head out onto the open road. I know that, Lora, Ski's wife, is not all that enthused about going on these excursions, but I think that if Ski wanted to jump out of an airplane, she would put on a parachute and jump.

On the trip we took a few years ago, we had stopped at this little diner and were enjoying our burgers, fries and beer, when Max said something that hit me harder than that load of buckshot. We were fooling around and I said something really stupid to Molly. It was something hurtful, and right after it came out of my mouth, I knew I should have never said it. She got that hurt look on her face and stormed out of the place. Lora went after her.

No one said anything for a couple of minutes, and then Max leaned over the table and said, "You know, Snake, you still don't have the sense of a tubeworm." I apologized to Molly and things smoothed over, but I never forgot what Max said.

The first chance I got to be alone with him, I confronted him about it. At first, he tried to make like he didn't know what I was talking about, but he finally admitted that what I had always thought was a dream was our first, real, encounter.

It seems that after our little talk, he did some research on bikes. He looked up plans and built his own bike, from scratch. Precious gems and metals being quite common where he came from, he used a lot of gold, platinum, and gems in his design. When he started to ride it, he said that he experienced all of the things that we had talked about: the feeling of power, of oneness, and especially, the feeling of freedom.

It was then that he decided that he wanted to be a biker more than he wanted to be an examiner. It was simple. He put in for his transfer, looked me up, and joined my club. He said that he never regretted his decision for one moment. The only thing he really had to give up was his immortality. It seems that where he was from was embedded somewhere in the fabric of time. When I was there, I was caught somewhere between life and death. My interview took place between heartbeats. In essence, he was interviewing a dying man and only his intervention saved my life.

By coming here, he became subject to new rules, and time suddenly became relevant. Once he removed himself from his environment, he became subject to mine. Where he was he was immortal, but here he was just another man.

Max pulled a clean rag from his pocket and wiped a bit of smudge from the chrome pipes of his latest creation. He pulled himself to his feet and stepped back to admire this latest marvel. A smile came to his lips and he placed his arm around my shoulder.

"You know, Snake," he said, "this is a life worth dying for."

"Yeah," I said, poking him gently in the ribs, "what did I tell ya?"

LORD TO THE RUTS

I remember sitting behind the wheel of my father's old, dark green Plymouth and pretending that I was driving, because, at nine, I knew that driving a car had to be the most wonderful thing that anyone could ever hope to do. In the middle of the steering wheel was a plastic emblem with an old sailing ship and something that looked like a rock. I knew that it was a rock because of Thanksgiving Day and the story of the Pilgrims landing at Plymouth Rock, which was probably where the car was made, and more than likely, by Pilgrims.

One Saturday we piled into the old Plymouth, my mother, my father, my sister and I, along with a picnic cooler containing a large casserole bowl and a green, two gallon, metal Thermos jug full of Kool-Aid . . . strawberry, or raspberry . . . it didn't really matter, as all tasted pretty much the same. We headed north to Morehouseville, New York, a little town nestled among the Adirondacks Mountains.

I sat in the back with my sister, not really wanting to be a part of this long ride north. My sister, who sat as far to the right as I was to the left on the long mohair seat, was looking forward to seeing our grandmother again. At the time, our only relationship was that we were related, which was hard to tell by looking at us. She was tall and thin, with long blond hair and a thin face. I was short, chunky, and a dark, chestnut color, from spending every possible moment out of doors.

Most of my time was spent with my friend Billy, along Limestone Creek, swimming, wading, fishing, and catching things in tin cans, such as small fish, crayfishes, and an occasional frog or two. I longed to be there today as I felt that the days of summer vacation were growing shorter. Soon school would start again, the leaves would begin to fall, and winter would, again, be upon us. I hated winter nearly as much as I hated school. Why couldn't I be like Tarzan, who lived in the deep jungle, talked to the animals, and only had to do something when some foolish explorers or some evildoers came into his domain? Even then, he would save the day in a short time, and Jane, Boy, Cheetah, and he would return to the tree house, and settle back into their life of leisure. Oh, how I wished I could be Boy, or even Cheetah, for that matter.

I stared out the window as the familiar landscape drifted by. We had been this way many times before. Why do grandmothers have to live so far away? I tried counting power poles, but lost tract somewhere around 500. They kept switching from one side of the road to the other and when we passed through a town it got even more confusing, with power poles, light poles, and telephone poles all combining into one big, mega wiring nightmare. I, then, started counting green cars, as our car was green, but even here there was a problem. There were light green cars and dark green cars, and some of the dark cars were so dark that they might even be considered black. Decisions had to be made quickly, as many would pass by in a flash; do you consider parked cars and those in garages?

There were a few diversions. There was that old Army tank in a kind of park, with a chain fence around it. Of course, there were the Burma Shave signs. My favorite was: "DINA DOESN'T—TREAT HIM—RIGHT—BUT IF—HE'D SHAVE—DINAMITE!" Then, for a real diversion there was the old, log bridge we had to cross over West Canada Creek. It was a long way down and there were big rocks in the creek and fast moving water. I used to close my eyes as we crossed, because keeping them open was too frightening. I could hear the logs moving under the wheels, but it wasn't anything I wanted to see.

Of course, my sister would make a big deal of it, because I had my face turned to the window so she couldn't see if I had my eyes closed or not. There would be much pushing and hitting and name calling, until my mother turned around or my father said, "Knock it off!" My sister and I would talk very little, because it only led to fighting. Occasionally, she might offer me a cracker, orange or apple. There was always something to eat on these long trips, because my sister and I both suffered from carsickness, the one thing we had in common.

After the bridge, the road ran through thick woods. It had only been finished the year before. Before that it was nothing but a macadam road that was often rough and full of deep mud holes. Power lines had been strung as the road was being built and my grandmother had power to her house, for the first time.

I say she had power, but it hadn't been connected to her house, yet, because there was nothing to connect it to. There were no outlets or wiring in the house. That would have to be done first. Grandma wasn't all too sure that she wanted it. After all, she had lived without electricity most of her life.

I didn't know how old grandma was, but she was wrinkly, had a pointy chin, and her mouth puckered inward, because she had no teeth. What always amazed me was the fact that she could eat steak and crunch potato chips as well as I could. She was also hunched over like she was just getting ready to pick something up. She must have been very old, indeed, maybe over fifty.

When we got to grandma's house, there were many cars parked in front and we had to park on the road. I don't recall there being a lot of kids. There must have been, but perhaps none my age. You see, there were too many years between my sister and I, so I knew that I was an *oops* baby. I never saw it as Planned Parenthood. Anyway, since must families have their kids in quick succession, I can see where most kids would have been more my sister's age, and no teenagers were going to play with a "maggot".

I contented myself with exploring the grounds around my grandmother's house; what there was of it. She had an old milk cow that was lazily grazing in a small enclosure, although it didn't look like there was much to graze on. There was a pigpen, but no pig, and an outhouse that must have been one hundred feet from the house. I opened the wooden door and the rusty hinges let out a grown of protest. It smelled funny inside and there was a large spider living in a web in the corner. There were two holes with wooden lids. One was larger than the other. I lifted the larger lid and looked inside. There was a wasp nest attached to the side and sunlight streamed in through the cracks in the boards. There was a deep hole in the center and the whole thing looked like it could be lifted up and moved to a different place. I was glad I did my number two before I left home. There is no way I could sit there with those wasps buzzing around below. I went outside, found a rock, threw it at the nest, and ran.

On the other side there was a small shed with a mangy looking horse peering out of the top part of a double door. I walked over and cautiously patted it on the head. It was swaybacked, tired looking, and had huge feet. It seemed to pay little attention to me, and was busy swatting at a large number of big flies with its tattered, encrusted tail. He turned around to get something to eat and I walked back toward the house.

The house was small, two stories, and looked taller than it was wide. The roof was steep, the kind that no one could possibly stand up on. A tall, narrow chimney jutted out of its peak. The back, where I was now, had a large, screened-in porch. Next to that, at a lower level, was a woodshed. The stairs were steep and had no landing. I had to climb the stairs, open the screen door and step back down, in order to swing the door open. There was one door that opened up into the kitchen from the porch.

Most of the grownups were seated around a long table, drinking coffee and talking. The kitchen was narrow, but it was as long as the house was wide, with a huge wood burning stove taking up a huge share of the cooking area. There was a wet sink and a hand pump set into the counter itself. A white pail set next to it with a ladle for drinking, I supposed, and priming the pump. I knew of such things because we had a well with a hand pump in the back yard at home. On hot summer days I would prime it and pump it for a while to get at the cold, crisp water.

"Stick around;" I heard my mother say, "we'll be leaving soon. Did you go to the bathroom? There won't be any place to go where we are going."

"Yes," I lied, afraid she might make me go back to that bug-infested, smelly outhouse.

Shortly, everyone filed out to the front of the house and piled into the automobiles. It seemed that everyone had a new car except my father and; although, my father thought grandma might want to ride with us, the rest insisted that she might be more comfortable riding in one of the newer cars. I know that my father must have been terribly embarrassed and ashamed, because I was.

The drive didn't last long as the lead car pulled off of the paved road and onto a dirt road. The road was rough and my dad's old car bounced around like the proverbial lumber wagon while the newer cars swayed and floated like they were strung on innerspring mattresses. The wheel was jerking in Dad's hand, as the narrow tires caught every rut and hole, and we were falling behind. My embarrassment turned to disappointment. I felt the same as I did when I was a kid, and we played "Farmer in the Dell" at school, when I ended up being the cheese; only I felt it for my dad as much as I did myself. After all, it was a matter of family pride.

The cars slowed as the lead car pulled onto what looked like a wagon trail. It pulled over and stopped and one of my uncles got out. The rest of the cars pulled over and everyone got out to see what the problem was.

"It's that bridge," my uncle was saying. "It doesn't look strong enough to hold the weight of a car."

My father walked down to a small wooden bridge that was built over a narrow stream. "It looks strong enough to me," he said.

It was decided that my father would be the first to cross the bridge. I don't know if it was because his car was old and it wouldn't be much of a loss if it did go through, or because it had those tall, thin tires they figured he could make it back across by driving through the stream. Whatever the reason, everyone pulled out of the way so my father could drive his car across the bridge. He had us get out and drove the car over alone. He stopped in the middle to show that the bridge was, indeed, strong enough. However, the road was nothing more than two wheel ruts, and when the first car crossed the bridge it didn't take long before it bottomed out. A bunch of guys had to push it to get it unstuck. The road only got worse from there. There were large rocks, deep mud holes, and a high dirt ridge in the middle that was higher than the bumpers on the newer cars.

It was decided to leave the newer cars behind and use my father's car to haul the food and stuff down the road to the lake, for the picnic. My grandmother was put in my father's car along with the food and people stood on the running boards while the old car putted down the rutted old road with plenty of clearance. My father even made another trip to bring down the folding tables and the lawn chairs.

Tables were arranged together and table cloths were laid over them and weighted down with rocks to keep the wind from blowing them off. Hotdogs and hamburgers were thrown on grilles and covered dishes were stacked on the table from one end to the other. One paper plate was sacrificed so that a rock could be used to hold the rest in place.

My mother had brought one covered dish. It was her specialty . . . potato salad. There must have been gazillion other bowls of salad on that table, but my mother's was the only bowl that was empty when we left.

The water was cold and the beach was too rocky for swimming. When the bugs started biting, I'm sure most people thought that this was not a very good picnic. To me, it was one of the most memorable days of my young life. Grandma rode back out in our car and when she was asked if she would rather ride back in one of the newer cars, she said that she was already in this one and could see no reason to switch cars, now.

"I'm perfectly comfortable in Rollie's car, riding back here with these two lovely children."

And we were, too; two lovely, well-behaved, children . . . at least until the ride home.

A Letter To Melinda

A steady rain still battered relentlessly against my study window. The shutters rattled and clattered as if shaken by some unseen hand. I found the weather to be most annoying, as the evening storm had caught me in hasty preparation of a most important legal case. The hour had grown late, and my desk lay strewn with manuscripts and legal papers. I pondered over volumes of law with lengthy passages that had long become so much meaningless prattle. I tried going over them again and again, but my ability to concentrate was waning rapidly. A knock at the door was as much a reprieve as a puzzle. *Who would be out in this weather, at this time of night?*

I left my study and stepped out into the dismal hallway. I had been so engrossed in my endeavor to complete my brief, I had failed to light the lamps. Through the opaque glass of the front door I could see the large, dark silhouette of a man. I was much relieved to find my dear friend Dr. Paul Sheldon standing upon my stoop. His hat and cape were drenched with rain, giving evidence to the fact that he had spent much time walking in this awful torrent.

"Come in," I said, closing the door against the wind and rain, "you look soaked to the skin."

"I hope I'm not disturbing you," he said, apologetically.

"Of course not," I lied, taking his coat and hat. They were heavily soaked with rain and immediately began dripping puddles of water onto the floor beneath the hall tree. "I always have time for an old friend."

He smiled, but somehow it looked out of place. I knew something was wrong, something serious. I put my arm around his shoulder. His suit jacket was damp as well.

"Come into my study where we may sit by the fire," I said. "You look like you could use a drink. I have just acquired a most excellent burgundy wine. It's a sassy Beaujolais one of my clients brought back from a recent trip to France. I think you'll enjoy it."

He followed me silently, like some shipwrecked sailor void of hope for rescue. I cleared some legal volumes from the chair nearest the fire, and offered it to him. He settled into the chair, his eyes were solemn and sunken, his mouth drawn and tense. I filled a glass with wine and offered it to him. He gulped it down hungrily. He stared at the contents as he turned the glass nervously in his hand. Not wanting to be the one to break the silence, I sat across from him and said nothing.

"I have come here, Warren," he began, his voice low and broken as if he were choking on every word, "because I need to talk to someone or I shall go completely mad." He downed the rest of the wine, then setting the glass a table near the chair, he clamped his head in his hands and began to cry.

"My God man, what is it?" I asked, immediately coming to his side.

"I'm sorry," he said, now wiping his eyes with his wet handkerchief, "I thought I was all cried out. I'm sorry I'm making such a fool of myself. Please give me a minute; I'll be all right."

Silently, I retrieved his glass, this time refreshing it with a little brandy. I offered it to him and he smiled and shook his head.

"Thank you," he said, lying back in the chair. He sipped the brandy slowly. "I suppose I'd better start at the beginning." He paused, as he brushed the damp hair from his forehead. "Twenty-five years ago, while I was a student in medical school, I met a young girl. Melinda was very beautiful, wild and so full of energy. I quickly got caught up in her world of dancing, partying, and drinking. I was young and impetuous. I was easily won over by her childlike charm and fell head over heels in love with her. This was before I knew you, and before I ever met Lydia . . . my dear sweet Lydia."

He paused to wipe a tear from his eye, and then, choking back a sob, he continued. "I married her over the protests of my parents who felt she was only after my money. I told them they were wrong; we were in love. What a fool I was. It was only a brief interlude. It didn't take me long to find out what kind of a girl she really was. She had an insatiable appetite for men. I went to a lawyer I knew at the time and got an annulment. It posed no problem. My parents offered her money. That was all she ever wanted from me, as she was incapable of loving anyone. I was so young and foolish, and so bound to have my way. I was fortunate that my parents were able to forgive what I had done so I was able to finish medical school and get on with my life."

He took a sip of his brandy. Pausing, he closed his eyes tightly and seemed to be looking deep into his own soul. It was as if I weren't even there. Suddenly he looked up at me as if he were seeing me for the first time.

"I met Lydia three years later," he continued. "She was so wonderful. So full of the qualities that I do so admire in a woman. She was talented, witty, charming, and full of such energy; it was all I could do to keep pace. Here was a woman, so giving and unselfish, how could I have ever thought I loved Melinda. Lydia and I were married the next year. Life could not have been better. My parents adored her."

"No one ever mentioned the fact that I had been married. It was as if it had never happened. I never wanted Lydia to know that she wasn't the first. I wanted her to believe that she was the only one that I had ever loved."

"About two years after Lydia and I were married, Melinda confronted me on the street. She looked old and her beauty had tarnished, but I still recognized her. She told me that she wanted to talk. I told her that we had nothing to talk about, and I started to go on my way. She grabbed my arm and said that she knew about my marriage, and about my wife's family and their reputation. She said that if I didn't listen to what she had to say I would be very sorry. We went to a small café on the other side of town, sat in a dark corner, and talked. She told me that she wanted money. She said that she wanted to be a lady and a fit mother to her small child. She said that she had talked to a lawyer who had told her that the annulment was not legal. She said that there were discrepancies, including the fact that she had been forced to sign it under duress. This is stupid. There had been no duress!"

"Why didn't you bring the document to me?" I ask. "You know that I am an expert on such matters."

"I didn't want my friends to know, not even you. I didn't want to take a chance that this would get back to Lydia. Besides, she agreed to a small allowance. 'Just enough,' she said, 'to get a better place to live, and to get off the street.' She said that her son was getting older, and she didn't want him to know that his mother was a nothing more than a common whore. I did feel some sympathy for her; even though

I never believed that the child, if he really existed, was in any way my responsibility."

"She would lie about a thing like that?" I asked.

"To get what she wanted," he informed me, "I believe she would. I, however, went along with her little blackmail scheme, thinking that it would only be temporary. Eventually, I would tell Lydia the truth, explain the circumstances, bring the documents to you, and you would tell me that all was in order. This would be, as they say, so much water under the bridge. The problem was I could never bring the subject up. I would always lose my nerve at the last moment."

He took another long drink of his brandy. I filled his glass.

"Thank you," he said. He picked up the glass, but only stared at it. "I just couldn't take a chance of losing Lydia."

"How much money did you give her?"

"Like I said, it was just a small allowance at first, but as the years went by, she demanded more and more money. It became increasingly harder to hide these growing sums of money from Lydia. At first, she believed me when I told her the money was for equipment and instruments for my laboratory, but with time I knew that she was becoming suspicious. She must have thought the worst of me, perhaps that I was even spending the money on other women. When I confronted Melinda with my wife's suspicions, she only laughed and told me that it was my problem, not hers. I then told her that I wouldn't pay anymore. I told her that I would go to the police. She only laughed, again. She knew that I wouldn't do that. I could see only one solution to my problem . . . I had to get rid of Melinda."

"You mean you meant to send her away?" I asked, afraid of what the answer might be.

"No, Warren. Quite frankly, I planned on murdering her. The problem was I didn't know just how to go about it. I am a surgeon. I suppose I could have taken a scalpel and slashed her throat. But then, there is always that fear of being caught. No. It had to be something much more devious and far less messy."

Again, he took a deep swallow of brandy. "The answer came quite by accident. In fact, at first, I didn't even recognize it as such. I was working in my laboratory, late one evening, when I discovered that one of my cultures had become contaminated. I didn't know how; perhaps I had been careless. I had been somewhat distraught, and my mind hadn't been entirely on my work. Lydia and I had had words that morning and tension had been building between us. I had taken to working later in my laboratory in order not to vent my frustrations on Lydia."

"I checked the bacillus under my microscope, and found it to be of singular form, of a kind that I had never seen before. Curious, I decided to test it further. I injected it into several laboratory rats. After four days, all of the rats died, apparently of heart failure. I found, after examining the rats that the bacillus had found its way into the muscle of the heart, and by robbing the muscle of its supply of oxygen, it had eventually caused the heart to fail. After further experimentation, I discovered that the bacillus could just as easily be transmitted through the lungs."

As he talked, a dark shadow seemed to form across his face. "At first, I was elated to think that I had discovered a new strand of bacillus," Paul continued. "I was willing to give it to the world as 'Incurcus cor morbus Shelden', but the more I thought about it, the more I realized that it could be the answer to all my problems. I knew that I had to test it on a human. I also knew where to find such a specimen."

"The bowels of the city are teeming with the vermin of mankind; the worthless refuse retched forth in boundless numbers on the fringe of society. All that was required was a few kind words, a bottle of whiskey, and the promise of some forthcoming riches. I had no trouble finding such a specimen."

"I put him up in a sleazy hotel, and gave him plenty of whiskey. I made sure that no one got a good look at me. I went back to my laboratory and prepared a dosage. When I got back to the room he was passed out on the bed. I merely had to pass the sample in front of his nose, a minuscule amount. I had to know its puissance. This was of the utmost importance. I was hoping that a small dosage would be sufficient. I was not disappointed. After a few days the man died. The papers listed the cause of death as heart failure. I believe his name was Fred."

"You had no remorse?" I asked.

"At the time, no, for my purpose had become so singular that the end justified the means."

"And now?" I asked.

He put his head down, as tears started running from his eyes. "Now, my heart could feel no greater remorse."

He handed me his empty glass, and I poured him yet another brandy.

"I had the means," he continued. "All that I required now was the vehicle. Actual contact with Melinda was out of the question. I needed a way to administer it remotely, in such a way as to not have any association with her at all. I came up with a simple solution. I would send her a letter. At first I thought of an advertisement, but then I thought that she might just throw something like that away. She would have to read it, to hold it close to her face. I had noticed, on our second meeting, that she was myopic. She had to hold the money close up in order to count it. Yes, it had to be a letter. A letter from an admirer; something she would want to read . . . a secret lover."

"I wrote the letter; passionate and sincere. I made believe I was writing it to my beloved Lydia. The words came easily. I signed it, 'Your secret admirer'. I knew that she was vain enough to believe that a woman, like herself, could have a secret admirer."

"How did you ever seal the bacillus into the envelope?" I inquired.

"Ah. I didn't. I added a very small amount of culture material to the bottom of the letter. I folded the letter very carefully and placed it in the envelope. Melting some sealing wax, I sealed all the seams. Finally, I injected a tiny amount of bacillus into the medium and sealed the hole."

"Weren't you worried that the seal might be broken before it was delivered?" I asked.

"I had thought of that, too. What I did was cancel the stamp myself. I copied the cancellation from one of my own correspondences. My intention was to hand deliver the letter myself, in the cover of darkness. I addressed the letter and placed it in the top drawer of my desk, in my study at home. After supper, that evening, I went to get the letter. It was gone."

"My God!" I shouted. "You don't mean?"

"Yes," he interrupted, "My beautiful, sweet, Lydia. She had been looking for a pen and had found my letter addressed to another woman. I found her crying in the bedroom, the letter still in her hand. It was no use trying to explain it to her. She wouldn't listen to anything I had

65

to say. She died four days later, despite all I could do. She died hating me!"

"My God, Paul! What have you done?"

"He looked down at his hands. "What I have done I cannot undo. My only wish now is that you will understand, and forgive me for being so foolish. You must also promise that no one will ever know what I have done."

"It will never come from my lips," I promised. "What are you going to do, now?"

"I must go home and await my final call. It has been two days, and already I can feel my heart growing weaker."

He rose to his feet, and I clamped him to my breast. "Farewell dear friend," I said, "but what about Melinda?"

He looked at me with a funny look in his eyes. "I have left her a package of a large sum of money, five hundred dollars. It will take her awhile to count it all." A faint smile came to his lips. "Perhaps it will take the rest of her life."

BENNIE

It all started out as a 4-H project. I got Bennie from a farmer down the road when I was about thirteen. He was the runt of the litter, and the farmer didn't have the time to give Bennie the special attention he really needed, so he sold him to me for ten dollars. I don't know exactly what kind of pig he was. The farmer explained to me about cross breeding boars and sows, and sows and boars, and how many times they had done this, but I just listened politely and pretended that I understood what he was saying. All I know is that Bennie was some kind of special pig, the kind they breed mostly for bacon.

Of course, I never had any intention of ever turning Bennie into bacon. He was, first, my 4-H project, and then my friend. I never had a dog, so Bennie quickly filled that void with the kind of companionship usually associated with the former. When he was a piglet, my mom let me keep him in a box on the back porch, but at night I used to sneak him up to my room. He would sleep at the foot of my bed.

When Bennie got bigger; however, my mom said that he had to go. My dad made a sty out behind the old garage, with a tin-roofed shelter where Bennie could go to get out of the weather. He didn't much like it, at first, and let us know about it with his constant caterwauling. But after a few days he settled in and things got back to some kind of normalcy.

As Bennie got bigger, feeding him became somewhat of a problem. I mowed lawns for extra money, in the summer, and in the winter I shoveled snow. There were other expenses too: vet bills, shots, dietary supplements, and worm medicine, just to mention a few. The bigger he got, the bigger my problems got. My dad wouldn't help me out. He said that Bennie was my problem and I had to learn responsibility. If things got too hard for me, he told me, I could always sell him to the butcher. I would never do that.

I guess all the real trouble started when Bennie got loose while I was at school. My mom and dad both worked. Mom worked days and Dad worked nights, so there was usually no one home when I got home. When my dad got up that day, he found Bennie in the vegetable garden. He had managed to rut up half of the garden, eating most of the carrots, all of the beets, and half of the potatoes. My dad went after him with a 2X4 and drove him back into his pen.

He shouldn't have done that. After all, Benny didn't know that he was doing anything wrong. He was just doing what pigs do, rutting for roots and stuff. Bennie didn't much like Dad after that. I could tell by the way he acted when my dad was around.

It was about two weeks later. I came home from school to find my dad's car in the driveway. My dad was nowhere in the house. I went out to the garage to see if he were there, and as I walked pass the pigpen I saw it. There was this huge amount of blood on the ground inside the pen with my Dad's shoes and clothes right in the middle of it. Bennie was lying next to his shelter; there was blood on his face.

"Bennie!" I shouted. "What have you done?"

` I already knew. When Mom got home, in about half an hour, there would be hell to pay. I knew that there was no longer anything that I could do for my dad, but there was something I could do to help Bennie. After all, I didn't want to lose Bennie as well as my dad.

I went into the garage and got a shovel to cover up the blood. Then I dug a hole and buried my dad's shoes and clothes in the section of the garden that Bennie had dug up. My next problem was how to get rid of the car. I had never driven a car before, but I had watched Dad do it. He had promised me he would take me down to get my permit and take me driving when I turned sixteen, but he never seemed to have the time. How difficult could it be? After all, girls do it.

I slid in behind the wheel. My dad was a big man. The seat was too far back and I could barely see over the dashboard. I fumbled around for the seat control. I had seem my mom adjust the seat every time she took Dad's car to go somewhere. It was just under the front of the seat, somewhere. I finally found it, but it took a lot of effort before the seat came slamming forward with a thud. I took a deep breath and looked at my watch. Mom would be home in twelve minutes.

I turned the key and the engine started. I looked out over the hood and it suddenly looked huge! I put the lever in reverse and pushed down on the accelerator. The car shot backward with such force it sent me into the dashboard. I slammed my foot on the brake and sat there for a moment with my heart trying to beat its way out of my chest.

Somehow, I managed to ease the car out of the driveway and onto the road. As I put the car in drive and eased it forward, a car came around the curve in the road, and since I was more on his side of the road than mine, his horn was blaring. I hit the gas, and before I knew it I was doing sixty. I took my foot off of the gas and hit the brake to slow down. I slowly began to feel comfortable at about thirty.

About a mile up the road was an old, abandoned quarry. I eased the car down the old, dirt road that led to it. It proved to be a bumpy ride. The quarry was half full of water so I just jumped out of the car and let it drive itself over the edge. There was a loud splash, some bubbling and it disappeared from sight. After the water had calmed down, aside from an oil slick, you couldn't tell it was there. The duckweed soon started moving back into the void, and before long it was hard to even notice the slick.

I ran as fast as I could, somehow managing to make it home before my mom. I turned on the TV and got a snack, just like I always did. After I caught my breath, I surprised myself at how calm I was. It was as if what Benny had done to my dad never happened.

The next day Mom was concerned, and she asked me if I had seen him. I told her, "No." I wasn't, actually, lying. There were still feet in the shoes, bits and pieces of bone and, of course, the blood, but who was to say that these things were really "Dad?" I don't know what happened to the rest of his bones, or his skull, but then I really didn't look very hard for them. Perhaps Benny had buried them or something. He was always digging holes.

Mom kept getting more and more concerned, and after supper, she started making phone calls to friends, family, the hospitals, and the Sheriff's office. Of course, no one had seen him. I was, almost, hoping that they had, that this was all just a bad dream and what I had seen was just the remains of some hound dog that was stupid enough to take on a huge pig and some of my dad's old clothes that had, somehow, found their way into the garden; maybe a scarecrow.

Of course, I knew what had happened. Benny had gotten out and was in the garden again. Dad decided to teach him a lesson and had gone after him with the two-by-four. Not a good idea when you dealing with a huge pig that is three times your size and hates your guts. I guess that was a poor choice of words, but you know what I mean. I imagine that Benny enjoyed his little snack, guts and all.

My dad worked nights at the foundry in Stockerton. It was about an hour's drive, and I remember him coming home, many nights, about one in the morning. Mom would get up to fix him a snack, sometimes; I think just so she could spend some time with him before she had to leave for her job at the supermarket. We might have gotten by with one car, if not for the fact that Dad had to leave for work before Mom got home. He was usually gone when I came home from school, so I really only got to see him on the weekends. Of course, this was the time I did all of my extra money jobs, so we really didn't share that much time together.

Perhaps this is why we weren't that close. I, actually, spent more time with Benny than I did with my Dad. I used to sit with Benny and stroke his head. I could tell him anything, and I think he really listened to me. Sometimes he would grunt and shake his head, like he really understood. To me, he was more than just a pet; he was a good friend.

My mom started to get all teary-eyed and started saying things like dad left her for another woman, even though she never had any reason to think that dad was cheating on her. She had to wait seventy-two hours before she could fill out a missing person's report. The Sheriff came to the house and asked a lot of questions. He even had a look around the yard and looked at the patch of garden that the pig had dug up.

He seemed like a really nice guy. He asked me about Benny: what was his name, how long I'd had him, and about how much he weighed. I told him Benny's name and all, but that I really didn't know how much he weighed, but thought it was well over five hundred pounds. I told him the farmer I got Benny from said that his pigs could get to be as much as twelve hundred pounds or more, but since Benny was a runt, he might not get to be much over one thousand.

He asked me what Benny liked to eat. I pointed to the garden and told him that he sure did a job on our carrots, beets and potatoes. I told him that I feed Benny mostly store-bought pig food that I mix with water and put in his trough. I told him that I had to work after school to earn enough money to keep Benny in food.

He told me that I must be a very responsible kid to take on such an undertaking at my age, and that he wished that there were more kids like me. He patted me on the back of my head and told me not to worry, that they would find my dad. I kind of, somewhat, doubted that. At least, I hoped they wouldn't. Because I buried my dad's clothes and got rid of the car, I was an accomplice to murder or something like that.

My mom got to feeling very distraught, so she took some time off from work to try to sort things out. I went to school, as usual, and stopped to do a couple of small jobs after school. I needed the money as Benny would soon be back to eating full rations, and hundred pounds bags of pig food don't grow on trees.

When I got home, Mom was working in the garden, replanting some of the things that Benny had dug up. While hilling some seed potatoes, she unearthed one of Dad's shoes, the one with his rotting foot still in it. I got there just in time to see her get sick.

"What have you done? What has that pig of yours done? My God! My God!" Tears were welling in her eyes and she clamped her hand tightly over her mouth. She threw down the shovel and ran for the house.

I followed after her yelling, "Mom. Mom." I didn't know what else to say. I had no idea what she would do next. Would she call the Sheriff? Would they come out and take Benny and me away? Would they shoot Benny? Would I go to jail for the rest of my life? The phone line . . . I needed to cut the phone line. I ran to the tool shed and grabbed the thing that my dad had used to trim the tree limbs. It had a long handle with a curved saw blade on the end, and a rope that ran to the lower jaw of a cutter. I ran to the house, slipped the cutter over the telephone wire, pulled down on the rope, and cut the wire cleanly in two. I threw down the tool and ran into the house, hoping that I was in time.

My mother wasn't on the phone. She had just unlocked the gun cabinet and was loading shells into my Dad's old, double-barreled, twelve-gauge shotgun. There were tears streaming down her cheeks, and she was having trouble seeing what she was doing. She wiped her eyes on the sleeve of her blouse, slipped in two shells, and closed the chamber.

"No, Mom!" I shouted. "You can't!"

"Out of my way, Tom," she said, "I will deal with you later, but for now that monster has to die!"

I grabbed for the gun, but she wrenched it away from me and pushed me down. I fell over a dining room chair, and by the time I got to my feet, she was out the back door. As I ran across the back lawn, she had reached the sty. She was only about six feet from where Benny lay under his lean-to. She wasn't aiming, but was holding the gun at her waist, but I knew at that distance she couldn't miss.

I threw myself at her and hit her in the small of her back. She fell forward against the fence and the gun discharged into the ground causing dirt and mud to billow up from the ground. The force of her momentum caused her to flip over the fence so that she landed on her back. I recovered the gun and turned to unload the second chamber.

Before either of us knew it, Benny was on top of her. He grabbed her throat in his huge jaws and ripped out a large section. She gurgled for a few seconds, her body twitched, and then she died.

I ran back to the house and up to my bedroom. I closed the door and climbed under the covers. I tried to close my mind to what was now going on in the sty. I knew what was happening to Mom, the same thing that had happened to Dad. It was just, that if I didn't see it, it wouldn't be so bad.

The next morning, before I went to school, I dug a deep hole and raked the blood and what was left of Mom into it. Benny didn't look so good. He lay in his lean-to, looking rather bloated. I went into the bathroom and got a half-dozen Alka-Seltzers, put them in a bowl of water, and set it in front of him. He lapped up the whole bowl and gave me a grunt that seemed to say, "Thank you."

Now, pretty much a seasoned driver, I didn't have as much trouble getting rid of Mom's car. I, also, took some duct tape and repaired the phone line. I came home directly from school that day. Right after I got home, the Sheriff arrived. He wanted to talk to my Mom, but I told him that she had gone shopping over in Glendisville and I didn't know when she would be back. He asked about Benny, and I told him that he was doing fine. He told me that he had been over to Mel Campbell's place, the farmer who sold me Benny, and looking at his pigs he had determined the Benny must weigh at least six, or seven hundred pounds. Mel had a show pig that didn't look any bigger than Benny that weighed that much. He told me that Mel had said that when I was ready to sell him for butchering, he would see to it that I got a fair price for him, but if I kept him too long I would lose my profit margin. He also told me that I should look for stale bread and cakes at bakeries and super markets to save money on pig food. I thanked him, but after he left, the thought of turning Benny into bacon turned my stomach. I had chips, Fritos, and ice cream for supper, but had trouble holding even that down.

Early the next morning, Betty Gramler, from the super market where my Mom worked, called and wanted to know if my mom was sick. I told her that she had the flu, and was sick in bed. She thought it was funny that she hadn't called in. I told her that my mom was too sick to even get out of bed. I also got a call, that night, from the place my dad worked. I told them that no one knew where he was, and everyone thought he had just skipped town. The woman said that it sounded like a typical "man thing", leaving my mom and me all alone. "Probably ran off with another woman," was her scenario. I really didn't care what they thought. I only wished that these people would leave me alone.

The next day was Saturday, so I got my wagon and went down to the feed store. I loaded up a couple of bags of pig food and paid them with some money from my mom's pocket book. I also stopped at the local convenience store and stocked up on hotdogs, chips, Pepsi, cookies, and corn chips. That afternoon, I took the money that was in my mom's pocket book, some money I found in the desk drawer, and the change in the can in the kitchen, and counted it all out. I came out to sixty-three dollars and seventy-eight cents, which included over eight dollars worth the pennies. I have grocery shopped with my mom enough times to know that sixty-three dollars doesn't go very far. Besides, Benny's food had gone up, and it wasn't cheap before.

Fortunately, Benny must have buried parts of Dad and Mom somewhere, because he wasn't into the pig food, like he usually was. This was good, because money would be tight from now on. I only gave him small rations and he was hardly touching that.

That evening the phone rang and startled me. It was my Aunt Maggie, from Portland. She wanted to know where my mother was and why she hadn't called her on her birthday like she always did. I told her that my mom was very sick and couldn't come to the phone.

"My God! Why didn't someone tell me," she said. "I will be there tomorrow."

I tried to talk her out of it. I told her that Mom was too sick for company. I told her that it was contagious, that it was some kind of plaque. She just said, "Nonsense," and told me to tell my mom that she was on her way. "She would do as much for me," she said, and then hung up before I could mention the flesh-eating virus.

She had come into money when her second husband died, and was always the one who sent me the best Christmas gifts. One year she sent me a RC car that did everything. It was my favorite toy until the battery gave out and I couldn't afford to buy a new one. She didn't waste any time. She hopped a jet, rented a car, and was at my door by ten a.m.

The first thing she did was insist on seeing my mom. I told her that Mom was sleeping, and that she had been up all night, hacking. I convinced her that Mom really needed her sleep. I offered to fix a pot coffee. When she asked if I knew how, I lied and told her that I had fixed it for Dad all the time.

I pulled out the thing on the coffee maker that you put the coffee into and put in a filter. I did know that much. However, I had no idea how much coffee to put in, so I only put in a half of cup. I filled the thing up to twelve cups, flicked the switch to "on" and got it perking. Meanwhile I snuck down to the basement and got the box of rat poison off of the shelf. I wasn't too sure how much to put in before she might taste it, so I only put four teaspoons.

When I served it to her she took a sip and said, "Oh my." I don't think it was because of the rat poison, though. It may have been a little rich, because she put in a lot of extra milk. She did sip it and smile politely; although, I got the impression she would have rather dumped the whole thing into the sink. I think she drank it just to be polite.

It wasn't long before she stood up, spilling her coffee, grabbed her throat, and started coughing up stuff. "You little bastard!" she yelled. "What have you done to me? What was in the coffee?"

Before I could tell her, "rat poison," her eyes rolled back into her head and she fell over backward. I left her there until after midnight, just to make sure, before I hauled her down the back steps, loaded her onto my wagon, to wheel her out to Benny. I found out later that it wasn't really rat poison. I had grabbed a bottle of plant food that was setting right next to it. I guess she must have died of a heart attack or something. I came back into the house and watched TV for a while, but when *Nightmare on Elm Street* came on, I went to bed. I didn't want to have any nightmares.

The next morning I cleaned myself up a little, put on my suit and went to church, alone. I had to leave early because it was two miles to town and I had to walk. I did think about driving my Aunt Maggie's car into town, but I didn't think that Slaughville was ready for that. People might wonder why I was driving a rental car. When I got back, I drove the car into the barn. I didn't know how deep the quarry was and three cars might put it over the limit as far as depth of the water went.

That afternoon I got out my dad's tools and began taking it apart. I went on the Internet, using my dad's user name: *studmuffin4969*, his birthday . . . how imaginative can you get? . . . and began selling car parts. I had no idea how much you could get for things like carburetors, headlights, and even windows. I was selling things even before I had them off of the car. I sold the engine block, the wheels and tires, and the front end to local people who came and picked them up. When they asked where *studmuffin4969* was, I told them that my dad was working, but that he left me a signed receipt and said for me to take the money. No one ever argued with that, after all, they had a receipt signed by my dad.

The money came in handy, because in about a week, Benny was back on pig food, again. Besides, the power company shut off the power and I had to pay them a bunch of money to get it turned back on. After that I started sorting through the big pile of letters that I had stuffed in a box in the kitchen. There were bills for just about everything, plus something called a mortgage payment that was now overdue.

On Monday I was too upset and too sick to go to school. When I figured everything up it was going to take most of the money that I had made from selling the car parts. I still had a few things left, like the rear end and the transmission, but what was I going to do for the next round of bills. I sat down and tried to figure out just what I could do without. The electricity? No, that ran the TV and the computer, and how was I going to make toast, in the morning? The cable? Definitely not! The phone? Well, I could do without the phone, but without a phone line I couldn't use the computer. The mortgage? No house, where would Benny and I go? The house insurance? Well, that didn't seem to be really important to me, but if things got really bad, couldn't I burn the house down and collect? The car insurance? Now, here was a place where I could save some money. Who needs insurance on two cars that are at the bottom of a quarry? Maybe I could claim that they were stolen, collect the money and then cancel the insurance? Nah, that wouldn't work. Who is going to hand some kid money and say, "Here, give this to your dad, *studmuffin4969*." Insurance people aren't as dumb as Internet buyers.

Things only got worse after that. The Sheriff came to the house to see my mom. When I told him that she was shopping he didn't believe me.

"I need to search the house," he said.

"Wait a minute," I replied, "you can't do that without one of those things, can you?"

"You mean a warrant?" he said. "I don't need one if I feel that there is something obviously wrong, here." He was standing in the doorway looking around. "I can see from here that a woman's hand has not touched this house in several weeks."

Perhaps it was the pizza boxes setting on the couch, or the empty cereal bowls stacked on the kitchen table that tipped him off. I'm not sure, but he pushed his way through the door and started calling my mom's name.

"Mrs. Davenport? Mrs. Davenport, are you here?" He drew his pistol and brushed me aside. "Don't worry, son," he whispered, "if there is something fishy going on here, I'll handle it."

He checked the kitchen, the closets, and the bathroom, and then started slowly up the stairs to the upstairs bedrooms. He pulled himself up by the railing, taking each step like a kitten stalking a bird. It was all I could do to keep from laughing. Only the fact that I knew I was in deep shit kept me from doing so.

As he made the landing and started up the second set of stairs I grabbed the poker from the fireplace and started after him. He couldn't see me because his head was above the landing. My bedroom was at the head of the stairs. He checked that one first. Then he walked to the end of the hall and checked the guest room. While he was inside, I ducked into my bedroom and hid behind the door. Having checked the guest room, he started down the hall to the master bedroom. As he passed my bedroom door I stepped out and let him have it as hard as I could.

He went down hard and lost his gun. When he pushed himself up on his elbows, I hit him again and again. After that he didn't move, but I hit him again just to make sure.

It had been fairly easy to drag Aunt Maggie across the tiled, kitchen floor and down the back steps, but the Sheriff was now lying on a carpeted floor, and although I tried as hard as I could, I couldn't get his two hundred plus body to move.

I went out to the barn and got some rope. I tied a length of rope around the Sheriff's legs, making several knots so it wouldn't come loose. I made a loop in another length of rope, went out to the sty and put it around Benny's neck. I didn't know just what Benny would do. I had never put a rope on him before. At first, he was reluctant, but slowly he began to yield, and finally, he began to follow me like an obedient puppy dog.

I led him to the house. He had a little trouble getting his huge frame through the kitchen door, and he seemed a little reluctant to navigate the steep stairs. I only got him as far as the first landing, but that was far enough. I tied a loop in the end of the rope that was around the Sheriff's legs and slipped it over his neck. I took the end of the other rope and led him back down the stairs, slowly.

The Sheriff's body followed along easily, his head bouncing on every step as he came. Benny wasn't even taxing himself; although, his hooves started slipping when he reached the tile floor of the kitchen. I never bothered getting the wagon. I just let Benny drag the Sheriff's body all the way to the sty.

I removed the ropes, the Sheriff's Western-style boots and his badge. The boots earned me thirty-five dollars, but I got sixty for the badge. The buyer gave me positive feedback and said that it was so good it looked real. It was a shame to have to burn his nice hat, but there was blood on it. I did get good money for the roof lights and the sirens. When I hauled the package down to the Post Office, the postman wanted to know what such a young man was doing with such a large package. Of course, he got a stupid answer.

Surfing the net, I learned that police car engines are special engines and that you can get good money for one if you go to the right people. I sold it to a guy from Millerland, who gave me eight hundred for it. Of course, it was setting in my red wagon, on the carport, when he got there to pick it up. He, also, got one of my dad's official receipts and, of course, I got the money in cash.

You may be wondering how I was handling the funds I got from the Internet. I always insisted on checks, I put them in the night deposit box at the bank, and the checks went out as usual. I practiced my parent's signatures, but I don't think I ever got either of them right. I don't think that anyone really looks at the signatures on the checks, do they?

Things were going pretty well for a while. I bought some tools from Harbor Freight, which made it easier for me to take the cars apart. I charged them to my father's credit card, which I paid with a check. I was going to school every day, and doing quite well. I forced myself to take a bath at least twice a week and actually started to do a little housework. The dishes were a must. It got a little discussing eating off of the same dirty plates.

It was a little scary sitting home alone every night, so I decided to let Benny sleep in the house. I thought of putting him in the spare bedroom, but he didn't like the stairs. I left the screen door unlatched so he could go in and out any time he wanted. He would pull on the outside handle; wedge his snout between the door and the frame, any time he wanted to come in. Most nights we would sit in the living room and watch TV together. On week nights I was in bed by ten. After all, I still had to go to school. Benny and I, well, we were family.

People called looking for Aunt Maggie. I told them that she had left right after my mom started feeling better. When they asked to talk to my mom, I would pretend to be her. If they thought that her voice sounded funny, I would just say that I had a cold. They came around, once, looking for the Sheriff. I told them that I hadn't seen him, but they could ask my mother if they wanted to wait until after she got out of the shower. It's funny how people don't like waiting. All I had to do was turn the shower on when I saw them pull in.

Once a bible salesman came to the house and pushed his way through the door. I don't think that he was really a bible salesman, but it didn't matter. Once Benny grabbed onto his leg, I knew that he wasn't going anywhere. Benny dragged him out to the sty screaming and yelling. I never even had to touch him. Benny even had a hole half-dug when I went out the next day. It only took me ten minutes with a rake and shovel.

It was last August when the checking account got overdrawn. It was right after I bought that video system that cost so much. Money was tight and Benny was running out of food. I was on this chat room and there was this weirdo who said he liked young boys. I sent him a picture of me when I was twelve and he sent me pictures. He was really sick. A couple of days later I invited him to the house. I told him that I would be home alone. I told him to bring some Peppermint Schnapps. There was some in the house after my parents, well, you know, and I thought it tasted pretty good. Being under twenty-one, there was no way I could get any more.

This jerk showed up about ten at night with the Schnapps. I yelled, from upstairs, for him to make himself comfortable and that I would be right down. He opened the bottle of Schnapps, poured a couple of shots in some glasses he found on the counter, and started taking off his clothes. Benny was watching from his favorite spot behind the couch. Before this guy could take off his shoes Benny had him by the foot and was dragging him, kicking and screaming, out the back door and into the night. I took a shower, downed the two glasses of Schnapps and went to bed knowing that Benny was good for a bit longer.

The next day I drove his late-model pickup into the barn. I got six dollars for his Levi's, four for the shirt, and twelve for his big silver belt buckle. Most of the truck parts I sold locally by listing them in the local paper over the course of the next three months.

There was this girl in my class. Her name was Brenda Fuller. I thought she was the most beautiful thing on the planet. Of course, the year before I thought that Pam Mason was the most beautiful thing on the planet, but Brenda was eighteen and had a nice body, while Pam had put on some weight. Besides, since I had turned eighteen and Pam was still only seventeen, this made her jail bait, and you know how that goes. The Senior Prom was coming up and I, somehow, worked up enough courage to ask Brenda if she would go with me. I never thought she would say yes, and when she did, it caught me completely by surprise. I pulled the transmission from the pickup and sold it to some shady dude who warned me that it had better be good or he was coming back for his money and a piece of my hide. I never gave the asshole a receipt.

The money paid for a nice corsage and stretch-limo. I went all out and rented a suit: the whole outfit, right down to the shoes and socks. All I knew was that I was truly in love, if not with Brenda then at least with her great boobs. She was five-two, with soft, blond hair, and the bluest eyes I had ever seen. Her lips were soft and pouting, and her large, even teeth challenged any I had ever seen on any movie star. Then there was her scent. All of the girls smelled like flowers, bathed in perfume, but not Brenda. Brenda had a gentle scent that transcended perfumes and hairspray. It was her scent and only Brenda smelled like that.

The limo and I arrived at her house promptly at eight. Her parents greeted me at the door and pumped me for information while I waited for Brenda to make her grand entrance down the long stairway that led from, what I had assumed, was her bedroom. I tried to imagine what it would be like. White satin sheets, a print bedspread, hundreds of stuffed animals, and the wall covered with pictures of famous rock stars, autographed with, "to Brenda with love," followed by some illegible scribbling that no one could decipher.

I fought back the urge to say something stupid, like, *"My pig ate my parents, and I'm here to pick up your lovely daughter . . . your pride and joy!"* Wouldn't that have made some great conversation? "My dad works at the foundry in Stockerton, and my mother works at the local Win-Dixie," I informed them.

"Oh, you little roach," they must have thought, *"you're not fit to kiss our daughter's foot."* Maybe not, but I didn't spend all that money on a limo to kiss their daughter's foot. I was aiming a bit higher.

Brenda finally emerged like an unfurling butterfly. Her dress squeezed her body in all the right places and exposed that soft cleavage that I had so grown to love. She floated down the stairway in her new high heels as if she had been born wearing them. I don't know how long my mouth lay open, but I remember closing it before I began to drool. Her father shot me a look, and I knew at that moment, if he could have found a way to justify it, he would have killed me. His parting smile looked more like a grimace.

When we danced the first dance I stared at her cleavage until I thought my eyes would burn. I found the soft, white flesh beyond the tan-line the most appealing. I admired the soft freckles and imagined them as tiny nipples. I envied them for being where I so wanted to be.

"I'm bored! Let's get out of here."

The sound was coming from her mouth, but it took a while to sink into my little brain. "What?"

She had me by the hand and was pulling me from the gymnasium floor. "You got anything?"

I reached into my pocket. "Gum?"

"No, you idiot, I mean like pot or something."

"Booze?"

"You've got some booze? What?"

"I have some Peppermint Schnapps."

"What the fuck is Peppermint Schnapps?"

"It's booze, only with peppermint," I explained.

"Can you get drunk on it?" Her eyes were beginning to look a little crazy.

"Well," I admitted, "a couple of shots gets me a little woozy."

"Where is it?"

"At my house," I said.

"And your parents are home, right?"

"No," I said, "they're away . . . for a while," I added.

"Sweet," she said, heading for the door.

"But we can't leave the gym," I argued.

"Yeah, sure!" She hit the handle on the emergency exit and pushed the heavy door open. An alarm went off. We ran to the nearest car and squatted down behind.

Someone came to the door and shined a flashlight around the parking lot. "Damn kids!" they said, and closed the door.

"The stretch limo won't be back for three hours," I uttered.

She bent down to remove her shoes. I caught a glimpse of even more forbidden flesh, and I felt my heart stop. "Then it looks like we're gonna to have to walk, doesn't it? Lead the way."

When we left the last street light behind I felt this closeness as the darkness fell in around us. She hiked her dress up so she could walk easier and I caught a fleeting glimpse of her panty hose. Teenage hormones were raging as we laughed and made silly conversation on the way to my house. We walked on the grass so she could avoid the gravel on the shoulder of the road. Her panty hose became torn and ragged from being snagged on the tall weeds. Finally, she stopped, removed her panty hose, and threw them into the bushes. It was then I saw her red panties and the hormones raged on even louder.

When we got to the house, I ran for the Schnapps and a couple of glasses. I moved some empty Fritos bags and a pizza box, and we sat on the couch.

"Your mother's not much of a house keeper, is she?"

"She has been away for a while," I said, "and she is sick a lot when she is home."

I poured some Schnapps into the glasses, and she took a sip. "Not too bad. Nothing I couldn't get used to. Fill up my glass," she said, "I'm not a social drinker."

She drank and I sipped. I didn't want to run out, and this was the only bottle I had. It was a 1.5 liters, but there were already a couple of shots missing, and I cursed myself for drinking them. She asked to use the john and I showed her where it was. Then I thought about Benny. I looked around and found him laying on the cool grass, in the back yard. I came back into the house and latched the back door. I didn't want Benny interrupting us at the wrong moment.

When she came back, she finished her glass and set it down amid the debris on the coffee table. "OK," she said, "I'm ready."

"Ready?" she caught me off guard.

"Yeah, Jesus, you've been staring down my dress all night. I figure you want these." With that she pulled down on the top of her dress and one of her breasts fell out, exposing the most beautiful, brownish-pink nipple I had ever seen up close. In fact it was the only nipple I had ever seen, in the flesh. "Where, the hell is your bedroom. I don't want to do it here, on this dirty couch."

What followed was two minutes of fumbling with garment and undergarments, followed by ten glorious minutes of groping, squeezing, licking, sucking foreplay, and finally ending with a messy climax that ended before I got it in.

I rolled off and she lie there laughing at me. "You are pitiful," she said. I thought you would be fun. Not only don't you have anything, but you shot all over me before you even got it in. Now, I have to take a shower before I can even go home. You do have a working shower? Never mind, I'll find it. You are, so, going to be the laughing stock of the whole, freakin' school."

I got dressed while she went to take a shower. After, I told her I would take her back home in the limo and she could pretend that nothing had ever happened.

"But, before we leave, I have something I would like to show you."

I took her out back to meet Benny. He was still lying in the grass where I had seen him earlier. This time I brought a flashlight. When I shone it on Benny she gave me a funny look.

"You brought me out here to see a filthy pig? You are weird!

She started to walk away, but I grabbed her arm. "No, I really want you to know Benny."

"Let go of my arm!" she shouted. "You're hurting me."

She should have never hit me. This time, I stayed and watched. I watched as Benny ate all those parts I had once been interested in. I wasn't interested anymore. To me, it was just one hundred and ten pounds of meat.

I got my baseball bat out of the hall closet and walked back to the school. I kept to the shadows and no one saw me. I walked out behind the dumpsters, ripped my clothes and hit myself, repeatedly with the bat; my arms, my legs, my shoulders, and, finally, my head. Just before I lost consciousness, I wiped the bat clean of prints with my shirt.

It wasn't until the next morning that anyone found my bloody, battered body. I was said to be near death, by the local paper. They rushed me to the hospital and I told a story, through swollen lips, of two men who had beatten me with bats and dragged Brenda off, screaming, in a black car. A Chevy, I thought, but it could have been a Honda. I admitted to having sex with her, but I don't think that was any surprise to her parents.

The whole story came out, about how my parents joined a cult and abandoned me because I wouldn't sell my soul to Satan and denounce the teachings of Christ. They had taken the two cars, but had left all of their worldly possessions behind because the devil wanted them as they had come onto this earth. I never told anyone, because I was too ashamed and also afraid that they would put me in an orphanage. I couldn't leave my pig, Benny. He was my only friend and the only one I trusted.

As I refined the story, the bleeding hearts swarmed all over me like rats on cheese. My uncle Fred came to live with me, but after a few months he left because he was afraid of Benny and me. He had good reason. He did; however, teach me how to drive and help me get a driver's license.

Funny, that after a few months, memories fade and bleeding hearts stop bleeding. Old news replaced by new news. I guess that is why they call it "news" otherwise they would call it "olds". Brenda's parents broke up and moved away. I guess they just couldn't deal with the loss of their sweet, darling, little girl. What they don't know is that Benny probably saved them from a life of grief, dragging her off the streets and out of crack houses.

People seldom wonder about who is living in the Davenport place any more. I'm twenty, now, and working at the same foundry where my dad worked. Benny can't get through the door of the house anymore, which is good, because he would, probably, fall through the floor. I still feed him well. On occasion, I'll invite a homeless person home for a few drinks. I talk them into taking a shower, and then I introduce them to Benny. Benny doesn't like them if they smell really bad. Benny gets so he does most of the cleanup himself, now; which is good. Benny is a really good pig. Hell, he's my very, very best friend; although, sometimes he even frightens me.

SLEEPING DOGS

"Good morning, Phil.

Phil Thomas had been restocking cigarettes, and hadn't seen Mr. Costello come into his store. Anthony Costello was a pleasant old man, with an aristocratic look, and the energetic gate of someone much younger. He was wearing a blue, pinstriped suit, and caring a silver-handled walking stick that he now laid, carefully, upon the counter.

"Are they in?" he asked.

"Why yes, Mr. Costello, they came in this morning." Phil bent to retrieve a box of imported, Italian cigars from beneath the counter.

"Would you open them for me, please, Phil?" Mr. Costello asked, as he fished his billfold from his jacket pocket. He laid a one hundred-dollar bill on the counter as Phil removed the wrapper from the box, and opened it up. Mr. Costello picked up one of the cigars with both hands as if it were a fine piece of jewelry. He ran it under his nose. "Nothing like a good, well-made cigar," he said.

"I wouldn't know," Phil remarked, making change. "I've never smoked. They claim smoking is bad for you."

"So they say." Anthony Costello had placed the cigar in his mouth, and was lighting it with a gold-cased lighter. "Myself, I've been smoking cigars since I was fifteen. Not always good ones like this, mind you, but still in all, I've smoked a good many cigars. I'm nearly seventy-five, you know, and if the good Lord felt fit to take me tomorrow, I wouldn't have missed a damn thing." He winked at Phil, "So you see," he said, pointing downward, "I'll smoke my cigars, and take my chances with the devil." He retrieved the change from the counter, placed it neatly into his billfold; picked up his cigars and his walking stick, and left the store.

"Strange old man," Phil thought, "him and his friend, Mr. Genoa. He always carries that walking stick, but I've never seen him use it."

85

Anthony Costello and Frances Genoa had come to Buckley about three years ago. They had purchased the old Hampton place, at the edge of town. It was the talk of the town for weeks. They paid for the house with cash, three hundred and fifty thousand dollars. The real estate dealer was afraid to carry it to the bank, but the two old men handed it over like it was just so much chump change. Of course, in a little town like Buckley, it was hard to keep anything a secret for long, even the fact that neither of the two men seemed to have a bank account, and always paid with cash.

But the town of Buckley had more serious things on its collective mind these days. Even this quiet little town had its share of bad people. The word was out that Wade Stigler had been released from the state prison. He was supposed to have served a fifteen-year sentence, but had been released early, mostly due to overcrowding and a revolving-door judge. This didn't set too well with the townsfolk. Wade's son, Billy, had disappeared nearly two years ago, much to the delight of everyone, including his mother, Molly.

Just as Wade had been, his son had become the town bully. Rumor had it that he was heavily into drugs, and was supporting his habit by stealing. There had been many break-ins around town, but none of them could be traced back to Billy; although, the local sheriff had no doubt that he was involved. Some of the townsfolk feared for the two new owners of the Hampton place, as a rumor was floating around town that the two old men kept large amounts of cash around the house. Many a concerned citizen was relieved when Bill decided to leave, some say, just ahead of the law.

Now, Wade would be coming back, no one doubted that. Few, if any who knew him, could ever feel that his cold, black heart could ever be rehabilitated. It was only two days later that all of their fears were confirmed. At three pm, that Friday, the person of Wade Stigler was seen stepping from a Sun Trail bus and onto the pleasant streets of Buckley.

Wade Stigler looked around for his wife. "Where the hell is that bitch?" he asked, aloud. "She knew I was coming in. The least she could do is be here to meet me!"

The bus driver handed Wade his bag, and pretended not to hear. "Here you are, sir. Thank you for traveling Sun Trail."

Wade picked up his bag and started on the long walk down the dusty road that led to the old, rundown house his father had left him. It was the only thing of any value that he still owned. It wasn't much; a small farm once, but under Wade's guidance it had become nothing more than fields of weeds. He had tried to make it work when he had first married Molly, but he was never meant to be a farmer. He took to drinking. He lost every job he ever had. The only things he was ever good at were fighting and stealing, and the latter had landed him in prison for the last seven and a half years.

"The bitch better have something ready to eat when I get there, or there will be hell to pay." Wade cleared his throat and spat. This town left a bad taste in his mouth. He was back, yes, but not for long. There was something that he had to do, but when that was done he would leave for good, with or without Molly.

Frances Genoa looked up from his flower garden as Anthony came into the backyard. "How does this look, Tony?" he asked.

"Jesus, Frank, you're a regular Martha Stewart. Want a cigar?"

"Kiss my ass, Tony! But, yes, I will have a cigar." He pushed himself to his feet, wiped his hands on his pants, and leaned backward to straighten his back.

Tony handed Frank a cigar. "You need to take it easy on yourself. At your age, you're gonna get down there, one of these days, and you won't be able to get back up."

Frank lit his cigar and took a deep drag. "You're forgetting, Tony; I'm two years younger than you."

Tony made a gesture with his hand. "You've lied about your age so many times; you don't even know how old you are."

Frank put his arm around his friend's shoulder. "You're probably right, Tony. Come on in the house. I made a nice paste salad, and some of that cannoli you like so well."

"I see your plan, Frank," Tony said, patting his stomach, "you're going to kill me with cannoli.

You remember the time I shot you in the leg? I thought you were going to kill me then."

"How could I forget, an inch higher and I would have been singing soprano. I would have killed you, too, Tony, but I was in too much pain at the time; you and that damn, hair-trigger."

"Hey. That hair-trigger saved my butt more than once."

As they sat down at the kitchen table, Frank picked up the paper and handed it to Tony. It was folded to an article on the second page. "Did you see this?" he asked.

"**Governor to dedicate new hospital wing?**"

"No, the article about Wade Stigler being released from prison."

"Should I know this Wade Stigler?"

"The kid, when we first came here?"

"You mean the little punk?"

"Yeah, that's his old man."

"Now that you mention it, I do see a family resemblance. Do you think this could be trouble?" Tony asked.

"It could be. I think we should be prepared for the worse."

"I always am," Tony said.

Wendy didn't notice, at first, that the couple seated at table two was Wade and Molly Stigler. Molly was seated with her hands folded in front of her. Wendy could see that she had a bruise and a fresh cut over her right eye. *The bastard!* She thought.

"What are you staring at?" Wade asked. "Give me a menu. I want a cold beer; make it a Bud draft." He looked at his silverware. "If it's not too much of a problem, could you bring me a clean fork?" He held it up so she could see it.

Wendy took the fork, but Wade didn't let go of it right away.

"I remember you. You're Wendy, right?"

"Yes," she said, "Wendy Parsons."

He was looking her up and down, and smiling broadly. "Well, Wendy, you sure filled out a might since the last time I saw you. You're a grown up woman, now. I remember how you and them other rug-rats used to come into Thomas's Store, lookin' ta swap bottles for candy. You were just a freckle-faced kid, then, with pigtails."

"Wade, please!" Molly said.

"What? I ain't sayin' nothing wrong. I'm just tellin' this young lady that she turned out right pretty." He looked up at Wendy. "Now, is there anything wrong with that?"

"No, sir," she said, nervously, "I guess not."

"See?" Wade said, reaching across the table and taking his wife's chin in his hand. "Even the young lady don't think I did nothin' wrong."

"Do you want me to come back?" Wendy asked, starting to put her pad and pencil back into her apron.

"No," replied Wade, not even looking at the menu. "All I want is a burger and fries." He leaned across the table, and looked into his wife's face. "And what do you want, sweetheart?"

"That sounds OK with me," she said.

"No, Baby," he was forcing a fake smile, now. "You can have anything your little heart desires." He reached into the pocket of his jeans, and pulled out a small wad of bills. "I got my mustering-out pay. I'm a rich son-of-a-bitch!" He picked up the menu and pretended to look it over. "Don't see no caviar on here, nowhere. Oh dear, maybe you will have to settle for a burger and some fries."

"Yeah," Molly said, softly, "that will be just fine."

Wade turned to Wendy. "Make sure that hers is well done. She likes them well done. Me, I like mine hot, wet and juicy."

He was running his tongue over his lips and Wendy had the feeling that he wasn't talking about burgers anymore. She left to get his beer and turn in his order. In four years as a waitress nothing had ever made her feel so uncomfortable.

Wade was looking around the restaurant. "Hey, honey, look over there; it's the Armstrongs!" He said it loud enough that everyone in the restaurant heard him.

As he started to get to his feet, Molly grabbed his arm. "Please, Wade, don't start anything!"

"Honey!" Wade pulled her hand from his arm. "I've been away for a long time. It's only proper that I socialize a bit with my old friends." He got up and walked to the table of an older couple who were seated two tables down. "Charley," he began, kneeling on the floor and leaning on the table, "how are you?"

"Please leave us alone, Wade," Charles pleaded. "We don't want any trouble."

Wade ignored him. "And you, Mrs. Armstrong, you're looking good in your fancy, smancy, new dress." He touched the sleeve, "What is this, satin?"

"No!" she said, pulling her arm away.

"Why are you doing this, Wade?" Charles asked.

"Doin' what, Charley?" Wade leaned closer. "I'm just being friendly. Sorry to hear about your granddaughter's abortion." He put his hand to his mouth and looked around. "Oops! No one was supposed to know, were they? Damn! Me and my big mouth! But ya know, here I am, over three hundred miles away, rotting away in state prison, and I heard all about it. So how much of a big secret can it be? If I remember right, you had a big hand in putting me in there."

"You stole my husband's coin collection!" Mrs. Armstrong shouted, angrily.

"Yes, I did, didn't I? I was a bad boy. But you did get most of it back, didn't you? I could have spent the coins, but no, I kept them all together, trying to sell it as a collection. Probably the reason I got caught. Here, you got most of your precious coins back, and I still got fifteen years. Now, is that fair?"

"It wasn't your only offence, Wade. You have no one to blame but yourself." Charles Armstrong was already sorry he had said that. Wade was giving him a look that chilled him to the bone.

"Yeah. Whatever." Wade was on his feet, now. "Maybe the next time we meet you two will be a little more sociable; maybe a little more giving, or forgiving. I did do my time, you know. I didn't see anyone bustin' their ass when my son, Billy, disappeared." He was looking around the restaurant as he said it.

"Your son left because the police were after him," Charles uttered, meekly.

"Yeah. I heard that rumor, too. But you know, Billy used to call me three, maybe four times a week. Suddenly, two years ago, the phone calls stopped. If my son was still alive, I would have heard from him by now. Do you think the cops give a shit? No! Have they been lookin' for him or his killer? No! Well, I'm here to say," he was raising his voice, and shaking his fist, "I'm goin' to get whoever did my son in. I know it was somebody in this stinkin' town." He was leaning close to Charles' face, now, "I ain't rulin' you out, either, Charley. Or anyone," he said to all that could hear.

Wendy delivered the two burgers to an empty table. The Stigler's had left before the police arrived.

A beer and a joint was all that was required to renew an old relationship. Ricky Taylor had hung around with Billy ever since Wade could remember. If anyone knew what had happened to Billy, Ricky would know.

Wade took another hit of the joint, and begged off. This stuff was a little stronger than the jailhouse shit he was used to. "So you and Billy were together the day before Billy disappeared?"

"Yeah, Pops," Ricky said, taking the last hit. He told me things were gettin' too hot for him, here, he needed to split. He said that he was fixin' to make a big score before he left."

"Do you know what he meant by that?" Wade finished his beer and was fishing a couple more out of the refrigerator.

"The only thing I can think of is this rumor that was goin' around that the old guys that bought the old Hampton place, had money just lying around the house."

"When did you see him last?"

Ricky popped the top from his beer and took a deep swallow. "It was about eight that night, I think. He said that he was going home to take a nap. Said he was probably going to be up late."

"Do you think he might have broken into the old guy's house that night?"

"It could be, you know, he was pretty good at breaking and entering. He showed me his tools, once. He kept them in the barn, under the floorboards."

"Why don't we go look and see if they're still there?" Wade got to his feet and went out the back door of the kitchen, toward the old barn. Ricky was right behind him, beer in hand.

The barn had been closed up for years. It smelled old and musty; cobwebs were everywhere. Ricky walked to the back wall and rolled an old truck tire out of the way. "Billy kept this tire on top of the board so his mama wouldn't mess with it." He pulled up the board. "Walla!" he said. "Billy's tools."

The tools were wrapped up in a plastic bag. Wade dumped them out on the floor, and examined them.

"These are good tools," he said. He held up a small package. "A good set of picks, like this, is hard to come by. Billy wouldn't have left without these."

Ricky's face took on a serious look. "So, what are ya sayin', Pops?"

"I'm sayin' that somebody did him in. Someone probably caught him breakin' in, and shot him. Whoever it was didn't even have the guts to call the cops. He's probably out there, somewhere, buried in some old creek bed, behind an old barn, stuffed down an old well, or maybe at the bottom of the lake. The only one who knows is the bastard that killed him, and before I blow his brains out, I'm gonna find out where Billy is. The least I can do for him is to see that he gets a decent burial."

Wade took a bar out of the tool bag and pried some boards off of the wall just above the workbench. He laid the bar down on the bench, and reaching down inside, he pulled out a canvass bag. Inside the bag, rapped in greasy rags, was a pistol.

"Damn," Ricky exclaimed, "where'd you get that?"

"Remember when Ken Brogan got shot?"

"Yeah, about ten years ago."

"Well, this is the gun I killed him with."

"Holy shit! You were the one who popped the deputy?"

"Yeah, and you'd better keep your mouth shut about it."

"Hey, Pops, I never had no love for that asshole. He busted me twice for possession, and once for DWI. As far as I'm concerned, you did us all a favor. Why'd ya do it?"

"He saw me loading cigarettes into my car after I broke into the local super market. He drew his gun. I was just a little quicker."

"But they found his body out on the old Willet road."

"It seemed like a better place than out in the middle of a damn parking lot. I loaded him into his car, drove him out there, dumped him in the ditch, and drove his patrol car into the swamp. As it turns out, it was a better idea. They didn't find his body for five days. By then it had rained so much, all the evidence was washed away, if there was any. As far as I know, they still ain't never found the car. It took me three hours to walk back to my car. By the time I peddled the cigarettes to a fence in Quarryville and got back home it was nearly noon. I hid the gun in this wall because it was the only thing that could link me to the shooting."

"What are you going to do, now?"

"Well," Wade said, as he removed the gun from the greasy rags. "While I clean this thing up, you're going into town and picking up some fresh ammunition."

"Why me?" Ricky asked.

"Two reasons, Ricky, my boy," Wade put his arm around his shoulder. "You're the only one who has a car, and if you do shoot off your big mouth you will, also, have a link to this weapon."

Sheriff Corbett caught the phone on the second ring before it woke up his sleeping wife. He looked at the clock. *Three o'clock; this better be important,* he thought. "Hello. Oh, hello Molly. What can I do for you?"

Molly was on the phone in the kitchen. She didn't dare speak loader than a whisper. "It's Wade, Sheriff. I think he's up to something bad. I overheard him talking to Ricky Taylor. He mentioned something about the old guys who live in the old Hampton place. I'm afraid he might be going to rob them, or something. You know how violent he is. I wouldn't want anything bad to happen to those nice, old men."

"Thanks for calling, Molly. I know how much courage it took for you to do this. Don't worry; Mel Volt is on patrol tonight. I'll see to it that he keeps a lookout for Ricky's car, and that he keeps a check on the old Hampton place. I'll go out there myself, in the morning, and have a talk with the old guys. I'd kind of hate to see anything happen to them myself.

Tony was just pouring his first cup of coffee when he heard the knock at the door. "Frank, there's someone at the door!" he shouted.

"OK! OK! I've got it. Well, hello, Sheriff," he heard Frank say, "what brings you all the way out here?"

"I just wanted to have a talk with you and your friend, if you don't mind."

"Of course not, Sheriff," Tony said, coming from the kitchen and greeting the sheriff with a warm handshake. "Frances and I just love to have company. Why don't you come out to the kitchen, I just put on a fresh pot of coffee."

"I really don't want to be any bother," the sheriff said."

"Nonsense," Tony assured him, "we don't often get an opportunity to entertain, and you certainly can't leave until you've tried some of Frances' delicious cannoli."

Tony led the way to the kitchen and Frank and the sheriff followed. Tony got out two more cups and filled them, while Frank brought out the basket with the cannoli. He removed the checkered cloth from the top and offered them to the sheriff.

"I shouldn't" the sheriff said, but took one, anyway, at Tony's insistence. He was glad he did. "My god," he exclaimed, "I think I've died and gone to heaven!"

"Good, aren't they?" Tony was also helping himself to one.

"Oh, come on guys, it's only pastry," Frank said, modestly.

"The sheriff was waving the cannoli in the air. "This is not just pastry, Mr. Genoa, this is a sweet piece of heaven." He took another bite.

"See? What have I been telling you, Frank?" Tony said, "Who would know better than a cop?" Tony made a motion with his hand. "Only kidding, Sheriff."

"No." Sheriff Corbett was wiping the cream from his chin with his handkerchief. "I was a cop in Philly for twelve years, before I came here. I practically lived on coffee and donuts. Believe me, I've eaten a lot of cannoli, but I've never had anything like this."

"When we first came here, I wanted him to open a bakery," Tony explained. "All he kept saying was that he was too old. He's two years younger than I am, and I'm not too old."

"You really ought to do something with this, Mr. Genoa." The sheriff licked the last succulent morsel from his fingers, and reluctantly washed it down with a sip of coffee. "You would be doing this town a big favor. Now, before I forget what I came here for, I need to warn you about this guy who was just released from the state prison."

"Is he a real bad guy?" Frank asked.

"One of the worst. If it were up to me, he would be rotting in jail. I think he had something to do with the death of one of my deputies, ten years ago, but I've never been able to link him to the crime. He was involved in a series of robberies, about eight years ago, and was sent up on a fifteen-year hitch. Some bleeding-heart judge let him off early. Now, I have reason to believe he may be up to his old tricks."

"What does this have to do with us?" Tony asked.

"Well, there was a rumor around town that you guys had a houseful of money."

Frank was the first to laugh, and then Tony joined in.

"We both pooled our life savings to buy this house," Frank explained. "We live a modest lifestyle on our Social Security. There's money left over for Anthony's fancy cigars, and an occasional bottle or two of good brandy, but drawers full of money, I assure you, we don't have."

"I just wanted to warn you. Whether you have any money or not, if Wade Stigler thinks you have, you could still be in danger. Keep your doors and windows locked at night, and if you hear anything suspicious at all, don't be afraid to give us a call." He fished around in his wallet for a card. "Here, this has my home phone number on it, in case you need to get a hold of me at night. I repeat, don't be afraid to call. Wade has already caused a stir at The Family Restaurant. I think I'll pay a visit to him on the way back to town and try to convince him that the best thing he can do, for all concerned, is get back on the bus and leave Buckley for good."

As the sheriff got up to leave, Tony snatched up the basket with the cannoli. "Why don't you take a couple for later?" he asked. He went to the counter, unrolled some paper towels, and began wrapping cannoli. "I'll wrap up a few for your wife. I assume you're married."

"Yes I am," the sheriff said, "I really appreciate it."

"We appreciate you coming all the way out here to warn us," Tony was now putting the cannoli into a plastic baggy.

"That's my job. I get paid to look out for the people of this town."

"Why don't you go out this way, Sheriff," Frank said, pointing to the back door of the kitchen, "this way you won't have so far to walk."

Tony threw up his hands, and rolled his eyes as Frank led the Sheriff out through the back porch and down the steps to the garden.

"Oh, what a beautiful garden you have, here," the sheriff said. "It must take a lot of time and patience to get it to look that good."

"I find it very relaxing," Frank said.

"Still in all, I've never had any luck growing anything. My wife says I have a brown thumb."

"The real secret," Frank explained, "is in how you prepare the soil. You have to work it over good, and add the right amount of nutrients. I don't believe in using chemicals and stuff. I always use natural fertilizers and compost. I even use table scraps. Tony's a big help. My back isn't what it used to be. He's a real pro with a shovel."

"Well, you guys sure did a nice job. What's in that new patch?" the Sheriff asked.

"Some flowers called Morning Mist. It's something new on the market. I've never worked with them before, but the picture on the package looked really nice. I'm hoping for the best."

"Well," the Sheriff said, smiling, "if it looks half as good as the rest of your garden, I'm sure they'll be beautiful." He looked around. "Even your vegetables are doing well; looks like you've got a little bit of just about everything. You guys really have a nice place, here."

"Why don't you take a couple of these zucchini, Sheriff?" Frank offered, "And how about some of these tomatoes? We'll never eat them all."

Tony hurried back to the house. "I'll get a bag," he shouted over his shoulder.

After the sheriff left, loaded down with a large bag of vegetables and his cannoli "doggy bag", Tony confronted Frank, angrily. "Why, the hell, did you have to bring him through the garden, Frank?"

"You know cops. If you flaunt the obvious, they'll overlook it. If I hadn't walked him through the garden, what's to say he wouldn't come poking around here on his own, when we weren't home? I satisfied his curiosity, and now that's over with."

"I just wish the hell he hadn't seen the fresh turned earth."

"Tony," Frank said, putting his arm around his shoulder, "How long were you a hit-man?"

"I don't know; something like 48 years."

"About two years longer than me, but then you're two years older than I am. In all those years didn't we always try to do the best for our marks?"

"I guess," Tony admitted. I always tried to make it as quick and painless as possible, and I always saw to it that they got some kind of a halfway decent burial."

Frank smiled, "Now, don't you think it's only proper that the father should be buried next to the son? And look at this spot. Even the Sheriff commented on how beautiful it looks. So, don't worry about it, Tony.

"Yeah, well where is he? I spent six hours softening that dirt up so we could get him in the ground quickly, and the S.O.B. never showed up."

When Molly Stigler answered the door Sheriff Corbett could see her swollen lip, the cut on her face, and the blood on her dress. "Is Wade here?" He asked.

"Yes, "she said, smiling. "He's in the kitchen."

When she smiled, Sheriff Corbett could also see that she was missing a tooth. *This*, he thought, *would at least get Wade some time for domestic violence.*

When they reached the kitchen Molly stepped over Wade Stigler's lifeless body and went directly to the stove. "Would you like some coffee, Sheriff; I just made a fresh pot." She didn't wait for him to answer, but poured a cup and set it on the table. "Cream and sugar?" She asked.

Wade's body lay on the floor, his head apparently struck several times with the cast-iron skillet that lay next to him. On the table lay a 32 Smith and Wesson; the same type of gun used to kill Deputy Brogan.

The sheriff took off his hat and scratched his head. He had thought for sure that Wade was buried in that fresh garden plot at the old guy's place. He dialed 911. "The coroner is going to take a while to get here. Do you like cannoli, Molly?"

The Preacher
And The Prostitute

She looked at her watch; it was 3:30 am. The rain had caught her out on one of her late-night walks. A bolt of lightning streaked across the sky, turning night into day for a second, but then the night turned into something even darker than before. She looked around for some sort of safe haven. Quickly, she ducked into a doorway. It was a brownstone apartment. She knew she couldn't stay there. The wind was picking up, blowing a steady drizzle into the narrow alcove, and even though she clung tightly to the corner nearest the doorway, it offered little protection. The flashes of lightning frightened her. Besides, if she were to be spotted here, she might be arrested for loitering, or worse. She was familiar with the routine; she had been arrested before; mostly for prostitution. After all that's what she was, a prostitute. On this night, she had no intentions of spending the night in jail, especially when she was only out for a walk.

Another sleepless night of tossing and turning had prompted her to go for a walk. She had made her "quota" for the day. Willy, her pimp, was satisfied. She should be in bed sleeping instead of wandering the streets this early in the morning. It wasn't safe, even for a girl like her. "Like her"? Why was she any different? She would be no different to a killer or rapist, would she? Oh, she might offer herself up, willingly, rather than have her throat slit, but that's not what those people are really about, is it? They're not after sex. They're after control, complete control. How many girls in her profession have already died? She knew two of them personally. Why was she out here walking these streets in the first place? This was crazy! She wasn't even familiar with this part of town. Sure, it was a safe neighborhood, but was any street safe at this time of night? Soon, people would be on their way to work. She suddenly didn't want to be found here.

The wind was blowing harder, now, and the rain increasing. Her skimpy outfit offered little protection from the sudden drop in temperature. Across the street there was a small church. The lights were still on and it looked inviting. A bolt of lightning struck somewhere nearby. This was all the prompting she needed. She put her head down and dashed out into the rain. Mounting the steps two at a time, she was pleasantly surprised to find the door unlocked. Downtown, the doors are always locked, even the doors of churches.

Pulling the heavy door open, she stepped inside. The lights inside weren't bright. It was almost like being in a theater. *Night lights*, she thought. The sound of her high heels echoed through the church as she made her way down the aisle to the front pew. The wooden seat was cold against her exposed back. She rubbed her shoulders and shivered in the semi-darkness.

Folding her hands, she offered a short prayer. "Our father, who art in Heaven . . ." It was the only prayer she knew. In fact this was only the second time she had been in a church since she was sixteen. That was when she had run away from home. She had come to the city by bus. She had no idea where she was going, or where she was going to stay. All she knew was that she had to get away from home. Her mother didn't understand or even care about her. At least, that's what she thought at the time. When she stepped off the bus, "Pops" was there. He was just waiting there at the bus station. He was nice, and he seemed to understand her. He knew she was hurting. He knew she was alone and frightened. He offered her food and a place to stay.

He must have been about thirty-five, tall, almost hansom, with a gentle smile and soft manner that put Angela at ease. It was easy to follow him. She was alone, frightened, and in a strange place. "Pops" was kind and understanding. He told her that there were other young girls living at his "place". He made it sound like a halfway house for runaways. There were other girls living there; some were her age, some were older. They all had the same look on their faces. At first, Angela thought that it was indifference, but it didn't take her long to realize that it was really the look of despair. He fed her, gave her soap and a towel, and when she had cleaned up, he showed her to her room, and he raped her. After, he sat down with her, and explained the facts of life.

"No one gets nothin' for nothin'," he told her. "If ya want to eat and have a place to stay, you'll have to earn your keep. Otherwise, I'll have ta put you back out in the street. You may think that I'm a bad person, now, but you'll soon find out that I'm not. There are people out there who are far worse than I am. Ask any of the other girls what it's like out there on the street. They find young girls with their throats cut every day. I did you a favor, Honey, whether you know it or not. A young thing, like you, on the streets, alone, is fair game for every weirdo with a knife. It wouldn't have been long before they'd found you in an alley with your throat cut. We're a family, here. We take care of each other. I take care of you, and you take care of me. The other girls will show you how."

It didn't take her long to learn the ropes. "Pops" was more of a user than a father image. For the first couple weeks she was "Pops" main squeeze, until the novelty wore off, and then a new runaway was recruited. She was sent out on the street to earn her keep. He set quotas, and if a girl didn't make her quota, he would slap her around. Angela had no trouble making her quota. It wasn't long before she had her own following. She was young and pretty. It wasn't just the "Johns" that noticed, either. One or two of the local pimps also had their eyes on her.

Pops often lost girls to the pimps. He warned them about talking with them. "You think you got it bad, here?" he would warn them. "Those pimps treat their girls even worse. They beat them, and if they don't do what they're told, they cut them."

It wasn't long, though, before Angela was wooed away by a man named Russell. Russell was a smooth talker. He offered her a nice apartment, clothes, and money. He worked on a percentage, he explained to her, and that's all. "Pops" wanted it all, and would dole it out, reluctantly. It didn't hurt that Russell was tall and good looking.

At first, Angela didn't mind setting up housekeeping with him. He took her places, wined her and dined her. Even though she was a minor, they still served her at some of the finest nightclubs, no questions asked. She was with Russell and that's all that mattered. She felt really safe for the first time since she had left home.

It didn't take long before she began to see the down side of being with Russell. When he was drunk, which wasn't often, he got mean . . . really mean. He would slap her around at the slightest provocation.

One night, when he was especially drunk, he hit her so hard that he drove her teeth through the corner of her lip. Angela felt the scar on the side of her mouth as she remembered the incident. He felt bad about it after, but Angela thought it was more because she was now damaged goods, than from any real remorse. After that, she fell out of favor, and Russell found a new girl, named Elese who was a year older. Her relationship with Russell became one of strictly business, and that was fine with her.

He was good at his job. He took good care of the girls in his charge. There were twelve, at the time, a pretty large harem for one pimp to control. There were others watching and waiting to pounce on him like so many hungry jackals. It was only a matter of time before something happened. It was the week after Angela eighteenth birthday that the news came down the street that Russell had been found dead. His body had been found in a back alley. His throat had been cut. She cried for three days. She couldn't even eat.

Willy "Boy" Brown as the prime suspect, but it seems he had an iron clad alibi. At the time of the murder, he was having dinner with his mother and some friends, in Waukegan, nearly forty miles away. Before that, no one even knew he had a mother. It wasn't long before he was coming around recruiting the girls Russell had left behind, including Angela. Willy Brown was the quintessential pimp. He lived life large with big cars, flashy clothes, and a lavish lifestyle. He was tall, black, arrogant, and walked with a cocky gate. Nevertheless, the girls seemed to like him. He was firm, but he was never abusive, and he didn't like other pimps, who were. He didn't want to be called a pimp. He considered himself more of a manager. He provided a service; saw to it that the bills were paid, watched over the girls, and took his percentage. He slept with some of the girls, but it wasn't a requisite. If there were a problem he would take care of it; any kind of a problem.

There was this time when some John, who was high on acid, cut up Maria. Willy saw to it that she got the best medical treatment. The John ended up on a slab with his throat cut. Willy was visiting his mother that time, too. He even sent Maria to a plastic surgeon. He called it a "body shop", and said he would do the same for his car. No one would want a whore with scars all over her body. They knew that it was just his way of showing how tough he was. He said that his mother once told him, "If you don't take good care of them girls, Willy, I'm gonna come down there and cut off your nuts!" The girls wondered if his mother even knew what he really did for a living, or perhaps, who was really in charge here.

The sound of a door closing brought her abruptly back from her thoughts. She stood up and looked around, wondering how she was going to explain her presents if she was confronted. A sudden chill overtook her, and she shivered, uncontrollably.

"You must be cold."

"Oh! My God!" The man who now stood beside her startled her. He was about her height, in his early thirties, but with a boyish quality that transcended his years.

"Did I frighten you? I'm sorry. I've been watching you, I must confess. We don't get many visitors this time of night. I was curious to know just what you were up to. I decided that you looked harmless enough." He handed her a tan, wool blanket. "Here," he smiled warmly, "you do look cold."

She accepted the blanket and wrapped it around her shoulders. "Thank you." There was "USA" printed in large letters on one side. He noticed that she was looking at it.

"Army surplus, "he confessed. "This church is a safe haven in case of a storm, invasion, or pestilence." He laughed. It was a gentle laugh that made her feel at ease.

She sat back in the pew and pulled the blanket tightly around her. "How about rain?" she asked.

"That'll work, too," he offered. He reached behind him, grabbed a folding chair and shook it open with one motion. Turning it around, he straddled it backward; resting his folded arms on the back and his chin on his arms. He seemed to be studying her. "You're not from around here, are you?"

"That obvious, is it?"

"Working girl, right?"

"Most people would just call me a whore, or a slut. The nicest thing anyone's ever call me, until now, was a prostitute. 'A working girl', that's cute. I haven't heard that in a while." She put her head down.

He reached over, put his hand under her chin and raised her head. "Rather hard on yourself, aren't you?"

She chuckled, nervously, "Whores are not that highly regarded in our society, or haven't you heard?"

"So you feel, then, that you have fallen from grace? Do you feel that you have fallen from God's graces, too?"

"Of course." She bowed her head again.

Again, he raised her head with his hand. "Do you really think that any God could be so shallow? Is what you do so awful? You give of yourself, so that others may find pleasure. Not every woman is capable of doing that."

"You make me sound like some kind of Florence Nightingale. There is no charity involved, here. I do it for the money. I'm a prostitute; I sell myself to anyone who has the right price."

"And aren't we all prostitutes of a kind? As a society, we sell our time, our pride, and sometimes even our souls, for money. We all give up a part of ourselves for cold hard cash. So why are the rest of us any different from you?"

"What have you sold, Preacher? What have you given up for cold hard cash?"

"Perhaps, a bit of my free spirit, as I tie myself down to my church, my God, and my congregation. I stand here every Sunday, preaching to my flocks, of truth, of love, of understanding, as if I know all the answers. I am a pure phony! If they could look inside my soul, they would see that I am just as frightened and confused as they are. I prostitute myself to God! I prostitute myself to my congregation! I smile when I want to tell them to go to hell! I listen to their petty problems, as if I really care. I do it for pride. I do it for respect. I do it for dignity. I do it for money." He took her hand in his, and stroking it softly, he kissed it.

She looked up into his soft blue eyes. There were tears forming. "Now, who's being hard on himself?" she asked, smiling.

"Sorry," he said, suddenly getting to his feet. "Would you like a cup of coffee?" He reached out his hand. "We have a small dining hall in the back where the coffee pot is always on."

She accepted his hand, and removing the blanket, she got to her feet. "Don't you ever sleep?" she asked.

"And miss a chance to have a cup of coffee with a beautiful, young woman? Are you daft?"

He led the way down a narrow hallway to a large room filled with long tables and metal, folding chairs. He flicked on a switch, and Angela shielded her eyes, as a battery of florescent lights came to life. In the back of the room was a small table that held several coffee makers, a stack of Styrofoam cups, several containers of sugar and creamer as well as a box of donuts, the preacher had warned, may be a bit stale.

He offered her one, but she declined. He filled a cup and handed it to her. "You'll have to do your own fixin's," he said, "By the way, I don't know your name."

"Angela," she replied. "Angela Hall. My friends call me Angie."

He poured himself a cup of coffee, and then extended his free hand. "Pleased to meet you, Angie," he said. I would certainly like to be your friend. My name is William Bencher. My friends call me "Preacher Bill", but just plain, old Bill is fine with me."

"Pleased to meet you, too, Bill," she said, taking his hand.

He motioned toward one of the tables. "Shall we take a seat?"

She took a seat at the end of the first table, and he sat across from her. He had the box of donuts in his hand. He took one and bit into it. "Not too bad," he informed her, "a little crunchy, but still good. Are you sure you won't have one?"

"No, thanks."

"Got to watch your figure, right. With a body like yours, you must have to be careful what you eat"

"What do you mean by that?"

"Well, let's face it, nobody wants a fat whore."

"You come right to the point, don't you, Preacher Bill?"

"I mean no disrespect. Let's face it. I sell God; you sell your body. The nicer I can make God look, the easier he is to sell. The better your body looks, the easier it is to sell. That's just business."

She put her hands on her sides, and leaned back in the chair. "You know, I just can't figure you out. You really don't sound like a preacher."

"When was the last time you went to church, besides today?"

"OK! You made your point. Maybe things have changed since I was fourteen."

"My God! Has it been that long?"

"Since before I left home."

"So you were a runaway?"

"Yes. I just couldn't get along with my mother."

"How long has it been since you've seen her?"

"Nearly ten years."

"Don't you think she must have been worried sick? Don't you ever wonder how many nights she must have cried herself to sleep? How hurt she must have felt, thinking that it was all her fault. Have you ever gone to see her, or called her to tell her that you're still alive?"

"I tried a couple of times, but I just couldn't get myself to do it. What would I say to her, 'Hi Mom, it's your whore daughter, I want to come back home'. Somehow, I don't think she would have welcomed me with open arms. Now, it's been ten years. I know it's too late. I could never go home."

Bill got to his feet and poured himself a warm-up. He held up the pot. "Want some more?"

She put up her hand, "No more for me."

He slid back into the seat, cupping both of his hands around the cup as if to warm them. "A mother's love is the strongest kind of love there is, you know. It's stronger than that of a man and a woman, stronger than the love of man for his God, and even stronger than the love for one's own country. A mother's love knows no boundaries, and has no limits. If you honestly think that she doesn't still love you, then you're a fool. Somehow, I can't see you as a fool."

"What do you know about a mother's love?" she asked.

He took a sip of his coffee and stared down at the table. His face got very sad for a moment. "I had a mother, once. She died when I was fifteen."

"I'm sorry;" she apologized, "that was cruel of me."

He looked up at her, again. "No! It was a fair question. I know how strong a mother's love is because I was probably the worst kid that ever could be. I was always in trouble. Just before my mother died, she made me promise that I would straighten myself out."

"Is that when you decided to become a minister?"

"Hell no! I did six months as a juvey, after that."

"Is that what straightened you out?"

"Not really. It was after my father came back into my life, and I saw what I could become, that I finally saw the handwriting on the wall. He was a two-time loser, heading for his third hitch and life imprisonment.

I saw how much alike we were, and it scared the fucking shit out of me!"

Angela leaned back in the chair and laughed, hardily.

His eyes narrowed, "You find that amusing?"

"No! I'm sorry! It's just that it struck me as funny to hear you say 'fucking shit'."

"You mean coming from a preacher? Let's not play games, here. I know all the 'bad' words; I grew up with a very explicit vocabulary. I also know that you know all the 'bad' words, and I'm sure you've used them all at one time or another. So, who, the fuck, are we kidding."

"Wow, Preacher! Is this what I've been missing by not going to church? Is this some sort of 'new wave' preaching? If so, I think it's fucking great."

"I think you're missing the point. I'm not trying to shock you into going back to church. That is something you have to decide for yourself. And no, this is not the new format of the modern church. What I'm trying to communicate is that what we are, is not as important as who we are. Deep down inside, we're not all that much different."

"Oh, bullshit! Here you are, safe in your nice church, with everyone looking up to you. I'm out there in the street, peddling my ass. No one ever looks up to me. My pimp always has his hand out, the cops are always harassing me; I've been beat-up, arrested, stabbed, strip-searched, and, believe it or not, raped. So where do you get off, sitting there on your little pedestal, saying that we're anything alike, Preacher?"

"Please call me Bill. Tell me Angela, do you like your job?"

Her brow was wrinkled, now, and it was obvious that she had taken on a defensive posture.

"What, are you crazy? Hell no, I don't like my job!"

"Are you good at what you do?"

"What kind of question is that?"

"An honest question."

"Yeah! I think I am. At twenty-six, I can still bring in as much money as some of those pimply-faced teenyboppers, with their cute little asses."

"So you must take some pride in your work."

Angela grabbed her purse, threw the strap over her shoulder, and got to her feet. "I think I need to get the fuck out of here!" she shouted. "One minute you're a preacher, and the next minute you're talking dirty and asking me how I like being a whore! Why do I feel I've been here before? The next thing you'll be asking me if I give out free samples! Well, the answer to that is, fuck no!"

"Sit down!" His voice was low and authoritative.

"What?"

"I said, sit down!" He was on his feet, now, and there was a funny look in his eyes.

She sat down hard in the chair and slammed her purse on the table. She looked at her watch. "Look," she said, "it will be light soon, I need to call a cab and get back to my apartment."

"What you need to do is shut up and listen! You came in here for a reason."

"It was raining. I came in to get out of the rain."

"Bullshit! There's a phone booth on the corner. You could have called a cab. As for wanting to have sex with you, I must admit that I do find you very attractive. You have a great body, and very nice tits." He got to his feet, pulled his wallet from his back pocket, fished out two one-hundred-dollar bills, and threw them on the table. "I'm not a man of means, but I am sure that I will be able to come up with the price of a good lay. If the two hundred isn't enough, I could cut you a check. I assure you that I have excellent credit. If this is how you really feel, then let's get this out of the way. I'm up to it if you are. The table may be a little hard, but I promise not to take long. The truth is; I may have neglected my sex life too long. I may be a tad out of practice." He started to unbutton his shirt. "OK! Let's get it over with, so we can get back to the real issue at hand."

"You're not serious, are you?"

"Not really. The truth is I don't perform well when I'm pissed off!"

"Sorry. I just wasn't sure where all this was going. So, what is the issue at hand?"

He reached across the table and took her hand, again. His eyes were softer, now, warm and friendly. "Why you of course. You're stuck in a job you hate. The question is, why?"

"That's simple," she offered, the tears now running from her eyes. "It's all I've ever done. I don't know how to do anything else."

"Have you ever thought of being a model?"

"With this?" She pointed to the scar on the corner of her mouth.

"A minor flaw only adds to the charm of a pearl."

"Well, that's very kind, but I'm afraid the modeling industry wouldn't share your views. I'm damaged goods. No one wants damaged goods."

"You know what your problem is? Your problem is you. You're only twenty-six. It's not too late to start over."

"Doing what? Do you have any idea what I make as a prostitute? With my skills, where am I going to find a job making that kind of money?"

"Did you start out making big money?"

"Hell no! I started out selling my body for twenty or twenty-five dollars, a shot!"

"So, you'll just have to be content with starting at the bottom, again. The important thing is how you feel about yourself, not how much money you can make. You did it once; you can do it again. You're not stupid. I can see that. If you really apply yourself, you will be able to accomplish anything. Find a job; any job. Maybe something you could like. Start at the bottom and claw your way to the top. It will be hard. You're a woman. You will have to be able to accept disappointment, prejudice, and rejection, but I think you're up to a good fight. There are a lot of women out there who have started out with less than you have to offer, who have made it. You owe it to yourself to at least try. After all, what do you have to lose? You could always go back to what you're doing now."

He looked at his watch, pushed back his chair, and got to his feet. "Now, if you will forgive me the doors open, officially, in one hour. I need to shave, shower and change my clothes. If you wish, I will call you a cab."

"Thank you." She gathered up her purse, got to her feet, and straightened her clothes. "It looks like I need to do the same." She offered him her hand. "Thanks for the coffee, Bill. We'll have to do this again some time."

They stopped at his office while he called for a cab, and then he walked her to the front door. "I wish you would think over what I said."

"I will," she assured him, and kissed him softly on the cheek.

Bill Bencher toweled himself off, selected a pair of blue boxer shorts from the neat stack in the top drawer and put them on. From the closet, he picked out a light brown suit and a white shirt. He stepped into the suit pants and fastened the snap. They were a little big, but there was an extra hole in the attached belt. He donned the shirt, tucked it in, and snugged up the belt to the new setting. He then selected a green tie from the rack. He had to tie it three times before he got it right. He smiled at his reflection. "Looks like you're a little out of practice, Billy Boy," he said to himself. He smoothed the tie against the shirtfront. He seemed pleased at what he saw. He slipped on the jacket, and then stepped back in front of the mirror.

"Tah-dah! Now, all you need, Billy Boy, is a briefcase, and you'll look just like any other commuter in the rush-hour traffic. I think I saw one in the office. Good-bye, Reverend Bencher. Hello, successful business-man." He saluted his reflection.

Ellen Johnson tried her key in the front door. It was already unlocked. *The reverend must have already unlocked it,* she thought. She often came early on Wednesdays to help clean the church. The reverend and his wife usually slept late. Ellen had her own key so she didn't have to disturb them. It was an arrangement they had enjoyed for years. She would never vacuum before nine. By that time they would be up, and about. She pushed open the doors, setting a box of donuts in the back pew while she removed her sweater. The reverend always made the coffee, and she would always bring the donuts. She looked at her watch; it was eight. An hour would be plenty of time to do what dusting needed to be done.

She went to the dining hall, and set the donuts on the table in the back. She notice the two used coffee cups on the last table. This seemed weird to her. The reverend was always such a neat freak. It wasn't like him to leave dirty cups lying around. She gathered them up to put them in the trash. On one of the cups she noticed a heavy lipstick print. "Curious," she thought, "Mrs. Collen almost never wears lipstick, and never anything this dark."

As she passed the door that led to the Minister's apartment, she noticed the door was open, slightly. When she reached to close it, her hand came away damp. When she looked at her hand, she saw what looked like blood. "My God!" she said, out loud. "Has someone injured themselves? Hello!" she shouted, through the open door. "It's me, Ellen, are you alright?" Not invoking a response, she yelled louder. "Hello, Reverend . . . Kate, are you in there?" Cautiously, she opened the door and entered the apartment. The living room was in complete disarray. The coffee table was overturned and papers and broken glass was scattered all over the floor. She put her hand to her mouth, disbelieving what she was seeing. The door to the master bedroom was opened wide. She stuck her head through the doorway. The bloody sight that affronted her eyes caused her knees to buckle and the blood to rush from her brain. She fainted.

Angela climbed aboard the bus, and took the third seat so she could have a window seat. She clutched an over-night bag in her lap and smiled to herself as she thought of her conversation with her mother. Four hours, they had talked. It was going to be one hell of a bill, but then, Willy will have to worry about that. Let him consider it her going-away present.

"He's gonna be pissed, when he finds out I'm gone," she thought to herself, *"but he'll get over it."* She still wasn't sure she was doing the right thing. She just couldn't believe how understanding her mother was. Angela told her everything . . . everything. She cried; her mother cried. Most of their conversation was trying to talk between sobs. They had let it all out, both of them. She couldn't believe how good it felt just to cry. They would need time to get to know each other again. The little girl she had been before she left home, no longer existed. Maybe this was a good thing. If her mother was willing to give their relationship a try, then so was she.

The man in front of her unfolded the morning paper. A headline caught her eye. **"Dangerous, homicidal killer escapes from mental institution."** She read the first few lines over the man's shoulder. *William Bencher,* she read to herself. *Now, why does that name sound so familiar?*

THE RED CARPET

Zavior was standing in the doorway of the moon deck as Gonog arrive home from work. How lovely she looked, her pale, blue skin glistening in the bright glow of the twin moons. Gonog did so admire his helpmate. How eloquent she was, how majestic her stature, how effortlessly she would glissade across a room. Words as to how he felt about his life partner, the mother of his child, were not within his vocabulary and Gonog spoke over 560 languages, fluently.

It was part of his job as Social Coordinator of sector eight. Listening to the petty complaints of regional potentates, calming tempers, and reassuring each that their views would be taken into consideration, sometimes communicating in four to six different languages and dialogs, simultaneously, took a certain flair and savoir faire that few possessed. Those, whom had once been predator and prey, pest and host, itch and scratcher, now, under the new order of the Confederacy, were required to live in harmony.

A Marvonian diplomat, named Borganoz, once asked him how any synthetic food could ever replace a large, succulent slice of fresh-killed Swack, thrust onto a spit and simmered in its own juices over an open fire. Gonog, being a strict vegetarian, had never tasted meat. The mere thought of devouring flesh was less than appealing to him. He suggested that perhaps the thrill of the hunt was what the Marvonian really missed. He suggested that automatons, representing prey, could be developed and the hunt resumed. He also suggested that the Swackian diplomats be persuaded to join the hunt. Perhaps they might find that they had more in common than they thought.

He was surprised to hear that Borganoz had taken his advice, and the hunt was scheduled for the cycle of the solar flares, about the time of the vernal equinox. What surprised him the most was the fact that he had been invited to join the Marvonian party. He, of course, accepted. Someone had to be there to make sure that the overzealous

Marvonians didn't end up hunting down the Swackians and cooking them up, anyway.

All went well until the hunt was over. Borganoz had planned a big surprise. The post-hunt festivities would include a huge barbeque. However, when it was announced that the main course would be synthetic Swack, the silence that followed was deafening. Marbro, the Swackian leader was the first to break the silence. His roaring laughter reverberated off of the surrounding mountains like fulminating thunder.

"I never realized, my dear friend, Borganoz," he said, "that you Marvonians held us Swackians in such high esteem. We would be honored to partake in your most punctiliously prepared victuals," he spread his arms to indicate the tables filled with prepared foods, "but only on one condition. Next cycle," he said, pointing a long, yellow digit at Borganoz, "we Swackians will provide the food. It will be one of our most cherished dishes, Marvon wieners."

The silence was repeated. This time it was Borganoz who burst forth with his resounding roar of laughter. Coming forward, he clamped his left, upper arm, soundly, around Marbro's shoulder and pulled him close.

"I do so love someone with a sense of humor who can appreciate a good joke," he shouted. "We Marvonians will be looking forward to next cycle's hunt and smorgasbord with the utmost anticipation!"

Gonog didn't remember when he started breathing again, but apparently it was soon enough to keep him from fainting dead away. The event became an annual event, and was enjoyed by Marvonian and Swackian alike. It helped bolster a slow time in the Marvonian calendar, helping the economy, and providing the holiday loving Morvonians with yet another excuse for a segment of celebration. On the other hand, the Marvon wieners, so impetuously mentioned at the first regale, were in fact just a figment of Marbro's imagination. However, upon returning home, he convinced his greatest chefs that it might be prudent and advantageous to come up with something that tasted better than they did. The resulting product is now being sold to Marvonian and Swackian alike in quantities measured in galactic tons. The sweetest part, to Gonog, was the fact that the festival was named in his honor.

Not everything has gone as well as this. Most days were filled with endless complaints, breaches of contracts, political frays, and infringements of all kinds. Smoothing over conflicts, while keeping the Confederacy running on an even course, was a full-time job. That's why tonight; as he set his briefcase down for the last time . . . at least for the next two sequels . . . his mind was drifting far from the workplace and to thoughts of a well-earned vacation.

"You haven't been listening to a thing I've said, have you?" His wife was standing before him, now, colorful brochures clutched in each hand. "Do I have to make all the decisions around here? Your two sequels will be up and I'll still be stuck here in Lamport. Lamport, Lamport, Lamport!" She turned and looked out the window. "I'm sick of looking at the same sky, the same mountains, and the same purple landscape. I want to go to someplace exciting this year."

Gonog looked down at one of the brochures in her hand. "How about Maylox 5?"

"We went there three cycles ago," she said, shaking her head. "Don't you remember the leaches? I so abhor those creatures, constantly asking if they could suck our blood, I think they're disgusting!"

"They're Porbonites, Dear, not leaches. One of my associates is a Porbonite. They're really not that bad when you get to know them. It's just that it's hard for them to break old habits."

"I don't really care!" she shouted, storming into the food preparation area, and throwing the brochures on the counter. "I just want to go to someplace . . ." she was waving her arms, looking about the room, as if she were looking for some sign that would give her the right word, ". . . new!" Her eye caught something setting next to the door. "What is that?"

"What, dear?" Gonog had decided to move his briefcase before she threw it, also.

"What is this *thing* on the floor, next to the portal?"

"Oh, that. I'm not sure, dear. I must have picked it up on the beltway, coming home. It was stuck in the intake of the Star Sprinter X-3. Some sort of space debris, I would presume."

"Have you looked at this? Look at the drawing on this plaque. Were, in the galaxy, would the female humanoid be shorter than the male?"

113

Gonog set the object on the counter and looked closely at the plaque. "Well, there you are. Look at the planets, dear. It's a whole different solar system, maybe a whole different galaxy. Apparently this piece of debris wandered out of its own space and into the traffic lanes. I'll drop it off at the Transportation Department before we leave and let them dispose of it."

"You'll do nothing of the sort, Gonog," Zavior said, asserting her feminine authority. I think it's one of the nicest things you've ever brought me. I think that this plaque would look very nice on the south wall. Take it off the debris for me, will you?"

Gonog went to the shop to get his tools. When he got back, his daughter, Vissallia, who had just returned from college, was looking the object over carefully.

"Probe," she said, matter-of-factly.

"What makes you think it's a probe, Honey?" he asked.

"It says 'Pioneer 10' right here, daddy. Can't you read?"

"260 languages," he said, defensively, "but this isn't one of them. How do you know how to read it?"

"Oh, Daddy, don't you keep up with the latest things? Earth is all the rage, now. It's a small planet with one sun, and it's a pretty blue color."

"Not another blue planet." Zavior sounded disappointed.

"Oh, no, Momsy," Vissallia explained. "It only looks blue from space. Bimbaly and Izala went there two cycles ago, and said that it was actually a lovely green color."

"Green?" Zavior's eyes grew brighter. "Oh, Gonog, you know how much I love green! Why can't we go there this year? I find green to be so relaxing."

"You know we can't visit a foreign planet without an invitation," Gonog informed her. "It would be a direct violation of the 'Intergalactic Non-invasive Act'."

Zavior was looking the plaque over closely. "Take a close look at the plaque, Dear. Do you see how the subordinate male has his hand raised in a gesture of friendship? Now, wouldn't you consider that a friendly act; maybe even an invitation?"

"Gonog nodded his head. "Well, I guess it could be."

"What about the map?" Zavior pointed out. "Surely that is an invitation."

"I never thought of it that way, but now that you mentioned it, if they didn't want us to go there, why would they send us a map?"

Vissallia was truly excited. "Then we're going to Earth!" She kissed her parents on the cheeks. "I'm going to start packing, right now!"

"How far is this Earth place, honey?" Gonog yelled after his daughter.

"About 200 grimslas, Daddy."

"200 grimslas! Pack lightly," he yelled, "we'll need to conserve fuel."

Making sure that his bike was stable, Snake urgently made his way through the scrub brush. He unzipped his jeans, targeted a resting tumbleweed, and relieved himself. As he shook himself dry, he thought he heard the sound of something moving behind him.

"You must be fond of that plant," a female voice said, "but I fear that you're too late to help it much."

Snake spun around to see three blue creatures standing before him, all over seven feet tall; two of them females. He was trying unsuccessfully to pull up his zipper.

"Let me help you with that," said Zavior, stepping foreward. "Vissallia sometimes has the same trouble with her suit." She tucked in his manhood and successfully closed his zipper. "There," she said, "now that wasn't hard, was it?

"Should you be touching that, dear?" Gonog asked.

"It's all right, honey." She held up her hands. "I'm wearing invisable gloves."

Snake just stood there, his mouth agape. "Jesus!" was all he said.

Gonog stepped forward and extended his hand. "Pleased to meet you, Jesus. My name is Gonog, this is my life partner Zavior, and my daughter Vissallia. We're from the planet Lamport in the galaxy Esquro. Have you lived here long?"

"In Arizona?" Snake asked.

Gonog spread his hand. "I mean on this little planet. Ert, I believe you call it."

"Earth, Daddy," Vissallia corrected.

"Oh yes, Earth."

"Where else would I live?" Snake asked, still in a state of confusion.

"Why, I understand you have twelve other planets in your solar system. Haven't you ever visited any of them?" Gonog inquired.

"Hey, man," Snake said, "even I know we only have nine planets; eight if you don't count Pluto

"Thirteen," Vissallia corrected.

"How does she know all this shit?" Snake was taking offense to the fact that some foreigner would claim to know more about his own solar system than he did.

"I have a straight 1000+ average in school," Vissallia informed him. "I'm at the head of my class."

"Yeah?" Snake wasn't paying any attention to Vissallia's boast; his attention was captured by the huge craft looming up behind the visitors. "Wow! That's a real beauty," he said, walking toward it to get a better look. How fast does it go?"

"The Star Sprinter X-3? About eight, flat out," Gonog explained.

"That don't sound like much," Snake commented, scratching his head.

"That's eight light years per segment," Vissallia explained. "We're moving hundreds of times faster than the speed of light. That's why no one saw us land."

"It must take a lot of fuel to run it."

"Actually," Gonog explained, "it gets 48 inter-solar, and 53 interstellar, depending on the traffic. That's light years per capsule."

"What-the-hell's a capsule?"

"One of these,' Gonog said, producing a small canister from his pocket.

"You're pulling my leg," Snake said, taking the canister from Gonog's hand and looking it over. "How's it work?"

"Well, the problem is, you have to dissolve this capsule in 200 tolags of water before you can use it. The water is what costs the most."

"And how much is 200 tolags?"

Gonog looked around. "Say that you were standing in water up to your neck, and you reached your arms out as far as you could in all directions. That would be about the volume of 200 tolags."

Snake's mouth dropped. "Holy shit, that's about a thousand gallons! I wonder if it would work in my bike. If it did, that much could run my bike forever."

"Bike? What's a bike," asked Vissallia.

"A chopper, hog, scooter, a motorcycle.

"A what?"

"Never mind," Snake said, "come here, I'll show you."

They followed Snake through the bushes to where he had left his bike. The bright sun was now glistening off the custom paint job and the chromed Springer front-end that Snake, now, proudly polished with the bottom of his shirt.

"This is my ride," he said.

"Oh daddy!" Vissallia exclaimed. "Isn't that just so adorable? But doesn't that thing dig into the ground while it's moving?"

"The kick stand? No, you kick it up when you get ready to ride."

"I understand that while this thing is moving centrifugal force holds it up, but what holds it up when it's not moving?"

Snake threw his leg over the seat, avoiding the two-foot sissy bar with much difficulty. He leaned the bike to the left and kicked up the stand. "You hold the bike up like this," he explained, planting his feet firmly on the ground." He turned over the starter and the engine came to life. The pipes barked and popped as he twisted the throttle.

"Oh, how primitive!" Vissallia shrieked. "Please, Daddy, can I go for a ride on it? Please."

Gonog couldn't remember the last time he had denied his daughter anything. "I suppose," he said, reluctantly.

Zavior shot him the look that is understood by all males all over the galaxies. It was too late; to rescind permission now would only admit that he had been wrong in giving it in the first place.

Vissallia, easily, threw her long leg over the sissy bar and settled into the seat behind Snake. The bike seat was designed so that a chick, on the back, could see over the head of the biker. She didn't need that advantage. As it was, her large breasts rested heavily on Snake's shoulders. He wondered how he would look cruising down the highway with a seven-foot, blue chick on the back. She did have nice eyes, though; sort of a cross between oriental and reptilian, and their purple color was in full contrast with her bright red hair. He gunned the engine, but instead of moving, the bike bogged down into the soft sand; too much weight on the back.

"How much do you weigh?" he asked.

"About one hundred and ten."

"Pounds?"

"No," she said, "dracnuds."

"How many pounds are one hundred and ten dracnuds?" he asked.

"I don't know, not as much as this machine, I don't think." She swung her leg over the sissy bar and got off. When Snake was off of the bike, she reached down and picked it up. "No," she said, "I'm much lighter than this." She set the bike down, carefully, and then reached down and picked up Snake. "Just a little more than you, I believe."

Snake was caught off guard. Here was a broad who could lift a bike that he knew weighed over eight hundred pounds like it was nothing more than a sack of potatoes. For the first time in his twenty-two years, he knew that he was really in love. He pushed the bike out to the hard pavement, and they both remounted.

"Where do I hang on?" she asked.

"You'll need to hang on to me," he said, as he kicked the bike into gear.

She reached down and grabbed him by the inside of his thighs.

"Ah, I think it would be better, if you just put your arms around my waist," he said, wincing with pain.

Actually, with her height, it was more natural to put her arms around his chest. He sped off down the highway, cranking the bike up to seventy-five.

"This is great," she shouted above the noise, "but can you go fast?"

He turned the throttle all the way. On a good day, with little wind, this bike would do one hundred and twenty, but with all the extra weight, and wind resistance, he was lucky to get ninety. The road was straight, and there was little traffic, so he had all of the room that he needed. He looked in the mirror. There was something coming up fast behind him. He reached over and steadied the mirror to stop it from vibrating so he could get a better look. There were two blue people, coming up behind him, in something that looked very much like a large, silver bedpan. Two of the four cars that it passed went off of the road.

He was to meet the rest of the club at a bar about two miles up the road, so he just kept on going. He wasn't too sure what he was going to tell the guys when he got there. He would have to play it by ear. It was a nice day, so he slowed down to fifty-five. She didn't seem to mind. She was holding her long hair out of her eyes with one hand and looking intently at the scenery. There really wasn't a whole lot to see: cactus, Joshua trees, cows, fences, desert, now and then a gas station, house, or well-worn billboard.

"Where is the green?" she shouted. "There was supposed to be green."

"This is the desert, Sweetheart," he informed her. "There is a lot of green when you get out of the desert."

"What are the four-footed creatures?" she asked.

"Cows!" Snake shouted back.

"They seem nice. Do they talk?"

"No," he said. "They just eat, fart, give milk, and then we cook them up and eat them."

"Oh! How horrible! You mean that you still do that, here."

"That's what they're here for, to eat."

"I'll bet Daddy could talk to them," she said. "All creatures should live together in peace."

"Whatever," Snake said.

They arrived at the Lazy Moon just before noon. There were over thirty motorcycles lined up in front, in three rows. Vissallia, immediately, began looking them over carefully. She pointed out three that she liked, including one with a radically extended front end.

Snake (aka Jesus) was fascinated by the little craft Vissallia's parents were driving. It had no wheels, made no sound, and settled down on three legs that suddenly appeared when the thing stopped. Inside there was enough seating for four people and the instrument panel was so simple and uncluttered that even Snake thought he could, eventually, figure it out. There was a clear top that was now down, that somehow slid into the outer skin. That was another thing. The shell didn't feel hard, yet it wasn't actually soft, either.

"It's inflatable," Gonog explained, matter-of-factly. "It's called a Landfloater."

"You're kidding!" It caught Snake off guard. "How do they do that?"

"It is constructed from a plastic, malleable material that has two distinct neutral shapes. Heat it to a certain temperature and let the air out and it reverts back to its compact shape. Heat that to the same temperature and you can inflate it to its present shape. The whole thing can be reduced down to something that is no larger than a full-grown mucklark."

"A what?"

"About the size of that man's helmet."

Snake turned around to see the whole gang standing there, mouths agape, staring at the two blue people. They hadn't noticed Vissallia, yet, because she was behind the bikes, bent over, admiring the exhaust system on one of the machines.

"Jesus!" It was Grunt who first said anything.

"These must by your friends, Jesus," Gonog said, smiling broadly. "My name is Gonog, this is my life partner, Zavior, and that . . ." he pointed behind them, "is my daughter, Vissallia."

The whole gang turned around to see this shapely, blue-skinned, red-haired dolly sauntering toward them. Her gold, metallic outfit fit her like it had been painted on and except for the blue makeup and the over-dyed red hair, she was a knockout. They, simultaneously, emitted a collective sigh.

"Blue's a nice color," Grunt commented.

It wasn't until she started to get closer that they realized that she was either getting taller, or they were all shrinking.

"I like that one," she said, pointing to a red chopper in the first row. "Is it for sale?"

"You don't know much about bikers," Grunt said. "They would rather give up their old ladies than their bikes"

Weasel stepped forward. "That's my bike, and I don't know, for a quickie I might just considerate it."

"What is a quickie?" Vissallia asked, innocently.

"I think he is talking about sex, dear," her mother informed her.

"Oh. OK," she said, waving her finger at the group of bikers, "will that be just him?"

Immediately, several hands shot up.

"That doesn't rub off, does it?" Weasel inquired.

"What?"

"Hey!" Snake yelled, coming forward and grabbing Vissallia's hand. "That's my girl!"

"Sorry," Grunt said. "We didn't know fer sure."

"Well, I'm tellin' ya, fer sure, now. You get yer own girl, Weasel."

Vissallia pulled her hand away. "I don't know what the fuss is all about, Jesus, he only wanted some quick sex, not a lifetime commitment."

"Yeah," chimed in Weasel."

"You stay out of this, Weasel! In the first place my name ain't, Jesus, damn it!"

"It's Dammit?"

Snake was obviously upset. "No, it ain't Dammit, or Jesus, it's Snake! Actually, it's Charles Edward Harlington the third!" He suddenly realized what he had just said. "But don't any of you jokers ever repeat that! As far as anyone is concerned, it's Snake, just, Snake! Is that clear to everyone?"

All the bikers were shaking their heads and grunting, while Gonog, Zavior and Vissallia looked on in disbelief.

Vissallia couldn't understand how he could get so excited over something so trivial, when there were more important issues to explore, like the eating of cows. And where did he get off saying that she was *his girl?* She was nearly a head and a half taller than he was, besides being a female, which clearly made her the dominate one. He could be *her guy,* but she was, definitely, not *his girl!*

Grunt stepped forward. "You'se people are gonna hafta go," he began. "We got something going down here in a little while. The Fire Riders think that they are gonna kick us Gray Ghosts out of the Lazy Moon and make it their place." He turned around so they could see the Gray Ghost colors on the back of his jacket. "That ain't gonna happen."

"Too late, Grunt," Weasel said.

The combined roar of about thirty bikes could be heard in the distance, as the glitter of chrome proved, proof positive, that it was the Fire Riders.

"Just stay out of the way," Grunt said, "this is gonna get nasty."

The gang donned their gloves, and grabbing chains and clubs, they formed a line between their bikes, the Lazy Moon, and the incoming horde.

Zavior hit Gonog on the shoulder, "Do something, Gonog, someone could get hurt."

"What do you want me to do?" he asked.

"I don't know," she said, curtly, you're the Social Coordinator."

The aggregation came to a halt on the other side of the road. Bikes were precariously tethered, as weapons were hastily procured, and the no longer snorting beasts were left to their own fate. The leader, Rogue, the biggest and meanest of the lot, was the first to start across, but a large, blue giant quickly stepped in his path.

"Out of my way, clown," he said, his voice rough and gravely.

"I think we need to talk," said Gonog, "before this goes any further."

"I think not," informed Rogue, swinging a large chain at his aggressor.

Gonog grabbed the chain in mid-swing and easily pulled it apart, like one of those paper chains that you make to adorn the tree at Christmas time. He picked up Rogue by the back of his jacket and transported him across the road as if he were a small child. Snatching up Grunt in the same manner, he returned to the center of the highway. Everyone just stood there, mesmerized, as if frozen in time, not knowing what to do about this blue monster.

"Now," said Gonog, as he set them both down, "what exactly is this problem that you think is worth fighting over?"

"Well," said Grunt, "they want to take over the Lazy Moon."

"By *take over* you mean that they want to purchase the place?"

"No. No. They want to hang out here, like we do, but without us."

"And you," Gonog said, turning to Rogue, "don't want them around because you don't have anything in common with them, right?"

"Well, no," Rogue hesitated, "we are all bikers, an some of them jokers used to belong to a club that some of us belonged to, once."

"So you," he was now turning to Grunt, "are concerned that the owner will not want the extra business. You are being considerate."

"Well, no, I'm sure that Sam could always use a little more business, it's just that, well, ah, hell, I don't know."

"You know," Gonog began in a slow even tone, "the way I see it is like this. You have two small clubs that have nothing better to do than look for trouble. What if you had a mission?"

"Like what?" asked Rogue.

"Oh, I don't know. I'm new around here and don't know what needs to be done. Maybe some community work, charity work; something involving lots of guys who might just be bored, and need something to occupy their time."

"Hey, you know, I'll bet that all of us could throw a house up in nothing flat, for some family what ain't got a place to live," offered one of the Fire Riders. "I heard that there are organizations that do that kind of stuff."

"I bet we could collect gifts, at Christmas time, for kids that don't have much," offered one of the Gray Ghosts.

"Sound like good ideas to me," Gonog offered. "Why don't we all go inside and put our heads together over a few drinks. Who knows what we all could come up with?"

The rest of the evening went well. They even took a vote and decided to become one club. The final accord was that the name of the club would be the Ghost Riders and that the colors would depict a skeleton on an extreme chopper, with lots of fire. This seemed to make everyone happy. They even voted for a leader, but the surprising thing was that the new leader was neither Rogue nor Grunt, but a tall, good looking, clean-cut young man by the name of Nathan. Perhaps they thought that if they were going to be doing social work they needed a new image.

Things between Vissallia and Snake improved as *Snake* became *Charley* and he learned to say, "Yes ma'am and no ma'am," more frequently. Gonog discovered that flique, commonly used as ballast on Star Sprinters, was known here as diamonds, and large chunks, especially those the size of your thumb, brought considerable Earthly wealth. He was able to rent an entire hotel in an area that was not only green, but had a large blue-green ocean lapping at a private beach. It easily accommodated Gonog, Zavior, Vissallia, their sixty guests, and even their guests.

Gonog parked his Skimmer III in his designated parking spot. As he exited, Minquam, a co-worker with the Standardization Department, greeted him.

"How was your vacation?" he asked. "I heard you went to Earth."

"What vacation?" said Gonog.

"Why, what did you do?" Minquam asked.

"Same thing I do here," Gonog replied, "Social Coordination. It seems that the Earth people have as many problems as we do. It took me nearly a week and a half just to convince them that eating creatures called 'cows' was wrong and that 'moo' meant 'no'. Somebody called Mack Donald complained, because he said it would put him out of business. It seems something called a 'ham' burger was, actually, made from cows. Fortunately, Zavior is an expert at synthetic cookery and was able to come up with a concoction of soybeans, sorghum and wood fiber. By the time they added a bun, some things called tomato, onion, pickle, lettuce, and their usual condiments, none of them could tell the difference."

In the meantime a funny looking contrivance had pulled up next to Gonog's Skimmer III and a rather small creature was now leaning against it.

"Who is this with you?" Minquam asked.

"That is my daughter's new boyfriend," Gonog informed him. "I've gotten him a job with the maintenance department. He's rather good with tools."

Minquam put his hand to his mouthpart and leaned in closer. "Rather puny and pale, isn't he?"

"You get used to it," Gonog whispered back.

"So, I take it you're not going to go back to Earth on your next cycle," Minquam said, his fluctuating gills denoting a bit of sarcastic attitude.

"Oh, yes, we're definitely going back," Gonog stated. "By the way, you work in Standardization. Tell me, I just purchased a new Star Sprinter X-5, just how much ballast can it handle?"

STATUS QUO

Sarah stood before the Comptroller, her hands nervously pulling at the hem of her dress. She wore her pleated mini, the one with the red flowers.

"I'm sorry, Miss Brownshaw," he was saying. "There is no way we can grant you human status when you are clearly well past the eighty percentile. You clearly understood that this would happen when you elected to terminate your ninety-five-year-old façade for this exquisite model. Four-fifths of your brain had to be converted to digital, requiring you to sign off any rights to being considered human. It is just standard procedure."

"I know that, but I've changed my mind. I no longer want to be like this."

"Surely you understand that the only other alternative is . . . well . . . to no longer exist. I know that there are groups who believe that this is a good alternative, but I see no logical reason for electing such an extreme choice when one is able to extend one's life in such an exquisite manner. Might I say you don't look a day over twenty?"

"As a machine? How can you call this living? I want to terminate my life. I want to be buried with my husband. I should have listened to him. He did the right thing."

"Yes, Mr. Brownshaw belonged to one of those right-wing groups."

"It was called a church."

"Putting your faith in invisible entities has long gone out of style, Miss Brownshaw."

"That's <u>Mrs.</u> Brownshaw."

"There is no longer any logical reason to carry that moniker, Miss Brownshaw, as only something like fifteen percent of that former person still exists. You are free to marry, although you can no longer have children, but many childless families go on to live happy lives. Think of the advantages. You are free of pain, diseases, bad habits, and obesity. When my time in life arrives, I will have no problem making the same decision."

Sarah looked down at the Comptroller sitting before her in his high-back, swivel chair. He couldn't have been much over forty. He seemed pompous, arrogant, so all-knowing, yet he knew nothing of what she was going through.

"I feel as if I'm trapped inside this machine. I have no feelings."

"Oh, come, come, Miss Brownshaw, I understand that the sense of touch is quite remarkable."

"I find no enjoyment in petting a dog. I'm afraid to hold a kitten for fear I will crush it. There is no pleasure in sex; it's as if I am looking through the eyes of someone else. Life for me ceased when they put what was left of me in this cage."

"But, Miss Brownshaw, think of the alternative. Surely you must find some pleasures in being alive, being able to work, go to a movie, watch the sunrise, and knowing that this will continue until that one-fifth of your brain finally decides to expire; five or six hundred years from now. You will never be any older than you are now. Surely that has to stand for something."

"Yes, that's what I thought at first, but my life has lost its sense of purpose. Now I only exist to exist. Where is the urgency? What I don't accomplish today can wait until tomorrow, or next year, or ten years from now. I no longer have to exercise. In fact it is discouraged; I'd be wasting fuel cells. I had to go back to work to pay for this . . . shell, but not in my life's work, because the creative part of me was in the other part of my brain, the part of me that was still human."

"The human status is only for legal issues. You are still as human as anyone else, except when it comes to things like voting, or making legal decisions. You must see that we certainly can't have the digital part of your brain making what would normally be 'human' decisions."

"You mean like euthanasia, terminating my own existence?"

"You must realize, Miss Brownshaw, that the 'shell', as you call it, cost the government a sizable amount of money, and until it is fully paid for you really have no say in deciding whether it is to be shut down or not. In fact, the government can make things very unpleasant for those who feel that they can refuse to work off their indebtedness."

"Non-humans."

"Precisely. I assume that you have the forty-year plan?"

"I have twenty-five years, six months, and eighteen days left, accounting for leap-years. I can no longer remember the touch of my husband's hand, but I could calculate the volume of this room by counting the floor tiles. It is no longer a brain, it's a computer."

"People strive their whole life; never achieving that level of genius."

"It's not real. It's not mine. I once could bake a cake from scratch without having to read it out of a book, or measure ingredients like a chemical formula. I could watch a butterfly without even noticing the scales on its wings. I could get involved in a mindless soap opera. Now, my clothes are arranged by the days of the week, my checkbook is always balanced, crossword puzzles are no longer a challenge, and I see birds as nothing more than something that craps on my car. Where is the quality?"

"Miss Brownshaw, now you're being a bit melodramatic. I believe it was Shakespeare who wrote something about bearing what ills we have, rather than fly to others that we know not of. Choosing death over life is contrary to human nature."

"Unlike you, Mr. Clemmons, I believe that there is someplace better, and I grow anxious to go there. I have seen hell. It is here and now. If I wish to go there, now, who is to suffer other than myself?"

"Even if I agreed with your madness, Miss Brownshaw, there is still your financial obligation."

"And if I find the funds?"

"I am an open-minded person. I might be willing to sign your status form, but only upon proof of full payment."

She grabbed the papers from the desk. "Believe me, Mr. Clemmons, I will hold you to that. Good day, sir."

The Comptroller watched as she crossed the room to the door. "Nice model, "he thought. "When I convert, I just might marry one of those."

It was raining hard when Dora Brownshaw left the building, but she made no effort to find shelter. She crossed the parking lot and climbed into her car. The only thing on her mind was how she was going to acquire three hundred sixty-two thousand, five hundred and eighty-seven dollars, and thirty-eight cents. The eighty-seven dollars and thirty-eight cents would be no problem, but the rest could represent a formidable obstacle.

With the population of the United States just topping six hundred million, she thought, *she would only need to sell something to every other man, woman, and child that would earn a profit of only one cent each, and I could make over three million dollars. Most people, today, wouldn't even bend over to pick up a nickel, and yet one penny could hold the key to my very existence, or to be more specific, lack of existence. But why would anyone send me a penny, or even everyone other one?*

She pondered this as she drove into the pouring rain. She even thought about crashing her car, but then thought better of it. She was titanium. The car was steel. She could very easily survive the crash. The car wouldn't. She would be without a car. Cars are expensive. Being without a car was nearly as bad as being trapped in her shell. She was not even allowed to harbor an irrational thought.

She took the next day off and went to the library. She was looking for some niche that would earn her that evasive penny. She decided to check the laws to see exactly what kind of enterprise non-humans were allowed to engage in. On page three, under "Eighty Percentiles" she found something very interesting.

The next day she called work and told them that she quit. She spent the next week constantly walking, talking to herself, and calculating volumes of useless data. It was a constant battle with her own neurons; messages like "Why? Is this necessary?" and "Will you shut up?" constantly bombarded her little piece of fleshy, human mind. Within seven days she completely exhausted her monthly supply of power packs, and she collapsed on the street like a string-less puppet.

They took her to "Recovery" where she kept uttering things like, "Two and two are nine, scissors brakes water, flocks of flying penguins, and Jack to King five."

Doctor Milton was shaking his head. This was one of the worse cases he had seen in over five years. "Chronic Dementia, I'd say. Not much use to society. It's too bad; she could have had another five hundred years. Get it ready. We'll be able to remove all the brain matter and sterilize everything. At least we can save the unit. Someone will need to run the paperwork over to the Comptroller and get it signed before we can terminate the donor. Of course, it can't be reused in this country, but if it isn't used for parts, someone in some third world country would be happy to take it off our hands. I have a great-great aunt who has this model. She has to be at least 150 and doesn't look a day over twenty."

A nurse placed a new paper on his desk. Comptroller Clemmons looked at his watch. Perhaps he had time for one more before lunch. There was this place that just opened on Fifth Street that was supposed to have the best synthetic steak in town.

"What is it?" he asked.

"Termination papers," the nurse was still in her scrubs and had another hour before she could go to lunch.

"Dementia, huh? I don't see too many of these, anymore. Terminal?"

"Doc Milton doesn't believe there is any hope." She made a gesture with her hand. "Nutso."

He picked up his pen. "If you're only working with less than twenty percent of a brain, I guess there really isn't much you can do with it." He never even read the details; his mind was less focused on the paper before him than on the thought of enjoying the best synthetic steak in town. He scribble his signature in the space allotted for "Comptroller", pressed the official stamp into it and handed it back to the nurse.

As the nurse crossed the room to the door, the Comptroller called after her. "Hold on a minute," he said, "I need the name for my docket."

The nurse looked at the paper for a moment, "Sarah Margaret Brownshaw," she shouted back.

"Who?" The comptroller had suddenly lost his color.

"Sarah Margaret Brownshaw," the nurse repeated.

There really was no need for her to repeat the name. He heard it clearly the first time. *"That bitch!"* he thought. *"That freakin' bitch!"* He made his way down to the sandwich shop. With the bitter taste he had in his mouth, nothing was going to taste good, today. That steak would just have to wait.

So Grows The Tree

He awoke from the horror! The look of panic that at first dominated his eyes slowly turned to dismay. The icy fingers of fear, still clinging fast to his spine, caused waves of shivers to consume his entire body. As if in contradiction, beads of perspiration formed on his wrinkled brow. His tongue darted about his mouth as if trying to cleanse it of some bitter thought. The horrors of his dream now gave way to the greatest terror of all: to awaken from your worst nightmare to find it only the reflection of reality.

John Norris sat up and fumbled for the bottle of whiskey beside his bed. He didn't need to look. It would be there. It was his friend, his ally, and his only comfort in these impossible times. The world had gone mad! Passion and greed had overruled reason, and the sanctity of life had somehow become the lowest denominator. He swallowed the whiskey hungrily, not really caring for the taste, only its effect. The sun poked briefly through a cloud filled sky that had hung there so long, for so many weeks. The heavy rains of the day before had now become a steady drizzle, but even its cleansing effect could do little to diminish the sweet smell of death lingering as a constant reminder that this was not just another warm summer day.

He slammed the window closed as if to shut out the world. The world he could have loved. The world he could have cherished. The world that had gushed forth with all the things he could have loved and should have loved with impunity; the world that now weighted heavily in his heart, with the guilty feeling that he had once taken it all for granted.

He lay back on the bed, sipped his whiskey and thought of better times, times of home, of family, and the times before the madness. They were times of struggle and uncertainty, of hard work and sacrifice, of pain and disappointment, but they were good times, the best times. He had a pretty good job, and his wife was working. They had a small house in the suburbs. His daughter, Becky, had just turned eighteen and was in her first year of college. She had started to date this boy, Michael. It had been a little too serious, as far as he was concerned, and he worried about her.

That was before the war, the bombs, and the breakdown of governments. Before countries and cities fell to decay. Before the death, the stench, the disease, and the bands of outlaws that now roamed the land, raping, looting and killing. His face winced with pain as he recalled the day he first saw the body of his daughter, laying bloody and lifeless on a dark, city street. She had been dumped there, after being murdered by one of the roving outlaw gangs. They were kids, gone wild, who had no regard for human life or law and order.

She had gone out that night, to meet her boyfriend. He had been the one who found her . . . only too late! All those years, he had sheltered her from the world and protected her from the dark side of life, all those years, for what? "Get what you can out life, Honey, look out for yourself, and trust no one," he remembered telling her. That was good advice.

If she had only listened to his advice, she might still be alive. Why hadn't she listened? A girl, walking the streets alone, she was just asking for trouble. She must have seen them coming, walking toward her. Why didn't she run? Did they call to her? Did she know some of them? Why had she been so trusting?

`Maybe it was his fault. Maybe if he had instilled in her mind the need to be careful. Maybe if he had watched her more closely. Perhaps he would have caught her trying to sneak out that night. Perhaps; but then there would have been other nights. If only he had left the city like most of his friends and neighbors. Why had he stayed to try to eke out a living from the dying city? It would have been safer to take his family and run. He thought, at the time, there was a chance that things would turn around and life would get back to some sort of normalcy. He realized now, it had just been hopeful wishing. How could he have been so stupid? It was his fault. The whole fucking mess was his fault!

His thoughts drifted to the day his wife had died. She had died in his arms, in the cold, damp basement of a burned out building; sick and hungry. Driven from their home, they had been reduced to living like animals: scavenging for food and shelter, and hiding from the gangs and the madness. She was not a strong woman. The cold, the rain, and the lack of food and shelter had done much to weaken her body, but disappointment was the real killer. The loss of her home, her life, and her lovely daughter had stripped her of her will to live. He missed her so much. He missed them both.

After his wife died, he headed north, zigzagging to avoid all cities, towns, and people at all cost. He slept in caves, cribs, and barns whenever he could, always moving, never staying in one spot very long. He gleaned the fields for food and learned to eat weeds and bugs with almost as much relish as an occasionally liberated can of peas or sauerkraut he might find in a burned out house or building.

Death was everywhere, its sickening scent so dominating his sense of smell; he would hold wild flowers beneath his nose to block it out. Rotting corpses were everywhere. People were killed for their meager belongings, or for defending their loved ones. Groups of people banded together for protection, but it had become increasingly harder to tell the "good guys" from the "bad guys". In John's mind, it was best to avoid them all.

He had moved north for nearly a year before stumbling on this small cabin at the edge of nowhere. He had assumed it must have been a hunting cabin. Perhaps it had been owned by some city dweller; abandoned now and long forgotten. Perhaps the owner had become one of the benevolent mainstays of the city's growing army of well-fed rats. He only hoped the owner would never show. It could make his life somewhat complicated. He jumped to his feet holding the bottle in front of him.

"Here's to you, my anonymous benefactor," He raised his bottle toward the ceiling, "May we never meet. May I never have to blow your fucking brains out!" He took a long drink.

Not that he was sure he could. This was one part of his survival he had never had to put to the test. Could he really take a human life? Even after all the death he had seen, life was still sacred to him. It was a test he hoped he would never be put to. He knew he was being naive. His luck was bound to run out sooner or later.

"Luck!" he shouted. "Funny, I don't feel lucky."

The sun had disappeared behind the clouds and the world was again bathed in a kind of twilight. He walked to the window and looked out across the weed filled yard. He let his eyes follow the narrow, empty, rutted road that ended abruptly at the rolling hill and appeared again as a thin band, some distance away. The trees were full and the wild flowers grew in mass profusion, occupying places where they had never been allowed to grow before. Another time he might have enjoyed the view.

He held the bottle up in front of the window. He took another sip and capped it off. The bottle was half full and he needed to conserve it. No telling when he might find another. It might be never. He turned to place the bottle next to the bed when he caught something out of the corner of his eye. He thought he had seen a movement! Yes, behind a tree, just up the road and to the right! There, it moved again. He could see it through the brush!

He grabbed the rifle that was leaning against the bedroom wall. It was an M-1 carbine, with a full clip, compliments of the late owner. He left the bedroom and crawled on his hands and knees beneath the large window in the front of the cottage. He worked his way through the kitchen and carefully opened the back door. Sliding out the door, he slowly crept along the back of the cottage, keeping himself between the structure and the trees.

"There he is!" he almost shouted aloud.

A chill crept through him as he felt the veins pounding in his neck. He dried his sweating palms on his shirt and took a deep breath. The figure moved again. A rifle came into view.

Oh my God, he thought, *an assault rifle! If I shoot and miss, I'm dead!*

He lay back against the wall, wiping his forehead with the bottom of his shirt. First he thought of running, but where would he go? There was too much open ground; he would be spotted before he got very far. Besides, this was the best place he had found. There was food here, water, and shelter. He wasn't about to give it all up that easily. If he was ever going to take a stand, it might as well be here, and it might as well be now!

He leaned out and chanced another quick look. *He's too far away*, he thought, *I might not hit him from here. What if I miss?* The last thing he wanted was a shoot-out.

The figure crossed the road and ran to the tree near the front of the cottage. John couldn't see him from where he was. He knew he would have to move around to the other corner of the cottage. Slowly he moved, inch by inch, cursing every twig and leaf. His feet were like lead and his heart was beating so hard that he thought for sure that he was going to have a heart attack. Nevertheless, he managed to make it to the other corner and paused to catch his breath. A gust of wind blew the rain into his eyes, as he peered around the corner, and made it hard for him to see.

The figure was there, crouched beneath the large window, bobbing up and down; much like a boat on a rolling sea. He seemed as if he were changing direction, without really stopping. His clothes were heavy with rain. A hood, pulled tightly around his head, cloaked his face in darkness, exposing only chance bits of unruly hair. He held an assault rifle tightly gripped in his hands, while across his back was a knapsack, dripping from the morning rain. The rain was becoming heavy now and the intruder paused to wipe the water from his eyes. This was John's moment of opportunity! He jumped forward and carefully took aim! He couldn't shoot!

"Drop the gun!" he shouted. "Don't move! Don't even breathe!" He knew he was being redundant. His voice was breaking and his commands were not quite as forceful as he would have liked.

Nonetheless, the intruder quickly obeyed. He dropped his gun and raising his hands slowly as he turned toward John.

"Now step back away from the gun!"

The intruder stepped back slowly, pulling back the hood with a thin, white hand. Long strands of wet, blond hair fell gently about a soft, white neck, and flowed abundantly over slender shoulders. Deep blue eyes flashed in the faint light. A faint smile emerged from soft, full lips. The intruder was a young girl!

"Hey be cool, man! I was only looking for something to eat."

She was young, rather pale and petite despite the balky clothes she wore. She wore no make-up and the soft, pink glow of her cheeks reminded him of his own dear, sweet Becky. A shy, nervous smile melted his heart.

"Gun's not loaded," she offered. "I only carry it to scare people. I'd never use it. Don't even know if it works."

"It's OK," he said, dropping the muzzle of his rifle. "Come on inside. I'll get you something to eat. You look like you're soaked through to the skin."

"Thanks, man," she said. "I'm starved. I haven't eaten in two days and that was just some dried corn."

They walked to the side door of the kitchen. He led the way. The kitchen was small and dirty. The kitchen table was littered with empty cans and dirty dishes. Leaning his rifle against the counter, he began to rummage through the cupboards.

"Pardon the mess," he said, making a motion toward the kitchen, "I wasn't expecting company. Are beans OK?"

"Sure," she replied, removing her jacket and hanging it on the back of the chair. It dripped puddles that flowed into streams, which swiftly formed a large, muddy lake on the dirty floor. She stood there, her dirty "T" shirt clinging to her slim, young body, giving more than the illusion of nakedness. She sat down and unzipped her knapsack.

"Would you like a dry shirt?" he asked, averting his gaze. "There are some clothes in the bedroom closet. They might be a little big on you, but they're dry."

"Not now," she replied, "I really would like that can of beans."

"No problem," he said, pleasantly. It felt good to have someone to talk too. He hadn't been around another human being in well over a year. He turned and found the can opener on the cluttered counter, and opened the can. Finding a clean spoon, he placed them before her, carefully, as if a sudden movement might frighten her away. She attacked the beans with savage delight. He had almost forgotten what it was like to be that hungry.

"Why are you staring at me, man?" she asked. She was looking up at him, her eyes wide and childlike.

"I'm sorry," John said, "I didn't mean to upset you. It's just that you remind me of someone. She was about your age, with blond hair and blue eyes. It's just that the resemblance is uncanny. You have the same smile, the same dimples, and even the way you hold your head is the same."

"Was she pretty?" she asked.

"Oh yes. Very pretty."

"Were you in love with her?"

"Very much so, but not in the way you're thinking. She was my daughter."

"Yeah, I have a lot of older men tell me I remind them of their daughters. Mostly, they just want to get close enough to cop a free feel. Hey, if that's what turns you on, man, go ahead." She placed her hands beneath her breasts and pushed them up. "I don't mind."

"No, please." He turned away shyly. "You misunderstand. I really mean you remind me of my daughter. Would you like something else?" he asked, changing the subject.

"Sure." She was picking away at the bottom of the can.

He rummaged through the cupboard once more. "How about some canned peaches?"

"Sounds great." She ran her fingers around the inside of the can and sucked the residue from her fingers. She attacked the peaches with equal enthusiasm and with the same flagrant disregard for good, table manners. She licked the last of the sweet nectar from her fingertips and looked up at him, her blue eyes wide. "If you've got something to drink, we can take it into the bedroom, and I'll pay you for the food."

"What do you mean, 'pay me'?"

"You know, man, have sex with you. Isn't that what this was all about? You give me food; I give you a piece of ass. Fuck, man, I ain't got nothing else worth anything."

"God! Young lady, I'm old enough to be your father! You're just a baby. You're much too young for that!"

"I haven't the time to be young!" she replied, sharply. How do you think I've managed to survive this long? Besides, if I don't give it away some asshole will just take it anyway! Where the fuck have you been, man, on the moon? People bargain for everything. If you ain't got nothin' worth bargaining for you might just end up dead."

"You're probably right, Sweetheart. I'm not too sure what's going on out there anymore. I've been avoiding people for a long time. There are too many crazy people running around. I'm just glad it turned out to be you and not one of them. I'll get you something to drink. You look like you need it. But no need for sex, your company is payment enough."

As he left for the bedroom her eyes followed him with a look of disbelief. He returned shortly with the half empty bottle of whiskey. He fumbled in the cupboard for a couple of his cleanest glasses and filled them partway. Setting one of the glasses in front of her, he turned to retrieve his own. When he turned around again, there was a handgun leveled at him.

"Are you crazy?" he asked. "What are you doing?"

"I figure, if you don't want to screw me, I might as well get it over with," she said coldly, "Nobody's ever turned me down before. Maybe you're just too fuckin' old to get a hard-on. I don't know, man, and I don't fuckin' care. All I know is you're giving me the willies."

"Give me that gun, young lady! There's no need for any guns here. I'm not gonna hurt you." He stepped forward slowly and held out his hand. When she squeezed the trigger the force of the impact felt like he had been punched by an unseen hand. He grabbed his chest and steadied himself against the counter. His hand came away bloody.

"Why?" he asked, this one word requiring all his breath.

"Before my Daddy was killed, he told me, 'Do and take whatever is necessary for your survival, honey, and trust no one!' I can see you've got a nice place here with a couple weeks' supply of food for the two of us. That's enough to last me four or five weeks. That's four or five weeks I don't have to worry about. Ain't no sense in keeping you around. You're right, you are too old. I ain't that hard up. Besides, how do I know you won't try to kill me, once you're tired of having me around, and the food starts to get low? A piece of ass ain't worth an empty stomach. I don't know you. I don't trust you. Better you than me."

He was growing weaker as his knees buckled and he slid to the floor. Blood gushed from his mouth as he spoke, "You've learned well, Sweetheart; may I at least, ask your name?"

"Sure. It's Rebecca. Rebecca Thomas."

She was indifferent to his death; it was something she had seen so many times in her short life. If there was one thing she had learned, it was that dead people couldn't hurt you. She had no problem disposing of his body in the garden behind the house. After all, she had had to bury her parents and her little brother. She would have been dead herself, if one of the gang hadn't wanted her for himself. The stupid bastard got careless with his assault rifle, or she might not be here today, either. She had taken three of them out, making good her escape. Her only regret was that she had only killed three. The rest of the bastards ran. The fuckin' cowards!

No, she was no stranger to death. It was his smile and that look of contentment that she just couldn't understand. It had been frozen there, his death mask, as he mumbled something about destiny and fulfilled dreams. *He was just some crazy old fool,* she thought. She tried to block it out of her mind, but she could see his face every time she closed her eyes. Even the whiskey didn't help much. The whole ordeal made her feel so uneasy, even a bit remorseful. It was like, somehow, she had just killed her own Father.

"Fuck it!" she shouted, swallowing the last of the whiskey and smashing the empty bottle against the wall. She lay on the bed now, staring at the ceiling. She was beginning to feel the effects of the alcohol. "Maybe he was legit and maybe he wasn't, but then a lot of good people have died for no good reason," her words were slurred. "Including my family," she added. Tears formed in the corners of her eyes and she quickly brush them away. This world had no use for tears. Slowly sleep overtook her, and the moonlight streamed in through the open window bathing her naked body in its soft light. She twitched and jerked about in her drunken sleep, as the nightmares returned to haunt her dream world as well.

HOMELAND SECURITY

Now, I don't know about the rest of the country, but here in Parkersville, we were doing just fine. "Homeland security" was doing so well and we were just about as safe as we could possibility be. Why, we hadn't had an incident all year. Of course, we never had very many incidents before, as I recall, except that incident when Huge Rollins got a bit too heavily into the hard cider and drove his Chevy pickup into Parson creek.

Our postmaster personally checked all the incoming mail, as well as every package that came through, each week. He checked for high explosives, anthrax, and contraband, such as that girly book that young Tom Holcomb tried to smuggle into our fine community.

Now, Jeb Pearlman, the postmaster, turned the contraband over to me, Mayor Rutherford Collins, once he had determined, after close scrutiny, that it was indeed "objectionable material". The Town Council also had to make a judgment; as did our local clergy, Reverend Hall; the town clerk, Frank Bronco; the local judge, his honorable Thomas P. Horton; the Sheriff, Tim Langley and his deputy Fred Tupelos; the head of the Ways and Means Committee, Hank Croswell; the principal of the school, Oscar McCarty; the Cub Scout leader, Forest Reed; the Boy Scout leader, Wendell Patton; the high school coach, Phil Barbados; the local Inn keeper, Clause Holt, as well as all of the patrons present; the members of the local chapter of the Elks Club; as well as the members of the local Rod and Gun Club.

In fact, the only male, over twenty-one, who did not see this piece of evidence, was Olson Christian, who is eighty-six and legally blind. However, many of the pictures were described to him and some of the articles were read in his presents. He later thanked us for our candor and retired to his abode to reflect on what he had heard. He seemed greatly disturbed.

It had been suggested that the local librarian, Miss Gobble, be allowed to examine this piece of evidence, but the council deemed the material too offensive for her sensitivity. In fact, it was unanimously decided that this filthy material was too offensive for any decent woman to view; although, Bill Holland did admit that he showed it to his girlfriend, Phyllis Comstock, but stated, emphatically, he would never expose his wife to such debauchery.

The document, having been duly judged immoral contraband by a majority of upstanding citizenry, was filed under **Abominable material** and placed in the top file at the Town Clerk's office, the file nearest the men's room. It had become common practice for certain members of the local society who could find time to pull themselves away from their busy schedule, to further scrutinize this piece of evidence upon retiring to the adjacent privy. Whereupon, wholly do to an oversight I'm sure, the said document failed to find its way back into the appropriate file.

After a week, the document took on a deplorable appearance, as the pages became smudged and started sticking together. The janitor, who had no idea that this magazine was indeed the infamous evidence, disposed of the book in the trash; however, two of its most explicit and demeaning pages had been preserved and were, eventually, placed back into the file.

Shortly after that, the Parkersville Town Council, as well as the United States Post Office, and I, as mayor, were named as co-defendants in a lawsuit initiated by the law firm of Bristow, Hampton, and Clark, on behalf of one Thomas Henry Holcomb. The summons stated that we were in violation of his first and fourth amendment rights. A court date was set for August 15, in the Federal Courthouse in Wizenburg, the county seat.

This did cause a bit of a hubbub; although, as most of us agreed, it seemed to be more of an inconvenience and a frivolous action, to say the least. After all, Jeb Pearlman, as a duly sworn member of the United States Postal Service, was obligated to confiscate, by virtue of federal statues, anything that was deemed to be of an obscene nature. The decent and moral citizenry of Parkersville had determined that this magazine was indeed nothing more than degrading and immoral filth depicting women in a demeaning and immoral manner, and we were going to prove it in a court of law. Judge Horton, who had had a long and successful career as a trial lawyer before he took over from Judge Fetcher as Town Judge, agreed to represent our case; in fact was looking forward to it.

On the fifteenth we stood in the courtroom as Judge Wheeler, an old acquaintance of Judge Horton, took the bench. He smiled at Judge Horton and nodded his head. They were old golf buddies and members of the same country club. The judge leaned over and whispered in my ear, "It's in the bag."

Tom Holcomb's lawyer was some young upstart from upstate. The judge commented that he still looked "wet behind the ears". I couldn't help but notice his fancy blue suit, silk tie, and patent leather shoes. He may have been wet behind the ears, but he certainly looked like he was doing all right for himself. His name was Cavanaugh.

"The case at hand is Holcomb v. Mayor Rutherford Collins and the Town of Parkersville," the judge began. "The defendants are accused of violating Mr. Holcomb's first and fourth amendment rights by illegal seizure of certain personal material. How do the defendants plead?"

"Not guilty, your honor," Judge Horton said.

"Very well," the Judge removed his glasses and looked up. "I will now hear opening statements, first from the plaintiff."

Now, for some reason, the postmaster, Jeb Pearlman, had been dropped from the suit. Judge Horton figured that the United States Post Office had decided to settle out of court.

The young lawyer got to his feet. He seemed cocky and self-assured, which made me feel a bit uneasy. "Robert Cavanaugh, your honor, I am here to represent my client, Thomas H. Holcomb. I will prove, by preponderance of the evidence that these dependants did, on or about the first of August, illegally seize a magazine addressed to my client, and with malice aforethought, expunged this periodical after indulging their own interests. We are suing for punitive damages in the amount of $20,000, as we feel that compensatory damages are relevant, as this has been a blatant violation of my client's first and fourth amendment rights, and should be duly punished as severely as the law will allow."

Judge Horton jumped to his feet, "I strongly protest to these implications of any wrongdoing. As the governing body of the Town of Parkersville we had every right to confiscate this sick and perverted literature that was illegally transported through our local postal service."

"I see," said the Judge. "Do you have any evidence to present?"

Of course, all we had left, after the janitor had disposed of the magazine, were the two pictures that had survived. These, being the crème de la crème of debauchery, would still be very damaging, as the name of the periodical and the date was printed on the bottom of every page. Horton handed them to the bailiff, who gave them to Judge Wheeler.

The Judge looked them over with much interest, and then removed his reading glasses. "Mark this as 'exhibit A'," he told the clerk, and it was done.

Cavanaugh was on his feet holding a paper in his hand. "I would like to submit this piece of evidence, your honor; it is a picture of the front cover of the magazine in question."

The judge looked it over and had it marked as "exhibit B".

"As you can see, your honor, there is nothing obscene on the cover of this magazine. There may be hints of female, frontal nudity, but all of the pertinent areas of the female anatomy have been covered by printing, rendering them no more scandalous than what you might be expected to view at a public beach."

"Yes," said the Judge, "I will agree with that."

"But, your honor," Horton blurted out, "as you can see, what was inside was of a very sexually explicit nature."

"Perhaps, but the front cover was not of this nature," Cavanaugh reiterated. Therefore, there was no reason to break the seal and look inside. This was a blatant violation of my client's fourth amendment right against unreasonable search and seizure."

"There was, however," Horton interjected, "a reasonable assumption of what this particular magazine contained. The name, over the years, has become synonymous with pornography. Therefore it was reasonable to presume what may lie beyond the covers."

Cavanaugh glanced down at his papers. "Has my illustrious colleague any proof of this allegation, or is he relying purely on his own personal observations?"

By this time Judge Horton's neck had turned red and it extended all the way to the tips of his ears. Still, he managed to maintain his composure. "Inasmuch as this is not the only issue of this repugnant publication, we could have easily, strictly for the purpose of enlightenment to the possible filth that might be available to our innocent flower of youth, had the opportunity of perusing its pages at some other occasion."

"And," Cavanaugh pointed out, "Committing the same act of, so called, "prurient interest" you accuse my client of performing."

"Purely for ethical reasons," Judge Horton insisted. "Know thy enemy."

"I suppose that passing my client's magazine around the whole community was for 'ethical reasons'?"

"As you know there is no such thing as 'ideological' obscenity. In order to reach an opinion we had to do so by consensus."

"Are we talking about a true consensus, here, Judge Horton, or merely a quorum? I understand that only one *woman* in Parkerville actually got a look at the magazine in question." He flopped open the file on the desk. "Your honor, I would like to call Phyllis Comstock to the stand."

The court became quite noisy, and the judge had to bang his gavel a couple of times to restore order. All watched as Phyllis Comstock swayed down the aisle in her short skirt and tight blouse. She swore on the bible, slid into the chair, tossed back her long hair, and crossed her legs. Every eye in the courthouse was on her, for various reasons.

"Tell me, Miss Comstock," Cavanaugh began, as he stood before her, slapping a thick folder softly against his leg, "did you, by any chance, get a chance to look at the magazine in question?"

"I sure did," she answered.

"May I ask what you thought about it?"

"I thought it was very interesting. In fact I thought it was very educational."

"In what way, Miss Comstock?"

"Well, for one thing, I never knew that men could be so huge, if you know what I mean."

This started the courtroom buzzing, and it took the bailiff several minutes to get it calmed down again.

"Would you say that you are a prurient person?" Cavanaugh asked the pretty Miss Comstock.

"I don't understand what you mean."

"Are you lascivious, promiscuous, to put it bluntly, Miss Comstock, are you a slut?"

The thirty-one-year-old blonde, tossed her hair, uncrossed her legs and smoothed out her dress. "Hell no!" she replied rather angrily. "I'll have you know that I have been faithful to the same man for the last three years, which is a hell of a lot longer that he has ever been faithful to his wife. Hell, he's cheated on me twice that I know of."

Bill Holland slumped down where he sat; his face had turned red. His wife was now looking at him in a way that no man wants his wife looking at him. Many of the men were wondering what kind of a fool would cheat on woman like Phyllis Comstock, or even Bonnie Holland, for that matter?

"Would you say that you are sexually normal?"

She smiled at the young lawyer in such a way it made him blush. "I've never had any complaints."

Judge Horton was on his feet, "I object, your honor! Everyone in Parkersville knows what kind of a woman Phyllis Comstock is.

"Jesus, Judge, are you crazy?" I whispered, loudly. "We can't afford a defamation suit on top of this!"

"Would you care to make a statement in regard to this woman's character?" Judge Wheeler asked.

"She ah, she ah, is of fine character, Judge." Horton was sweating profusely; wiped his face with his handkerchief. "I merely wanted to object to this line of questioning."

"I have no further questions for this witness, your honor," Cavanaugh announced, calmly.

"Do you have any questions of this witness?" the judge asked Horton.

"Yes," Horton said, stepping forward, "I have one. Tell me, Miss Comstock, did you find anything else "redeeming" in that magazine, besides the *sizeableness* of certain parts of men's anatomy?"

There was a snicker from the courtroom that was quickly put down by a look from the judge.

"There was this article on sleep disorders. Did you know, for instance, that when you are in

REM sleep . . ."

"Thank you, Miss Comstock," Horton said, cutting her short, "that will be all. You may step down. I would like to call Mayor Rutherford Collins to the stand."

I wasn't shocked. In view of the last testimony, a rebuttal was in order. After being sworn in, I took the stand.

"What was your opinion of this magazine, Mayor Collins?" Horton asked.

"Objection, your honor," Cavanaugh protested. "I believe that his testimony will be prejudicial, as he is one of the defendants."

"He is under oath, your honor," Horton countered, and he is the Mayor of Parkersville."

"Although I am inclined to agree with you, Mr. Cavanaugh, I would still be interested to hear what the Mayor has to say in the interest of clearing up this matter."

"Thank you, your honor," Horton said. You could tell that he was finally feeling sure of himself. "Now, I would like to ask you, again, Mayor Collins, what you thought of this magazine."

"I thought it was very pornographic, full of debauchery, and extremely degrading to women." I was at this time feeling very self-righteous.

"And the articles, did you read any of them?" Horton was pacing the floor, his hands behind his back, looking very much like Parry Mason.

"There were very few articles, mostly lascivious stories, full of bad language and poor syntax, obviously published without any concern for literary value."

"I see," he said, "and the pictures, were they of any artistic value?"

"No," I replied. "Like I said, it was just pure smut."

"In other words, would you say that this magazine was without any redeeming social values, and went far beyond any contemporary community standards for decency?"

"I would say that is a correct statement. Yes."

"Thank you," Horton said. "I have no further questions.

Cavanaugh got to his feet. He rubbed his chin and looked around the courtroom. "No redeeming social values," he said.

I took it as a question. "Yes," I replied.

"It went far beyond any contemporary community standards for decency."

I also took that to be a question. "Yes."

"Tell me, Mayor Collins, what exactly are contemporary community standards for decency?"

"Why family values, I would say." *Who could argue with that?*

He picked up one of the two pictures that was part of "exhibit A". "What would you say was the theme of this particular picture?"

It was a picture of a man and a young woman engaged in sex. She was lying across a table and he stood in front of her grasping her by the hips. "Sex, I would say. Vulgar sex."

"Vulgar sex," he repeated. He paused as he walked back and forth in front of the courtroom. "Vulgar sex," he repeated again. "Is all sex vulgar?" he asked.

"No, of course not," I answered, already feeling trapped by my own words.

"Would you say that sex between a husband and wife is vulgar?"

"Absolutely not."

"How about two consenting adults who are not married? Would that be vulgar?" he asked.

Suddenly the words, "defamation suit" crept through my mind again. I thought of Phyllis Comstock and answered "No."

"Judging by this picture, they may or may not be husband and wife, but they are, indeed, consenting adults. So if the act of sex is not 'vulgar' then why is a picture of the act of sex so 'vulgar'? Please explain why you find the human form so disgusting."

"I don't," I said.

"So you find this picture disgusting. Vulgar . . ." he was holding it up, now, strutting back and forth in front of the crowded courtroom. People were straining to get a better look. ". . . and beyond contemporary community standards of decency. Is it entirely possible that two married people, or two consenting adults might actually engage in this exact form of lovemaking without it being beyond contemporary community standards of decency?"

I caught a look at the judge. He looked amused. Horton looked devastated. I was unable to answer.

"Mayor?"

"Yes," I finally admitted, in almost a whisper, "it's possible."

Cavanaugh turned to the judge. "I rest my case, your honor."

Judge Thomas P. Horton has retired, and has taken up chicken farming. Jeb Pearlman is no longer Post Master. In fact, the Post Office closed the branch office in Parkerville. Jeb was allowed to stay on as a mail carrier at a reduced pay. He still has twelve years before he can retire. It tears him up, on the first of the month, when he has to deliver Tom Holcomb's girly magazines. Tom Holcomb can be seen driving around town in his fancy convertible with a couple of those "naked lady" mud-flaps on the back. Phyllis Comstock is no longer Bill Holland's girl; she's been dating that big-shot lawyer, Cavanaugh, for two months now. Bill's wife filed for a divorce about the same time. With Phyllis Comstock out of the picture, Bonnie Holland has become the toast of the town and has been seen, on several occasions, riding around in Tom Holcomb's convertible. Bill is looking pretty down-in-the-mouth. He hasn't had anyone to cheat on for over two months.

I'm still Mayor, at least, until the next election a month from now. Things move slowly in this town, but these folks have long memories. I'm not going to run again. I couldn't win even if I was the only one running, like I was last term. There is a good chance that Tom Holcomb might run; after all, he is the most popular man in town. At least, he had the common decency to keep the money circulating about town. He bought the car from *"Fair Dealing" Bo Hatcherson's Used Cars*, a big screen TV from *Joe's TV Shop*, and the mud-flaps from Dickey Collin's garage sale. As for that "Homeland Security" crap, save that for the big cities. I'd rather take my chances with the bombs and the anthrax. At least with them you know where you stand.

DEATHDAY

"Ludicrous, huh?" Bill took another sip of his beer. "That's what I thought when I first heard about it. I got this from a good source. The Senate is voting on it this week!"

"You're crazy, Bill!" Yancy was shaking his head, rolling his eyes, and doing that little chuckle he always did when he thought logic was being replaced by stupidity. "First of all, genocide is against the Constitution and, secondly, that would be discriminating against people because of their age. Even the government can't do that, Bill."

"That's what you think, Yancy!" Bill had set down his beer and was now shaking his finger at his drinking buddy. "Congress makes the laws and they can change them any time they want!"

"I thought you said it was the Senate?"

"Senate, Congress, what's the difference? What I'm saying is, the government is going to decide who is going to live and who is going to die, and there's not a damn thing we can do about it."

"I can just vote the bastards out, Billy. That's what I can do." Yancy took a long drink of his beer and slammed the bottle down on the table. "I'm an American citizen and I have my rights. There is no one going to tell me when I'm going to die!"

"OK! OK, Yancy, just say for a minute that I'm right. Say that the government says that everyone will have one hundred years of life, and they will die about the same time that they were born, only one hundred years down the road. What the hell could you do about it?"

Yancy took a handful of popcorn and popped it in his mouth. This gave him time to think about Billy's question. "OK, Billy, let me ask you this question. Will the government do everything in its power to help keep me alive for those one hundred years?"

"Yeah. For argument's sake, let's just say that they will."

"Then, it doesn't sound like such a bad deal to me. I'd like to be guaranteed to live for a hundred years. If I don't like the quality of my life, I can just step out back and pop myself in the head with my 32."

Bill picked up one of the two fresh beers he had ordered as backups. He ran his hand around the top of the bottle before taking a drink. "That's bullshit, Yancy! What if they suddenly discover some new medicine that can prolong a person's life for maybe another hundred years, or so? Do you mean to tell me that you would be willing to die at one hundred, if you could live to be two or three hundred years old?"

Yancy sucked the foam from his bottle and started on a fresh one. "You talk about bullshit? What are the chances of that happening? Not in my lifetime."

"Yeah, but let's just say that it did happen, and they came up with some new drugs that could keep people alive, and in good health, and maybe even look younger for two or three hundred years. Would you still be happy with your one hundred years? You know that all those fat cats are not going to be terminated. All those brainy people, rich and powerful people, and big-shot politicians are going to be kept around forever, or at least while they still have power, or are useful. That's a given."

Yancy got up and snatched a fresh bowl of popcorn from the bar. While he was up, he ordered two more beers. He sat down and offered the bowl to Bill. "OK, Bill, if this happened I would be a little biffed."

"A little biffed?"

"OK. I'd be mad enough to bomb something, maybe. But what's your point? It ain't gonna happen."

"What if it is already happening? What if it's happening right now? What if the government has decided that you will have a 'death day' as well as a birthday? What if they have already decided that no one will live more than one hundred years, unless they have some kind of special skill or something?

"That's freaking bullshit, Bill, and you know it!"

The bartender set two fresh beers in front of the two men and picked up the empties. "Will you two keep it down, please? We have women in here."

"Sorry, Pete," Yancy said, handing him a five, "but Bill has some off the wall idea that the government is going to kill us off when we reach one hundred years old."

"I should be so lucky," Pete yelled over his shoulder as he turned to go back to the bar.

Bill swilled down the last of his beer and set the empty on Pete's tray as he passed. "Laugh if you want to, but I tell you, this is all going to come down; just like I say it will. The medicine and stuff is out there right now. The government has been suppressing it all these years. That's the reason they're doing this one hundred year thing. If people lived forever, can you imagine what that would do to Social Security or the economy?"

"So how are they going to do this? Are they going to round us up when we turn one hundred, take us to a large concentration camp, and gas us?" Yancy was shaking his head and rolling his eyes, again. "You're talking Nazi Germany, in the forties."

"Bill took a long sip of his beer and wiped his mouth. "Hell no! They're going to be a lot more sophisticated than that. Your death will look natural, or maybe it will look like an accident."

"Won't people get a little suspicious if people start dropping dead on their one hundredth birthday?" Yancy picked the last few pieces of popcorn from the bowl and washed them down with a long drink of beer.

"It probably won't be on their birthday. It might even happen a couple of years after they turn one hundred, or a few years before. This will all have to be scheduled. You know how the government works. There will be backlogs, paper jams, bungled attempts, and maybe even people that will get lost in the system. Maybe some people will get wind of what's going on and flee to South America, or something. Besides, the government has no control over accidents and natural causes. It will look like chaos, but it will be well planned."

"You're full of crap, Bill!" Yancy waved his hand and knocked over his beer. He got up and grabbed a handful of paper napkins from the bar and began to mop up the spill. He leaned forward so he could keep his voice low as to not alarm the women two tables away. The beer dripped off the table and onto his lap. He didn't seem to notice.

"I'm not full of crap, but I am full of beer." Bill pulled himself to his feet and staggered off toward the men's room.

Meanwhile, Yancy order two more beers and rescued another bowl of popcorn from the bar.

When Bill returned, there was a fresh beer setting next to his warm one. As he eased himself into his chair, he nearly fell over backward.

"I don't know Yancy," he said, his speech slurred a bit; "I may have reached my limit."

"I just got us two fresh ones. The tops are off of them, now. They won't take them back." Yancy's speech wasn't much better.

Bill drained the bottle of warm beer, and then, running his hand around the top of the fresh bottle, he stared at the label as if he were seeing one for the first time. "Never let it be said the Bill Moreland ever wasted a good beer." He put the bottle to his lips and took a long drink.

"I still say that you're full of crap about that 'death day' thing, but if it were true, what is that going to do to Social Security?"

"We're all going to have to work until we're eighty, man."

"Like hell! I, for one, have no intention of working until I'm eighty! At sixty-two I'm grabbing my pension and becoming a couch potato."

"Of course you won't. What people will have to do is come up with their own retirement plan."

"Like 401K?"

"Yeah, or something better. I can see the government phasing out Social Security all together."

Yancy washed down a handful of popcorn with a swallow of beer. "Y'know, I can see that happening. Social Security is about bust, anyway. Give me some good stock, some good investments, or maybe a small business that practically runs itself, and I know that I could do a whole lot better than Social Security."

"Ten-four, there, Yancy. I got into some computer software stock a few years back. I dumped that for health food, last year. It's been doing pretty good, but you have to keep your money moving; new things are always coming up." Bill got to his feet with a bit of difficulty. "Got to go, man. I've got to be at the office early tomorrow."

Yancy looked at his watch. "I had no idea it was getting so late." He downed the last of his beer. "I've got an early start, too." He put his arm around his friends shoulder, and as they staggered toward the door, he asked, "Do you really think that we are ever going to see one hundred?"

"I sure do," Bill assured him, "I have it from a very good source."

"Well, look at it this way, Bill. If we are all going to die on our birthdays, think of all the money we can save on cards and presents. You can't take it with you, right?"

Bill waved his finger at his friend just as he stepped through the door, "Speak for yourself, Yancy, I just bought this stock . . . ?"

One of the patrons leaned over the bar toward the bartender. "Who were those two clowns?"

"Oh, those two," Pete was mixing up a gin fizz for the pretty blonde at the end of the bar. "They come in here every Wednesday. The tall thin one, Yancy, works for the Treasury Department. The Big guy, Bill, works for the CIA."

"You're kidding."

"No. They both got really drunk one day and showed me their credentials."

"God!" the man's eyes suddenly got large. "You don't think that what they were talking about could be true, do you?"

"Who knows? Last week, they were arguing about aliens and UFO's, and the week before were terrorists infiltrating the Vatican."

THE CROSS
HAMMOCK CONSPIRACY

Cross Hammock is a chunk of real estate that few men in their right mind would ever want to navigate. It rises out of the swamp like some putrid, festered cyst, and for much of the rainy season is only navigable by creatures with webbed feet. Well, that and a few do-or-die hunters who would risk the daily torrents and soggy, musty abodes to hunt the elusive boar-hog; who itself would gladly forgo the pleasures of slogging around constantly in shoulder deep mud, but for the fact that it puts it on an even plane with the equally harried hound dogs. Of course, what the hounds lacked in mud-sloshable appendages, they make up for in pure determination. Between the hogs and the dogs it was pretty much a fifty/fifty proposition.

The hunters, themselves, are another story. Four-wheel drives get buried, boots become clogged with mud to a point that they become fifty-pound weights, and widening creeks and retention areas wash away scents, leaving the hound dogs mucking about in ever widening, muddy circles. Guns need constant cleaning; tent flaps, weighted down with rain, need constant attention; and red bugs, No-see-ums, and skeeters are always a nuisance. But as long as the beer and ice holds out, and the campfire keeps burning, these hardy "rednecks" still consider, what more sensible people would consider cruel torture, great sport.

Bill McGregor spit out the old dip and stuffed a fresh pinch under his lip. "Sure a lot nicer then it was last year," he said, changing position to avoid the smoke from the fire that had shifted direction for the third time in twenty minutes.

"Yeah," offered Cotton Belmonte, checking his watch before popping the top of a cold beer; not wanting to let his "drinkin' time" lap into his "huntin' time"; something no true sportsman would ever do. "Mud was much worse last year, and I about froze off my gonads sleepin' in that damp tent."

"Bubba" Lee Holman poked at the fire with a stick and got one of the bigger logs burning again. The resulting sparks, however, landed in his beard and caused him a few moments of grief before he snuff out the smoldering hairs. "Huntin' wouldn't be no good a' tall if it were too damn easy. Why every hunter in the area would be here huntin' them pigs an we'd be lucky if we got a shot at one."

"That is a fact," Bill said. "That sure was a beauty I almost got last year. Would of made a lot of good eatin', if the damn gun hadn't jammed. Toss me a cold one, will ya, Cotton?"

Cotton reached into the cooler and fished out a cold beer. "My old man used to say that nothin' tastes as good as something you've shot, gutted, and skun yourself."

"True that is," offered Bubba. "Them farm-raised pigs, what have never rutted fer roots or ate a rattler head on, don't have anywhere near the great flavor as a tough-natured, ole boar hog. I say that the meaner the disposition, the sweeter the meat."

"Damn, Bubba, now you made me hungry, again," Cotton said, fishing another fresh beer from the cooler. "Hand me that bag of chips, will ya?" His old yellow, Cur dog, Jack, nuzzled his hand and he scratched the dog's head. "Good boy," he said, "You're gonna find me a hog, tomorrow, ain'tcha boy?"

"Well, somebody better get one tomorrow," Bubba said, handing Cotton the chips. "We been here three days, already, and haven't got close enough to one to get a shot. Seems to me, last year, we got one the second day."

"It was old Tom who got one right off the bat." Bill was fishing a cold beer from the cooler. "Old Tom, who never drank, didn't smoke nor chew, didn't cuss, or have a bad word about anyone; died young."

"Forty-two is a might too young to be dyin' that's fer sure." Bubba had just opened up a bag of beef jerky and was passing it around. "They claim he accidentally shot himself cleanin' his 12 gauge, but I think his wife did him in when she found out he was diddlin' the neighbor's old lady. Hell, how many times did Tom clean his guns? I just couldn't see him suddenly getting careless."

"Yeah, well the coroner ruled it accidental, and ya can't hardly argue with that," Cotton stated, matter-of-factly. "I tend to agree with you, though, it seems that his old lady was more interested in collectin' his life insurance; especially when it was double indemnity for the fact that it was accidental and all. She barely stayed around long enough to get him in the ground."

"Yeah, well that ain't the whole of it, neither." Bubba drained the last of his beer and motioned for a refill. "I heard that the neighbor sold his house just after she did, and they met up in Miami and was living it up in some cozy, little cottage on the beach, somewhere."

"I never trusted Belle much." Bill had dug out three cans of Vienna sausage and was passing them around. "She always seemed a might stuck-up to me, her and those fancy clothes she used to wear. It seems to me that she was always showin' a bit more than was proper, if you know what I mean."

Cotton was passing around some more beer. He put in a couple more twelve-packs so they would have time to cool down. "I remember going there for a pool party and seeing her wear this skimpy swimsuit that, I swear, was letting hair show where it hadn't oughta show."

"Yeah," said Bill, "I remember that. That's when I learned that she was a true blonde."

They all laughed and took deep drinks of their beers. Bubba opened a can of mixed nuts and passed that around. Bill threw a couple more logs on the fire and Cotton's dog, Jack, turned his belly toward the flames and moaned contentedly.

"You got to admit, though, she did have it put together in all the right places, didn't she?" said Bubba not really asking a question nor expecting an answer.

"I know," said Bill, but she was Tom's wife, and it's just not right to look at a friend's wife that way."

There was a brief silence.

"Yeah, sure," said Bubba, and they all broke out laughing again. "Do you remember the one who worked at Barney's hardware? The one with those huge boobs that were pushed together so tight you couldn't drive a ten-penny nail between them with a ten-pound maul?"

"I sure do," said Cotton, fishing around for a cold beer. "If she bent down to get something off of the bottom shelf, I swear, you could see all the way to her belly button. If ya bought chain she stretched it out on the floor to get a measurement off the floor tile. If ya ever need any, I've got a couple hundred feet of light chain I'm never gonna use. I wonder what ever happened to her?"

"I suspect Barney had to let her go," offered Bill. "Barney probably never sold anything off the two upper shelves, unless he was there alone. Then again, Mama Barney might have had something to do with that, too. Not that I could blame her. If I were Barney I'd want to squeeze one of them, first chance I got. Maybe she got herself a job at Hooters."

"You're kidding, Bill, aren't ya?" asked Bubba. "You wouldn't cheat on Barb."

"I didn't say nothin' about cheatin'. Just because you sit in the seat and feel the upholstery doesn't mean you're going to be driving the car. Now, you tell me that you wouldn't want to grab one of those things and give it a good squeeze? I never said nothin' about jumping her bones."

Now, the word "bones" was familiar to Jack and he lifted his head when it was said, but no one seemed to be jumping up to get him a bone, so he just took it as people talk and laid his head back down. The thing about people is you never really know what they are saying. Now, when Jack said something, everyone knew exactly what he meant.

There was his night bark that usually got him in trouble, when something like that big cat next door came creeping around. That was his, "I'll get you one day, cat," bark. Then there was the morning, "I want something to eat" bark; the snarl for the meter man, who once sprayed him in the eyes with something that burned, when no one was home; the friendly yip for the mail man, who always stopped to slip him a treat; and the little moan when he wanted his belly rubbed, or his head scratched.

"Something like that could open a whole can of worms," continued Bubba. "She tells someone, who tells someone else, and the next thing you know my wife is filing for a divorce and I'm sitting' home alone paying for something I ain't getting'. Truth is, squeezin' one of them boobs can't feel a whole lot different than squeezin' a baby's butt cheek."

"You gotta be kiddin' me, Bubba," said Bill. "No one could get much of a thrill outa squeezin' a baby's butt cheek, unless he was one of those 'funny guys'."

"We've been friends a long time, Bill, but if you call me a 'funny guy' one more time I'm gonna cram one of these full beer cans up yer butt without even opening it!"

"Jesus, guys!" interjected Cotton. "We're all friends, here. No one is calling anyone a 'funny guy'. Not a good idea to have all this hostility with guns around. Besides, that would be a hell of a needless waste of a good beer."

"Sorry, Bubba," Bill said, "You know I didn't mean to say that you were a 'funny guy'. It was just the beer talking, speaking of which, I am pretty sure I am in need of another; another round for me and my friend, here, barkeep." He put his arm around Bubba's shoulder.

Cotton fearlessly plunged into the cold, icy waters and fished out a couple more beers, while the dog looked on with an intent look of concern, now having turned his cold nose toward the fire. Humans were so unpredictable, one minute they might be petting you and saying, "good boy" for taking a good, healthy crap, and the next time they might be kicking you in the butt for doing the vary, same thing. Grass, rug, what the hell is the difference?

It was dark, now, and the area around the fire was the only area that was illuminated. It was like being in a small circle in the middle of a huge, vast, black emptiness. If you thought about it, it could make you spine tingle not knowing what lay beyond the ring of light. The secret, of course, is to try not to think about it, and the cure for not thinking about it is, of course, copious amounts of beer. Snacks help, while tantalizing flavors titillate the taste buds for a fleeting moment, but still it requires copious amounts of beer to wash it all down. All of this required the expertise knowledge of someone none of our heroes had ever known, met, or even thought of, to make sure that the alcohol in each successive ice-cold can of popular, brewed, malted delight was kept, exactly, at 5.5 percent. As they slipped softly into the painless abyss of stupefied regression, I'm sure that none of this ever crossed their minds and Mr. Budweiser never got his just desert. However, loyalty did prevail within this group, and Mr. Budweiser's legacy would never be forsaken, not even for the sake of the few pieces of silver that might be saved by purchasing another. In this respect Mr. Budweiser would fare much better than Jesus.

The dog, however, thought that this was a good time to leave the area. Being around a bunch of staggering humans can only get you stepped on, or pissed on; besides, although dogs are quite familiar with the normal process of regurgitation, humans have a way of making it look quite disgusting. He took up his usual position on a thick bed of needles beneath a long-needle pine tree, and resumed his role as sole canine guardian of the camp; although, even he wondered if all the barking in the world would conger up much of a response other than, perhaps, a misguided shoe. Nevertheless, duty is duty, and Jack was never one to shirk his.

Jack was all alone this trip. Bubba's dog, Fire, had died of old age and Bill's dog, Cindy, was too young and inexperienced to be hunting boar hogs. It was too bad, too, because Cindy could sure make a cold night a little warmer. Dogs like Jack, who knew the ropes, best did this kind of hunting.

It wasn't long before the humans left the fire. One, as Jack could see from his silhouette, was pissing on the fire, while another was out of the firelight making strange, coughing and gagging sounds that made Jack wish that he had fingers so he could put them in his ears. It wasn't long; however, before the sound of multiple snoring reached his long, fluffy ears, and he rested with the knowledge that all was right with the world.

It was about this time that three of the biggest, meanest, ugliest hogs wandered in from the nearby prairie in search of subsidence. Coincidently, one of the trio was rather fond of Vienna sausage and the clear scent of half-empty cans of the same succulent treat tweaked his interest. Oblivious to danger, they swaggered into camp and discovered, in an old cooler intended mostly to keep out ants and small vermin, a virtual smorgasbord of Vienna sausage; potato chips; beef jerky; and mixed nuts: the good kind with lots of cashews and Brazil nuts. Getting the Vienna sausage out of the tiny cans was a laborious, but worthwhile challenge.

In the meantime, our friend Jack was certainly not being derelict. He was on his feet, showing his teeth and assessing the odds, which were not in his favor. The large tusks, gleaming in the fading firelight, gave credence to the fact that these were not your garden-variety piglets. There was no petting zoo material here.

They obviously didn't know that he was near, or they would have attacked him first and used the Vienna sausage and nut mix to flush the taste of dog from their mouths. Jack was smart enough to realize that even dog tastes good to pigs and maybe even humans for that matter.

He thought of barking, but since the humans had just gone to bed and the chances of waking them up after they had been drinking that funny smelling stuff that looked a lot like pee, was damn near nil, so he thought better of that. He thought of charging in and taking them by surprise, but then he thought that the only surprise would be seeing his entrails hanging from the mouth of one of the pigs, and this thought squelched any heroic thoughts of Rin Tin Tinism. This, he was sure, would earn him a decent burial and an "atta boy", before Cotton threw the first shovel of dirt over him.

Jack also had to think about the humans. If the pigs got into the tents, looking for more food, the humans wouldn't have much of a chance, either. Now, Jack was a whole lot smarter than most humans would give him credit for being. He concocted this brilliant idea.

He left, walking into the woods, away from the pigs. He slowly circled around until he was on the other side of the pigs, always making sure that he was downwind. He found his way to Cotton's old International pickup and jumped through the open window on the driver's side. It was always open because the thing that rolled the window up and down broke off about two years ago and Cotton never bothered to replace it.

Now this is the clever part. Jack knew that there was something on the dashboard that made the lights up front and on top light up. He had seen Cotton do it many times. He just couldn't remember which one. He also reasoned that before you could get them to work you had to turn the shinny thing that stuck out of the dash. He reached down and turned it to the right with his teeth. He heard a motor turn over and the engine start. Then, sitting on the seat, he reached down on the dash and pulled the first knob he found. The lights didn't come on, but the engine began to race. OK, wrong one!

He had better luck the second time, for the next one caused the light to come on brightly. The pigs looked up, but they weren't running; they seemed mesmerized. Jack jumped down from the seat and put his front paws on the dash for a better look. *Perhaps,* he reasoned, *a good bark would get them moving.* While he braced himself for one of those deep barks that come from deep in the diaphragm, his left-rear paw pushed against a lever sticking out of the floor. There was the sound of gears grinding and the truck shot forward catching the three pigs before they had time to run. Being in high gear, the truck stalled shortly after it climbed over the third, now lifeless, body as it came to rest against a tree.

Jack jumped out and took his position under his favorite tree. He was glad when all those bright lights finally faded and flickered out. They were keeping him awake.

The next morning, the three hunters awoke to see the three dead pigs and Cotton's pickup up against a tree, in gear, with the battery dead. They have still never been able to fully explain exactly what happened. There was talk that, perhaps, one of them was a sleepwalker, but this had never come up before. Besides, there were shotguns within reach, why would someone use Cotton's truck. Then they thought that maybe it was some kind of miracle, or even the work of the devil. They each took the meat to Father Petigue to have it blessed before they ate any of it; just to be sure. This cost them each a small portion of meat. It did cross their minds that someone might have been playing a joke on them, but then no one ever came forward and said, "Gotcha!" So what would be the sense? What really happened has always remained a mystery, and our three heroes never went hunting at Cross Hammock again.

Of course, no one talked about this matter with anyone else. As far as everyone else was concerned, they shot the pigs and that was it. The only witness was a dog named Jack and he wasn't saying anything . . . at least not in human circles.

OUT OF KANSAS

"Is anyone sitting here?"

I looked up to see the most beautiful illusion standing before me. She was clutching an overnight bag.

"No," I said, my voice breaking in the presents of such beauty. I couldn't look away from her eyes; they were the deepest blue, almost lavender. Maybe it was the lighting on the bus, or the way the sunlight came streaming through the tinted windows, but I had never seen eyes like these before. I removed my package from the seat and placed it on my lap. "Would you rather sit next to the window?" I asked, not knowing what else to say.

"No," she said, smiling, "this will be fine."

Her teeth were small and even, almost baby teeth. I grappled with my brain for something to say.

"You from around here?" I asked. *Dumb! Dumb! Don't ask personal questions. Do you want her to move to another seat?*

"No," she said. "I'm from Harrisburg, originally. Are you from here?"

"No," I admitted. I was just here to finish up some unfinished business. I'm heading back to New York."

"Are you from the city?"

She was the one asking the personal questions, now. "No," I admitting, "I come from a small town in upstate, New York that no one ever heard of."

"Me too. I always say Harrisburg because it's the nearest city."

"Yeah, I know what you mean. I usually tell people I'm from Syracuse. It saves a whole lot of explaining in the long run."

She laughed. I loved the sound of her laughter. How lucky I was. Of all the empty seats on the bus, she chose to sit next to me. I looked around. There were at least ten empty seats. Maybe she just thought I would be someone friendly. She does seem to like to talk.

The bus driver climbed into his seat and closed the door. He put the bus in gear and turned away from the curb. I heard the big diesel engine come to life as we pulled out into the traffic. Her face was turned toward mine and I watched as the sun flashed from behind the trees and the color of her eyes changed from blue, to mauve, to lavender. I turned toward the window, quickly. *I was staring, wasn't I? I mustn't do that.*

We watched from our lofty perch as the bus weaved its way through the downtown traffic and made its bid for the open highway. With a final roar of the powerful engine it took its place amid the endless stream of steel, flesh and tires. I was glad to be on my way. Glad to see the last of this town. Glad to be breathing free air again.

"Cookie?"

She caught me in deep thought. She was holding up a napkin with several cookies that she had removed from her overnight bag.

"Yes, thank you. Did you make them?"

"No, thank God!" she said, honoring me again with that wonderful little laugh. "These are eatable."

I laughed, too; a polite, cautious laugh. After all we were just strangers . . . nervous people just beginning to feel each other out . . . and laughing is just another expression of nervousness.

I took a bite of the cookie and realized that it was the first thing I'd had to eat since yesterday. I watched her nibble on her cookie, taking tiny bites with those tiny teeth.

"Pauline," she said, offering her hand.

I took her hand in mine, admiring the softness of it and the light hue of her skin. "John," I said.

"I hated that place," she said.

She caught me by surprise. It was hard to phantom that anyone so sweet and delicate could hate anything or anyone. "Never been too fond of it myself," I found myself saying." Well, after all, it was true. Fifty years I had spent in this God-forsaken place. I was glad to see the last of it.

The cookie tasted good, but now, something was gnawing at my stomach. Too nervous to eat supper last night, and too much in a hurry to leave to eat breakfast this morning. I looked at my watch. It was one of the cheap, digital things with the tiny window. I squinted at it, turning it in the light from the window. It looked like eight o'clock, another four hours until lunch. I thought of asking for another cookie, but quickly banished that thought from my mind. *She'll think you're a pig.*

"Pennsylvania must be nice, this time of year." *What a dumb thing to say. Of course it was, it's early fall. The leaves would be turning, it would be cooling down from the hot summer, and the birds would be getting ready to migrate.* A tinge of regret welled through my body. I was homesick.

"Oh, yes," she said. "It has been a while. I remember our vacations on the lake. We used to go canoeing, and how much I loved to fish with my father. So long ago."

I could see tears in the corners of her eyes. I, too, was feeling a bit depressed. I wondered if anything would be the same as I remembered. It has been so long. I wondered if you can, really, ever go back. She was shivering. "The air conditioning is cold. Let me by you and I'll see if I can find you a blanket."

There were dark blue blankets, neatly folded, in the overhead compartment. I noticed, as I handed one down to her, she was wearing slippers. *Now that's strange.*

"Thank you," she said, in that sweet voice, and all thoughts were wiped from my mind.

"Do you want to sit near the window?" I asked, again.

"No, I'm fine, here." There was that smile again.

I slid on past her, gathered up my bag and settled back into the seat. A large semi truck was passing, and I watched as the bus driver flashed his headlights on and off. The semi driver flashed his running lights, "*thanks.*"

They still do that? Maybe everything hasn't changed.

"Another cookie?" she asked as she, daintily, held the little napkin open for me.

"Oh, why not? Are you sure you didn't make these? They taste homemade to me."

She made a little girlish giggle. "Well, to tell the truth, I did help."

The cookie was a stopgap. The pain in my gut was getting worse. What I really needed was steak, medium rare, smothered in onions, a baked potato with sour cream, some creamed corn, a tall glass of beer, and the whole meal topped off with a huge slice of apple pie ala mode, with vanilla ice cream. After, I would sit back, sip on a cup of coffee and stare into those ever-changing eyes. Of course, the dinner wouldn't be complete unless she was with me.

"You married," I asked. It just rolled off of my tongue before I even had time to think about what I was saying. *None of your business, dummy!*

"I was, but my husband is dead."

It was nonchalant, rather mater-of-fact. "Oh, I'm sorry." I wasn't, really.

"I'm not," she said. "He was not a nice man."

Where do I go from here? Did I just open a can of worms that should have remained closed? "Oh." *Now, that's a brilliant comeback.*

"We were married for twenty years. He used to beat me, especially when he had been drinking. I finally got away from him and made a life of my own."

"I've heard of this before. You were very brave to do what you did. Many women are afraid to leave, and many end up being killed by their abusive husbands." In fifty years I had done a lot of reading.

The pain in my stomach was getting worse. I was beginning to feel sick. I reached over and tapped the bus driver on the shoulder. "Could you pull over?" I asked. "I feel like I'm going to throw up."

"We're not supposed to do that, sir," he said. "The bathroom is in the back of the bus."

"I'm not gonna make it to the back of the bus. Do you, really, want a mess to clean up?"

He looked into the mirrors, flicked on his turn signal, and eased the bus to the shoulder of the road. The air brakes came on and he opened the door.

Pauline was on her feet and helping me to get up. "I'm sorry you're not feeling well, John." Somehow her voice had changed. It didn't sound sincere.

The driver helped me down the steps and stood back while I turned my stomach inside out. There really wasn't much of anything to throw up, mostly mucous looking stuff and pieces of cookie. I could hear people talking. It was just a distant hum. Things were beginning to look fuzzy. When I had finished, I couldn't help myself. I fell into it, face-first.

When I came to, there were lots of cops and flashing lights. I could hear a laud, angry voice. It was Pauline. Two cops were taking her away.

She was kicking a screaming. "Bastards! You're all bastards! All men are bastards!"

As they loaded me on the gurney, I could hear one cop talking. "Pauline Winslow," he was saying. "She poisoned her whole family with cyanide. Not a good way to go. She's been locked away in a loony bin for the last forty-some years. Who would have thought she would go back to her old ways, once she got out."

"And this guy?" asked another cop.

"Thomas Spencer. Poor bastard just got out of Leavenworth, today. He did fifty years for shooting a guard in a botched bank robbery."

"Well, I guess he got his just desserts. Ya get it, cookies, desserts?"

"Yeah, Phil, you're a real cutup."

THE HAND
THAT FEEDS YOU

David Roche had never been a particular likeable guy, but after he lost his right arm in the service, he became downright detestable. Attempts to re-attach his arm had failed and he was forced to make do with a myriad of uncomfortable and awkward prostheses. He never liked the newer, less obvious models with the soft, pliable hand. He preferred the older, cruder model he referred to as "the claw".

He had little use for rehabilitation and physical therapy. Leaving the program early, he found his solace in whiskey, drugs, and self-pity. The creature he had become was so despicable; even he had learned to despise it. That is why, on this particular cold, rainy Tuesday evening, he found himself wandering the streets of New York, perhaps trying to get away from himself.

He was down to his last cigarette, out of drugs, money, and restraint. His next act was to walk into a liquor store, place a bottle of whiskey on the counter, and produce a gun that he held, awkwardly in his left hand.

"Give me all the money in the register!" he demanded.

The shopkeeper raised his hand. "Please don't shoot!" he pleaded. He was shaking badly and having trouble getting the money out of the till.

David was waving the gun now. "Hurry up, you oaf! I haven't got all day. What's the matter with you? Fuck it! Step back, you idiot!"

He shifted the gun to his right hand and clamped the heavy piece into the claw. He leaned over the counter, and with his left hand he began to grab money from the register. The gun began to slip, and as he tried to reposition it in his claw, the gun went off. The shopkeeper fell backward, a large hole where his left eye had been. Frightened, David crammed what bills he had into his pocket and ran from the store. On the way out, he lost his grip on the gun and it dropped to the floor.

The police caught up with him about three months later. His trial was brief; his fingerprints were all over the gun. Because of a long list of brushings with the law, including several assaults, he was given life in prison. This is only because, at that time, the death penalty had not yet been reinstated in New York. A few months later, with his priers, he might have been looking at a lethal injection.

They sent him to Attica to serve out his time. It was there that he became fast friends with a man named Linus Couch. He and Linus had many things in common: they were both detestable, both were there for committing a heinous murder, they had no friends or family, and neither one of them had their own right arm.

Linus, however, had a state-of-the-art, mechanical device. It could do almost anything that a real arm and hand could do, and more. David once watch Linus crush a metal cup with no more effort than it would have taken if it had been made of tinfoil. Linus used to love to show off by picking his nose with it. The arm had cost Linus a staggering amount of money. There was no way David could have ever afforded anything so extravagant and the VA would have never forked out that much money for one lousy prosthesis; especially not for a loser like him.

Oh, Roche had no disillusions about what he was. All his life he had struggled with an inability to deal with authority. They had always been against him: his teachers, his parents, the cops, the Army, and even the church. Had anyone ever taken his side? Hell, no! After all, it was a judge who suggested that he join the Army. "A tour in the armed forces might be just the thing to turn your life around." It was that or another year in "juvy".

Ironically, he had very little trouble with the discipline in boot camp. The sergeants were tyrannical and often brutal, but this kind of behavior he could understand and even appreciate. Hell, if you want people to do what you tell them to do, "pretty please" doesn't always cut it. It wasn't until after he lost his arm that he became so hateful, but not toward the Army, but for the judge that put him there. He swore that if he ever saw that judge on the street, he would blow his brains out. He hated that judge even more, now. He even blamed the botched stick-up on him. If it hadn't been for the loss of his arm he wouldn't have shot that guy, or dropped the gun. He had brought that fact up to his lawyer, but the bum had never mentioned it in his defense. There was another ass-hole that was out to get him, his own lawyer.

Linus had not been as lucky as David. He had been sentenced to death by lethal injection and the only thing that was keeping him alive were the appeals his lawyers had filed on his behalf. He knew that his appeals would run out, eventually, and that his number would be up.

David made no secret of how much he admired Linus' arm. He made Linus promise that when the time came, he would make sure that David got the arm. Linus agreed that he would have no more use for it after he was dead. He told David that he would have his lawyers make up all the paperwork, and see to it that all the arrangements were made. This made David very happy. He was never more anxious to see a man die; especially someone he actually liked.

On August 6th Linus Couch was given a lethal injection and paid his debt to society. Anticipation now entered the field of David's repertoire and his personality became even more obnoxious. He was involved in several fights in which he extracted full use of his clawed appendage, resulting in the removal and confiscation of his right arm.

On September 4th he was informed that he had a visitor. It turned out to be one of Linus' attorneys. He was wearing a blue suit that David figured never came off any rack. He opened his briefcase and placed a fistful of papers before them.

"You are David Tyler Roche?" he asked.

"Yeah," David answered, rather abruptly, "the one and only."

"I am here on behalf of the late Linus Couch. In his estate, he left instructions that you are to be the recipient of his Inprodico, model 463, prosthesis. This, Mr. Roche, is the good news. The bad news, however, is because of the nature of Mr. Couch's estate; the federal government has frozen all of his assets."

"So what does this all mean?" David asked.

"The operation involved in the reattachment of an artificial limb, such as this, is very costly. The limb may be yours, but the cost of reattachment cannot, at this time, come out of the estate of Mr. Couch. However, we have taken it on ourselves to find an alternative. There is a non-profit organization by the name of *Limbs for Life* that would be willing to perform the operation at no cost to you."

"So what's the catch?"

"No, there is no catch. *Limbs for Life* provides prostheses for those who have lost their arms at the shoulder, or their legs at the hip. In other words they cater to those who would receive little value from a conventional prosthesis. They receive some funding from the government, but most of their funding comes from donations from church groups and from the general public. They also distribute donated limbs from the families of deceased amputees."

"Great." David said, "When can they start?"

"All the proper forms have been filed. This, of course, will have to go through channels. It could take weeks; it could take months, or even years. With something like this there are no guarantees."

David got up to leave. "Yeah, well, one thing I've got plenty of is time."

The months rolled by, and David still didn't hear from anyone concerning his arm. Then, just before Christmas, he was informed that he had an appointment to go to the *Limbs for Life* clinic where he was to have a consultation with a Dr. Bixler. He was transported under armed guard, his legs were shackled, and his free arm was handcuffed to his belt. He had his claw back, but he was told to remove it. However, the guard brought it along just in case the doctor needed to have a look at it.

Dr. Bixler was a small man who David thought looked more like an accountant than a doctor. Nevertheless, he gave David a thorough examination, after which he presented David with several forms that he asked him to sign. "Why not," David thought. "What do I have to lose?" The operation was scheduled for February 15.

Dr. Bixler looked up from examining the paperwork. "Do you have any questions?" he asked.

"Yeah," David rocked back in his chair and attempted to push the handcuff farther up his wrist with the chair's arm. Handcuffs made his wrist itch. "Why do I have to wait until February 15?"

"We only have a small staff, here, Mr. Roche. Many of the doctors who perform these delicate operations have donated their time. Now, this particular model is very complicated and there are only a handful of surgeons in this area who are experienced at performing such an operation. We are fortunate that Dr. William Frankton has cleared his busy calendar for the fifteenth of February so he can be here to perform the operation. There is a patient ahead of you, and with Christmas coming, there is no way we could be ready for you much before the middle of February."

"Also," Dr. Bixler continued, "There is a breaking-in period with all of these models, consisting of two or three months; in which time the patient becomes familiar with the prosthesis and we, here at *Limbs for Life*, get to work out any 'bugs' in the system. You see, Mr. Roche, this prosthesis is primarily a conglomeration of synchronized components that work in conjunction with a system of hydraulics that serve as muscles. These will be tied into your severed nerve endings to provide the proper stimulation."

"Whoa, Doc," David tried to wave his left hand only to realize that it was still handcuffed to his belt. "You're talking to someone who never made it past the tenth grade."

"Well, let me put it this way, Mr. Roche." The doctor leaned back in his chair and folded his hands against his chest. He raised his right arm. "When you perform a voluntary operation, like raising your arm, impulses from your brain stimulate nerves that cause your muscles to respond. Do you understand?"

"Yeah, I can grasp that."

"Many of the movements you make with your arm and hand are involuntary and some are learned movements, such as catching and throwing a ball. There are also involuntary movements such as throwing your arm up to protect yourself or to swat at a mosquito. These all require minute electrical impulses from various sections the brain to take place. Your brain is still able to put out the appropriate signals; it's just that your muscles are no longer there to respond. The circuitry in this prosthesis is able to detect those minute electronic impulses, amplify them, feed them to relays that activate a series of solenoids, and these in turn open and close certain valves that operate several hydraulic units."

David looked over to the stump of his right shoulder. "In other words, what you're saying is that you're gonna attach a miniature, computerized backhoe to my right shoulder."

"Yes," Mr. Roche, Dr. Bixler was smiling, now, "that is quite an astute observation."

David looked over at the guard who was just filling the small cup that came with his thermos with hot coffee. "Ya hear that? The Doc thinks I'm astute, Frank. I bet you don't even know what that means."

"How long have you been without your arm, Mr. Roche?" the doctor asked.

"I lost it about fifteen years ago." David's face took on a serious look. "A damn mortar took it off. I got into a little trouble and the judge told me he would let me off if I joined the Army Reserves. Wouldn't you know it I got called up? We were the rear guard. It was supposed to be like a police action, you know, a mopping up operation. No one was supposed to get hurt. We were eating supper in the mess tent when, bam, those bastards dropped a rocket right on top of us. I was a luck one." He looked at his stub; "if you can call this lucky."

"You will have to learn how to use your arm all over again. It's a little like relearning how to ride a bike. You'll be surprised how fast you'll catch on. Of course, nerve ending are very tricky things to deal with. There are always bad connections; cross-connections, and maybe a few that won't be connected at all. These are all the bugs that we will have to work out, over time."

"Time is one thing I've got a lot of, Doc. I just don't understand why you guys are willing to waste all this time on someone like me; a lifer."

"Our organization is not here to judge, Mr. Roche. Perhaps, under different circumstances, things might have turned out differently for you. After all, you did put your life on the line for your country. I'd like to think that in a small way, we are helping to repay that debt."

"Yeah, maybe."

Dr, Bixler got to his feet. He came around the desk and took David's handcuffed hand. "I guess we'll see you again on February 15."

The weeks that followed filled David with mixed emotions. He was happy with the thought of having a useful right arm again, but the thought of a long and tedious operation frightened him. He kept to himself, reading a glut of smutty, torn paperbacks that circulated among the prisoners. When they came to shackle him for his trip, on the fifteenth, he was nearly ready to call it quits.

Despite his anxiety, the operation went well, and in the months that followed David surprised himself, again and again, with what he could do with his new prosthesis. There were a few bugs, at first, and three more operations had to be scheduled, but even this David took in his stride.

He wasn't ready to pick his nose, yet, but he could hold a paper cup without crushing it. This was more than he could do with his claw. Not having a sense of touch was a handicap, but David was slowing beginning to overcome this problem. He learned to sharpen his peripheral vision so as to more clearly judge the extent of his reach. It certainly wouldn't do to be seated at the table and have your hand resting in your neighbor's cream pudding, especially if your neighbor was big and had a short fuse. It was crowding the end of August before David successfully presented his cellmate with his first, prosthesis-held, slimy, green booger.

David was a new man. He was fun loving, cheerful, and fun to be around. The old David no longer existed. He had finally made peace with the world and with himself. When he was asked if he would like to participate in a program that brought young kids to the prison to try to "scare them straight", he agreed wholeheartedly.

His first session was on a Thursday. Tony Groacher was the first to tear into the unsuspecting youngsters. He was a big man with large tattooed arms that he now waved around menacingly.

"You are nothing but a bunch of punks!" he shouted, jabbing his finger only inches from one frightened boy's face. "You think I like it here? This ain't the Hilton, y'know. The food sucks, the bunks are hard, and the scenery never changes, nothin' but steel bars and concrete! You won't like it either, but this is where you're gonna end up if ya don't get your shit together! Tell em what it's like here, Roche."

David could see where this was going. He stepped forward and put on his meanest face. He slammed his mechanical arm down on one of the metal tables. It jumped from the floor with the impact and the sound reverberated around the room.

"You people are going to have to deal with people like me and Tony, here, and we don't like you punks, already!" He clamped his hand onto the heavy table and raised it off of the floor about an inch. Setting the table down, he raised his open hand into the air. "If I don't like you," he continued, "I might just grab you be the throat, like this." He put his hand on his own throat. "Then I might squeeze until your eyes pop out."

Suddenly, the hand tightened around David's throat and a strange look came over his face. His eyes rolled back in his head and he started gagging. Tony and the others started laughing and the kids joined in.

David pulled at the fingers of the prosthesis with his free hand, but his real hand was no match for the strong grip of the hydraulic units, and he slowly started to turn blue.

Tony was the first to realize that this was no gag. He ran forward and grabbed the fingers of the prosthesis in both of his strong hands. Others came to David's rescue, but the combined strength of three strong men could do nothing to break the grip on David's throat. The hand ripped away flesh and cartilage. David's lungs, long deprived of live-giving oxygen, sucked in blood and air, in nearly equal proportions through the open breach in his throat. All present stood in horror, as David's throaty gurgle became his final comment.

They were all at the inquest, the doctors, the lawyers, the warden, as well as the prisoners who were there that night. Judge Filbert presided over the inquest. He looked over all of the papers before him, and then he called on Warden Holmsman to be the first to testify.

"Was Mr. Roche under any kind of stress or unusual pressure?" the judge asked.

"No, your honor, he was in good spirits, and for the first time since he set foot in my prison, he was getting along with just about everyone. He had started to take some courses because he wanted to take the test for his high school equivalency."

"Then, Warden can you see any reason why he would want to take his own life?"

"Not at all; he was suddenly a happy camper, dedicated to improving himself, and helping those around him."

"Thank you Warden. Now, Dr. Bixler, you say in your report that the doctors and technicians could find nothing unusual, and that there seemed to be nothing mechanically wrong with the prosthesis. Has this particular model ever malfunctioned, like this, before?

"No, your honor," Dr. Bixler informed him. "We have had minor problems, but nothing like this. Sometimes, under emotional stress, or excitement, the circuitry does get confused and a certain amount of clumsiness will ensue, but nothing of this nature."

"I have been informed that this particular unit was a used prosthesis and that it was donated by a fellow prisoner who was executed," the judge looked down at his papers. I believe his name was Linus Couch. Is that correct?"

"Well no, your honor." Dr. Bixler fumbled around in his paperwork and retrieved a sheet of paper. "This particular unit was donated by the family of a man named Robert Whitman."

The judge removed his glasses and wiped them on his robe. "Would you please clarify this for the court?"

"Ah," Dr. Bixler fumbled around in his paperwork, again, "when we agree to accept a patient, such as Mr. Roche, any donated prosthesis becomes the property of the *Limbs for Life* organization. It is in the contract that is signed by the donator, as well as subsequent contracts signed by the recipient."

The judge looked over his glasses at the two attorneys that had represented Linus Couch. "Do you concur? He asked.

The two lawyers looked at each other and shook their head. "Yes, your honor," they said simultaneously.

"Very well," the judge turned again to Dr. Bixler, "please continue."

"The fact is that the Whitman family was still grieving over the unfortunate demise of their loved one and we did not want to pressure them into releasing the prosthesis, even though our recipient, a man named Cornell Horton was ready to receive it. He had given the organization a substantial donation and was extremely anxious to receive his prosthesis. We felt that because Mr. Roche was not, at the time, in the system, we were well within our rights to offer the Inprodico, model 463 to Mr. Horton and, when the Whitman prosthesis became available, we were prepared to offer it to Mr. Roche."

"I see," the judge said. "And both of these models are of equal value and proficiency?"

"Yes, your honor," Dr. Bixler, was pulling at his collar and beginning to sweat profusely. "Top of the line, state-of-the-art, except, of course, for that one minor problem I mentioned before. We didn't feel that clumsiness under pressure would be a problem under the watchfulness of a state prison system. In fact, we thought that it might prove to be an advantage. If angry, or excited, Mr. Roche would have trouble wielding a weapon."

"I see," the judge poured a glass of water and took a sip, "so you felt fully justified in switching this model 463 for, what was the other unit?"

The doctor sifted through his notes, again. "It was a Neton, model 26. It's manufactured by a Japanese firm."

"Did Mr. Roche know about the switch?"

"No. However, we did notify the attorneys for Mr. Couch's estate. We felt that since Mr. Roche was ignorant of the basic implementation of the device, the change in models would mean very little to him. As it worked out, he seemed very happy with the prosthesis. The warden informed me that there was a great improvement in his overall demeanor."

"When did this prosthesis finally become available?"

"Not until just after the first of February."

"And why did it take so long to get the Whitman family to release this prosthesis, Dr. Bixler?" the judge asked.

"The nature of the crime was extremely heinous, your honor. The man owned a liquor store and was viciously murdered at his place of business, in New York City, during a robbery, by . . . oh my god!"

"What is it, doctor?"

"Not that it's important, your honor; merely a coincidence," the doctor made a nervous chuckle, "but I have just noticed that the perpetrator was a man named David Roche."

LETTER FROM HELL

Hi Mom,

How shocked you must have been to see the envelope and from where it was mailed. Let's face facts; it must have been a shock just to see a letter from me. No, I didn't make up this letter while I was alive and have some friend mail it to you after I died. You know that I don't have any friends. Believe me; this letter is coming straight out of Hell. I have been awarded a few special privileges. Hey, with Dad, Cousin Ricky and Uncle Ralph as part of the alumni, I'm a full-fledged fraternity brother, already. Not only can I write letters, but I can also vote. Now, how scary is that?

It was hot when I got here, but then, "hot" in Hell is only a relative thing. You know what the first thing I did was? I bitched about having to stand in line. Think about it, why would you have to stand in line to get into Hell? I can see having to stand in line to get into the other place (We're not allowed to say, or write the "H" word). Hey, they have to measure you up for your wings and halo and to see in what key you want your harp to play. Here, you throw your clothes in a heap and you follow paths to wherever you think you want to go. It's a lot like Disney World, except there are not venders to sell you those overpriced bottles of cold water.

I was going to check out something called "The Eternal Wait", but the line there was too long, so I followed the path to "The Fiery Pit". I thought it was something that you just looked down into. I had no idea that they would throw me down into it. It was already full of people, which turned out to be a good thing as they broke my fall.

It didn't take me long to figure out that you were supposed to climb on the others to keep out of the flames. I was always a good climber. Remember the time I outfoxed the cops by climbing up on the roof?

It didn't take me long to get to the top of the heap, and while I was standing on this woman's face, one of the demons reached down and pulled me back up. He handed me a free ticket to something called "The Telemarketer", which turned out to be a booth full of speaker phones where sales pitches were coming at you from all directions; only you couldn't hang up on them. You would have been proud of me, Mom. I was so verbally abusive I had six of them in tears and eight more who put me on hold. For this I got a free ticket to something called "Trafficking" and some cotton candy. The cotton candy only made me thirsty.

At "Trafficking" they handed a bunch of us some drugs and said that the one who sold all of their drugs first would be the winner. They put us on some street where we had to interact with people who didn't seem all that real. I set up shop near an elementary school and was sold out in less than an hour. Those other fools were trying to sell to a bunch of dope addicts. Those people don't have any money. I even got to keep all the money, only I can't spend it here. I'll send it to you, and maybe you can buy me something nice with it, although I don't know how you would get it back to me. If there is a way I'll figure it out.

That earned me a ticket to something called "Grand Theft Auto". Here, I had to hot wire a car and try to get across the finish line before I got caught. The problem was, when I hit the street there was this huge traffic jam. I took to the sidewalk and went around much of it. Some people got in my way, and some didn't move fast enough. Tough! I rammed a few cars and even took the door off of one. This guy started chasing and ramming me until I found this gun jammed between the seats and fired a few rounds at him. I even got 5,000 extra points for firing into an occupied vehicle with children.

The cops started to chase me, but I lost them temporarily by driving the wrong way down a one-way street, forcing a few cars into the ditch and one off of a bridge. They caught up with me on the next block and tried to stop me with a spike strip. I avoided it by pulling onto the shoulder and taking out a couple of cops. I rammed one cop car and ran it into a tree. This damaged the radiator and the front fender, but it didn't stop me. It did wear out the front tire and cause it to blow. The engine overheated and seized just as I crossed the finish line.

When those demons pried open my door and helped me out, you would have thought that I was Mario Andretti, himself. My total score was over two million. Sixteen cars wrecked, including several cop car, and the one I stole. Three cops and forty-seven citizens injured or killed, including two children under twelve. Personal property damage over six city blocks was in the tens of thousands of dollars; no wonder they thought I was a hero.

The demons took me to a strip joint and fed me drinks. The thing is, the more I drank the thirstier I got. Then this one girl came out. She had all the right thinks in all the right places, and when she started to strip, it only got better. Now, I knew that this was Hell and enjoying yourself in Hell can lead to undesirable circumstances. I mean, she was right there, within reach. I could just reach up and grab . . . well . . . you know, but I didn't. I kept my cool. You have to remember that I was naked. There are not secrets in Hell. When I looked at her I thought of you. I kept thinking, *that could be my mom. That is my Mom. That is my Mom*, and it worked.

I, really, thought that the demons would be mad, but they weren't. After all, I had beaten them at their own game, but instead they patted me on the back and sent me off with another ticket. This time it was a place called "Bug Land". I knew, right away, that I wasn't going to like it. You know how I dislike bugs.

They sent me into this maze armed only with a can of bug spray. "OK," I thought, "how bad can this be? I've got the bug spray, and it looks like a good brand name."

Boy was I surprised. I came around the first corner and here was this giant ant holding a magnifying glass and trying to fry me with the sun's rays. I had to dodge and weave and run like hell. As it was, it damn near set my hair on fire. I managed to get the magnifying glass away from it and burn the hell out of its antennae. After that it lost its sense of direction and got lost in the maze.

Next, there was this huge fly that tried to pull my arms off. I gave it a shot of bug spray, and used the magnifying glass to fry its wings. It shook off the bug spray like a bad dose of teargas. It couldn't fly, but it could still walk, and it came after me with a vengeance.

As I rounded the next corner I saw a huge spider's web with a huge spider in the center. I found the sun, again, and flashed the beam into the fly's eyes. I stepped in front of the spider's web and shouted, "Nana-nana-na-na!" The fly charged and ran right into the spider's web. The spider came down, and while they were tussling, I slipped on by.

Around the next corner was a scorpion. It was on me in one bound. I held the large magnifying glass in front of me and warded off the blows from his tail. Suddenly, he stopped attacking me and jumped back. Then I realized that through the magnifying glass, I must have looked huge to him. I backed him around the next corner and into a huge centipede. The two of them started struggling while I worked my way past the centipede's tail end, and out the exit.

That was all I could handle for one day, so I got a weekly pass and checked into the Hotel Brimstone. They take stolen credit cards, but the room service really sucks. The beer is warm and the burgers taste like cardboard, just like all those burger places back home. At least the fries are never cold. You can order a milk shake but you'll never get it. By the time it gets to you it's boiled down to something resembling hot cold cream; or is that an oxymoron? I found out that you don't want to ask them to make the bed. The smell of their breath, while they are laughing at you, is enough to make your eyes water.

The Devil came to visit me, personally, today. He welcomed me and said that I would make a good addition to his team. He, also, said that he was impressed with my scores for the day, and thought that, even though I did well when I was alive, here I could be a prince. Prince Jacob! The Prince of . . . what? Prince of Darkness? I guess not; that's what they call him. I could be the Prince of Pain, the Prince of Fire, the Prince of Carjacking—Burglary—Shoplifting—Drug Dealing—Incest.

Oh, that's right. You didn't know about that. Why, the hell, do you think Marci hasn't talked to me since she was thirteen? I'll bet she didn't even go to my funeral. Hey, she was going through all that boy crazy shit, wearing those short skirts and padding her bra. Somebody would have porked her. It might as well have been me.

It wasn't my fault. She was thirteen; she didn't have to look sixteen. I was drunk and horny, and she was handy. It was just as much your fault. If you hadn't been out doing your Jesus shit, and had been home, it wouldn't have happened. It wasn't like she was my real sister, you know. After all, we don't have the same father. Who knows, if she had been a little older and hadn't fought so much, she might have even enjoyed it.

I know what you're doing, Mom. You're doing that thing with the rosary and saying all those Hail Mary's, that mumble jumble crap, and praying for my eternal soul. It's too late, Mom. I'm already here, in Hell. The bus doesn't even run to that other place that we are not allowed to mention. Even if I did go there, what would I be, and ex con, druggie, baby sister rapist? How much respect would I get there? At least, here, there are those who look up to me.

If you want to pray for someone, pray for your own soul. If you had been a little less forgiving, and kicked my ass once in a while, I might not have ended up becoming what I became. I'm not stupid, you know? When I was just a kid, I could lift a stereo in less than five minutes. When I was fifteen, I could hotwire any car and be down the road in less than three minute. I could talk people out of anything. I could have been a judge, or even a politician, if I had stayed in school.

That was your fault, too. You didn't make enough to support us. Someone had to bring in the money. The old guy who owned the furniture store would have married you in a heartbeat, but, no, you were too good for him. Jesus, he was old. If you had given him a few good years he would have died and left you everything. As it was, he ended up marring that sleazy whore down the block who took everything he had and left him high and dry. That could have been you.

But I didn't write you this letter to dwell on your shortcomings. I wanted you to know that I'm doing all right. Oh, and that Purgatory stuff is just a bunch of horseshit. When that drug dealer pumped the second slug into me, I went straight to Hell. It was like, boom, boom, and here I was at the end of the line, and then came this politician and his girlfriend, and then the drug dealer, himself, right behind them. His gun was still smoking. I had to laugh, though. He looked like Swiss cheese. I guess he must have tried to shoot it out with the cops. I've seen him a couple of times, but he must have done something nice in his life. The last time I saw him, they had just thrown him into the "Firy Pit". He's never been able to make it out.

I have to go, now. I have to go help stoke the fires. The work is hard, but somebody has to do it. It's not too bad; I work six hours on and six hours off. It's a lot cooler stoking than actually being in the fires. Things here run twenty-four/seven, and when I'm off, I mostly sleep, so don't expect another letter for at least another hundred years.

Your son,
Jacob

THE DEVIL'S NEMESIS

When I arrived at work that morning of August 5th there was a note on my desk from the editor. It seemed that someone named Gabriel Keane was being released from prison in Leavenworth, Kansas, and the editor wanted me to do a write-up about it. It was the type of work I was familiar with. Someone of note, either famous or infamous would again materialize to earn his or her second fifteen minutes of fame. It was the type of thing that would net me a two-line filler on page five, perhaps, or in the obituary, if the subject were recently deceased; surely the kind of article that people would, normally, glaze over on their way to the comics.

I gathered up the memo and made my way to the archives. In the files I found Gabriel Keane, but it didn't take me long to realize that I had the wrong man. According to the records, he was sentenced to ninety-nine years back in 1906. Perhaps I was looking for Gabriel Keane Junior, although I could find no such listing in the files.

I checked the microfilms for August of 1906 and found the trial of Gabriel Keane. It had already dragged on for four months before he was judged guilty by a jury in late September, and sentenced by the honorable Judge William Brannon on August 6th. The charges were numerous, and included the murder of one Charles McCarthy, who, according to eyewitness accounts, he shot down in cold blood during an altercation in Branigan's Saloon in May of that year.

He was only sixteen, at the time, and that is why the judge sentenced him to ninety-nine years instead of sending him to the gallows, as was customary at the time. The Judge refused to sentence a young boy to death; although, he stated that he would put Gabriel Keane away so that he would never be free to be a menace to the public again. The lithograph on the front page showed Gabriel standing tall and defiant in leg irons and handcuffs, with two guards flanking him on both sides, while the judge sentenced him. The caption read, "Gabriel Keane smiled and thanked the judge for his light sentence, before being led out of the courtroom."

"What are the odds that this is the same Gabriel Keane?" I wondered. *"After all he would be one hundred and fifteen years old. How many people have survived ninety-nine years in prison? There has to be two Gabriel Keanes."*

It would be easy to find out. All I needed to do was call Leavenworth Prison and asked when Gabriel Keane was first incarcerated. It was a shock to find out that he was indeed that Gabriel Keane. I asked the usual questions and got enough information to write my, usual, two-line story.

"Gabriel Keane, a convicted killer, was released from the federal prison at Leavenworth, Kansas today after serving what would normally be considered a life sentence of 99 years. It is not known, at this time, if he has any living relatives, or what he plans on doing now that he is a free man."

"Sources stated that he was in 'pretty good shape for a man his age', although at 115, he is, surely, quite feeble and probably will not be able to function in society without some sort of assistance. One would need to ask whether releasing him was the best thing for all concerned, including Gabriel Keane."

A week later, while I was busy trying to make my deadline for an article about a local model train show, I heard someone clearing his throat. I looked up to see a tall, elderly man standing in front of my desk. His shoulders were broad and rounded, his face chiseled from cracked, stained alabaster, and his sinuous arms strained the fabric of his rolled-up shirtsleeves. In one of his massive hands he held the folded page of a newspaper.

"You Kimble?" he asked. "Dwayne Kimble, the guy what wrote this article?"

"I'm Dwayne Kimble," I admitted, but looking at his face I began to wonder if admitting to be me was a good idea.

He threw the page down in front of me. I only had to glance at the headline, **"One hundred and fifteen year old man free,"** to know that this had to be about Gabriel Keane.

"I'm Gabriel Keane," he said, his steel-blue eyes now burning a hole through my retinas. He swept my desk clean with one swipe of his huge hand and mounted it like a pouncing tiger. There, supported by only the toes of his shoes and one hand . . . his left hand behind his back . . . he began to do one-handed pushups. "Someone had better get a camera," he yelled over his shoulder, "I'm a feeble old man. I can't keep this up forever."

Cameras flashed as people gathered around as a multitude of voices joined in with the count.

"Twelve . . . thirteen . . . fourteen . . . fifteen . . . sixteen . . . seventeen . . . eighteen . . . nineteen . . . twenty."

Gabriel jumped down from the desk. "If I do any more you'll just think I'm showin' off," he said, smiling. "Now, you pick out the best picture, Dwayne. You can put it with the retraction that states that maybe that 'feeble old man' ain't all that feeble after all."

He turned and left. People were cheering and patting him on the shoulders. I was nearly in tears, but mostly grateful that Mr. Keane wasn't looking for another 99 years.

GRAND THEFT AUTO

Roland Bradshaw had it all: a lucrative law practice, a luxurious house in Beverly Hills, an expensive sports car, and a cheating wife. Oh, it wasn't any secret to him. He retained one of the best private detective firms in the business. He was aware of her every move. He received reports daily. He knew who her latest conquest was, where she had picked him up, his age, weight, height, income and social standing. He kept a log on her as if she were a lab rat.

He knew that, to Paula, these young men . . . and they were young . . . were nothing but diversions, something to fill some sexual void in her life. When sex was the only thing that these men had to offer, it would soon wear thin and she would grow tired of them. Like a hungry shark, she was always looking for some fresh, young meat.

She took good care of herself. For a woman in her thirties, she was in excellent shape. She jogged every day, and went to the gym four times a week. Here, she would meet many of the young men who made up her retinue. They fell at her feet like toadyish thralls, and when she grew tired of them, she would dispose of them as easily as cold bath water.

Paula was well aware of her priorities. The first was to keep her husband happy, and the second was to keep herself happy, although sometimes the second priority became the first. She enjoyed all the things that her husband's position had to offer: money, prestige, power, and position. All these things were important to her, more important than all of her sexual conquests and daily liaisons. She love to shop, and Roland never denied her anything within reason. Even the bobbles she would purchase for her many lovers, Roland overlooked. Things like watches, bracelets, silk shirts, and even underwear, slid by his watchful eye as if they were normal household items. Gifts for her brother, she would tell him. He; however, doubted very much that her brother ever received any of these items.

Roland had his own reasons for not wanting to confront his wife with his knowledge of her goings-on. He had political ambitions, and a divorce was just the thing he didn't need at this time. A stable marriage, loving wife, happy home; these were all the things that make a candidate attractive to the public. To enter into a nasty divorce would be committing political suicide. There would be plenty of time for doling out justice after he was well established as a favorite son.

Besides, Paula had all the attributes of a good political wife. She was beautiful, intelligent, a great hostess, tidy, and a fashionable dresser. She had a winning personality that most people could not resist. There were even times when he felt close to her. When they were visiting family or having dinner with friends, it was almost as if they were the ideal couple. It was not until the next day, as he got ready for work and she prepared to embark on some new adventure, that Roland would realize that it had just been a clever façade.

It hadn't always been this way. There was a time when they really cared for one another. When he was struggling through college, she was always there to help him with his studies. When he landed his first job with a growing law firm, she had been his inspiration and most ardent supporter. Even when he had ventured on his own, starting a shaky law practice that might have gone either way, she was there, encouraging him.

After fifteen years, he still couldn't place his finger on the exact moment when everything changed. Perhaps it wasn't a quick change. It took place over a period of years. Perhaps so slowly that neither of them realized it was happening.

They had talked of having children, but in the beginning it was out of the question. They were both working, he was going to college; and neither of them had the time for a family. Then there were those struggling years: the long hours, the parties, the demanding clients, a quick peck in the morning, and many a night he would wake her up to kiss her good night. Children would have just been in the way.

Now, fifteen years had gone by; and they still had no children. They had discussed it, but at the time it seemed completely out of the question. Now, he was nearing forty, and she was thirty-seven. Was this really a good time to think about starting a family? He thought back. Perhaps they had started drifting apart when she began to wonder if she might be unable to conceive. She wanted him to undergo testing, but he had refused. What if the problem was his? After all, what would that solve? He really didn't want to know. There was some talk about adoption, maybe some older children, but aren't older children nothing but trouble?

It all drifted down to this ebb in their marriage, to the point where he no longer cared that she was having affairs. This only proved that there was probably nothing left to salvage. Whatever had been there in the beginning had now died. The whole charade had turned into a marriage of convenience and little more. Roland and Paula Bradshaw, the ideal couple, was nothing more than some hundred-dollar, papier-mâché, carnival front, propped up with bamboo sticks, for everyone to see?

"These eggs are runny!" Roland pushed his soft-boiled eggs away, and threw his morning paper on the table.

"I'm sorry, dear," Paula Bradshaw got to her feet and reached across the table for her husband's plate.

"Why are you sorry?" he asked. "Didn't Rosa cook breakfast this morning?"

"Don't you remember, dear? Rosa took the day off to go to her niece's wedding."

"That was today? Yes, I guess I'd forgotten."

"I'll cook a couple more for you, dear."

Roland looked at his watch. "No, I really don't have the time. I've got an early appointment this morning."

"Don't be silly, dear. You know how your stomach gets if you don't eat a good breakfast. The water is already hot; I'll just pop in a couple more eggs. It shouldn't take long to get it boiling again. I cooked these eggs for three minutes. I forgot that you like your eggs cooked longer. It won't take me long. Five or ten minutes, either way, isn't going to affect your schedule that much."

"Ok, dear," Roland said, picking up his paper. "If you want to play Suzy Homemaker, who am I to stand in your way?"

As Paula retreated to the kitchen, Roland thought about what had just transpired. Even in private, when there was no one around to see or hear what was going on, the charade continued. Paula was being pleasant, playing the domestic housewife, and Roland was enjoying it, even if it was just another ruse. Only once, in their fifteen years of marriage, had they had a real knockdown, drag-out fight. Now that he looked back at it, it appeared frivolous and stupid, but at the time there had been some real passions involved.

They had gone to a party, and both of them had been drinking. Their three-month marriage was just beginning to lose that fairytale sense of wonderment that often grips young couples that are truly in love. They were settling into each other's lives, and each was beginning to realize the other's "warts". Paula's biggest fault was her need to flirt, while Roland's was this jealous rage that only surfaced when he was under the influence, and unable to control it.

Her target, this night, was a young athlete by the name of Ted Crofton. He had a reputation for having a large sexual appetite and an eye for a pretty face, without regard as to whom that pretty face might be emotionally or legally bound to. He had all the assets of a sexual predator, except, instead of hiding in dark places to pounce on his victims; he confronted them head on and wooed them into submission with his hard body, winning smile, and his quick wit. Victims, used and discarded were nevertheless, left with a feeling of euphoria, and somehow grateful for the experience.

On this night, Roland saw his new bride as a potential victim. Of course, hindsight had now caused him to realize that the real victim might as easily have been Ted Crofton. Paula's appetite was indeed no less the Ted's, although, covert and latent at the time, Roland had no way of knowing. He plowed into Ted, with the inevitable result being Roland sustaining a "fat lip" and Paula had to drive them home.

The resulting fight was to be the worst confrontation they ever had. Certain rules were laid down; among them was the understanding that, if the marriage was to work, Paula could no longer flirt in front of him, and he was to realize that he did not own her. To this day, those ruled have never been changed or broken.

Roland had only known Paula for six months before they were married. They met at college, at a frat party. He had been drinking heavily for about an hour when he saw her arrive. He was just drunk enough and brave enough to ask her to dance. He had thought that she was the most beautiful thing that he had ever seen. Apparently a lot of the other guys thought the same thing, because it wasn't long before she was lost to him amid a barrage of admirers. He had retreated to a corner, and commenced to get blitzed on gin and tonic. When the tonic ran out, he switched to rum and Coke. When the Coke was gone, he started drinking Vodka, straight.

He didn't remember just when he had passed out, but when he came around, it was Paula who was standing over him saying, "Hey, fella, are you OK?" He had mumbled something, and she helped him to his feet. "I think you need some fresh air. Come on, big boy, you can walk me back to my dorm."

They never made it to her dorm, that night. Somehow, they ended up at his apartment. She made a pot of coffee, and they sat up the rest of the night talking. He had poured out his whole life to her as if he had known her forever. He told her of his fears, his loves, and his ambitions. In retrospect, he now realized that she had told him very little about herself. She was twenty, she was from a small town in upstate New York, she had a brother named Charley, her father's name was Robert, and her mother's name was Helen, she was here on a student loan, she played basket ball in high school, and the family dog was named Chip. Other than that, the rest of her life was a deep mystery.

Roland didn't care. All he had to do was look into her deep blue eyes and he knew that he was in love, if not with the girl, at least with the image. Of course, he also noticed the haunting promise of her deep cleavage, and the soft hint of smooth, white thigh that presented itself as she swung her crossed leg with undulating rhythms while seated next to him at the kitchen table. These thing, he had convinced himself, were not important.

After all, she was not like the chocolate bunny once coveted by his childhood self for its rich, sweet taste, to be devoured and forgotten. Long after he had tasted her physical attributes, he still retained a warm feeling in his heart whenever he thought of her; and when they were separated, he would long for just the sound of her voice. Was this not true love?

Now, as his wife made her way toward the kitchen, he wondered if in fact he had only been lying to himself. In retrospect, the taste of her nipples, the feel of her firm breasts, and the sweet smell of her soft hair against his face as he made his final thrusts, still excited him to this day. With the silliness of love out of the way, it was a wifely duty, preformed once a week, and with the absence of foreplay, it demanded little of their precious time.

Perhaps love had never really been a factor. Perhaps the whole thing had always been based on their physical attraction. What the hell is love, anyway? Isn't it just some chemical thing in the brain? Perhaps we are all born with some preconceived model of the perfect mate imbedded in our psyche. When the proper type appears before us, chemicals are dumped, our heart beats faster, and our hands begin to sweat. We call this love, but it just might be some kind of fucking virus. Maybe we're just sick.

Well if that's true, he said, under his breath, *then marriage must be the cure.*

"What, dear?" Paula set the plate before him. She had changed, and was now wearing shorts and a tight-fitting T-shirt that did nothing to conceal her nipples. "Did you say something?"

"Just talking to myself, Paula."

"You must be coming into some money," she said, smiling.

"The Blackburn account, dear," he announced. "It ought to keep you in T-shirts for a long time, maybe you can even afford to buy some bras."

She looked down at her breasts. "Don't be a fuddy-duddy, dear. Nipples are in fashion, they have been since the sixties." She placed her hands under her breasts and lifted them. "I'm certainly not ashamed of them, dear. I've worked hard to keep them this way, why not show them off? Which reminds me, I need to get going; my trainer doesn't like it when I'm late."

"Why," Roland said loudly, "is his dick on a schedule?"

"Now, why did you say that?" There was a pause; Paula put her hand to her mouth. "You've had me followed, haven't you?"

"What if I have?"

Paula stepped forward and slapped Roland across the face, hard. "You fucking bastard! You goddamn, fucking bastard! You've been spying on me. What gives you the right to spy on me?"

"I'm you fucking husband, for Christ sake!"

"I thought we had an agreement?"

"What, that you could screw anybody you wanted? What was I supposed to do, just ignore what was going on?"

"Yes, Roland, that is exactly what you were supposed to do. What do you think has kept this marriage going for so long . . . love? I don't know if I ever loved you, Roland. I hated college, you had potential, ambition, and your family had money. I knew that you were going places. I latched on to you like a remora, and went along for the ride." She stepped forward and slapped his face again.

"You fucking bitch!" Roland's right hand caught her on the side of her face and sent her hard against the china cabinet, causing part of her collection of antique dishes to go crashing onto the hardwood floor. He grabbed her by the front of her T-shirt; it ripped in his hand as he spun her around and slapped her again. She fell against the dining room table.

Roland stepped back, disbelieving what he had just done. He looked at his wife as she stood there, her hand on her face, her eyes reflecting her disbelief.

"I'm sorry!" he said. "I'm so sorry, Darling."

"Don't, *Darling*, me, you bastard! For fifteen years I've tried to be what I thought you wanted me to be. But I'm sure as hell not going to be your fucking punching bag. Did you forget the essence of our agreement? You don't own me, Roland, and if you ever lay a hand on me again, believe me, you are going to be so, fucking sorry! I think you need help, Roland. You're coming unhinged."

She turned and fled from the room, still holding her hand to her face. He heard the bedroom door slam and the sound of the lock turning, something she had never done in fifteen years. A little later he saw her emerge wearing a pink, formfitting top. She glared at him as she returned to the dining room to snatch her pocketbook from the table. He watched in silence, as she crossed the kitchen and went out the side door to the garage. There was the sound of the overhead door opening, a racing engine, and tires squealing, as she sped down the road in her Triumph.

What was he thinking? The problem was, he hadn't been thinking. Paula had the power to ruin all of his plans, not to mention the financial burden she could impose on him if she were to file for divorce. Jesus, he was a fucking lawyer! He knew the consequences of a messy divorce, especially one with the position and finances that they enjoyed. Roland was smart enough to know that he could kiss his political ambitions goodbye. There were other potential candidates that were qualified. His biggest trump card had been the squeaky-clean public image that he projected. He already had one strike against him, because of the kid thing. He had been thinking about adopting a couple of "rug rats"; foreign kids, maybe, Vietnamese or maybe Russian. The whole foundation would collapse if Paula chose to pull out.

Roland went to the kitchen and dragged the phonebook out of the drawer. He called the florist he had used when his uncle had died and ordered a ninety-nine dollar bouquet. Paula was usually home by three; he set it up to be delivered then, while he was at work. He felt that it would be less of a cop-out if she had time to appreciate the flowers before he got home from work. If he were there when they arrived, and she was still mad, she might just throw them in his face.

As he crossed the dining room he noticed the broken dishes on the floor. He got a wastepaper basket from the den and cleaned up the broken pieces. He put several of the larger pieces in his briefcase. There was a little antique shop he remembered seeing about twenty minutes out of town. Perhaps he could find some replacements there. At least, he could make an effort. It might help defuse the situation.

He grabbed his briefcase and headed out the side door to the garage. He looked at his watch; he was already late. He threw his briefcase on the seat, slid in behind the wheel, and speed-dialed the office number on his cell phone.

"Bradshaw, Carter and Wheeler, may I help you?"

"Carol. I'm going to be a little late. Tell Bob he'll have to see my first client this morning. I have some important business to attend to." He had backed out of the garage, and was now closing the garage door by remote.

"Very well, Mr. Bradshaw. At what time might we be able to expect you?"

Roland looked at his watch. It was nine-fifteen. It shouldn't take more than an hour. "I should be there no later than ten-thirty."

"Very well, Mr. Bradshaw. I'll inform Mr. Carter."

Roland left the upscale development, picked up I-405, then headed north on I-5. At Santa Clarita he veered west to route 14, toward Vincent. The traffic was heavy at this time of day, but as he got farther from the city, it thinned out considerably. At Vincent, he continued on toward Littlerock. The road was unfamiliar to him; he had been this way only a few times, and his wife had driven. The only reason he had remembered the little shop was because Paula had pointed it out to him as a possible place she might hunt for future treasures.

He was past the shop before he saw it. He had to drive to the next stoplight and make a U-turn. The little shop was part of a string of little shops including a fabric shop and a pawnbroker. A small bell jingled as he opened the door, and a woman, perhaps in her early forties, smiled up at him from her chair behind the counter. She had been reading a book that she now marked and set aside.

"Good morning," she said, getting to her feet. "Is there anything in particular I can help you with?"

Roland set his briefcase on the counter, opened it up, and spread out the broken pieces of plate.

"Exquisite piece," she said, picking up one of the pieces. She turned it over. *Capodimointe*, she said, pointing to the crown and "N" symbol on the back. "How unfortunate that it got broken." She picked up the other pieces, one by one. "This one was a *Royal Doulton*, also a very nice piece, and this one," she held a piece of border into the light that streamed in through the window, "may have been a *Meissen*, but I'm not sure. Someone has excellent taste."

"They are my wife's, or should I say, they were." Roland was feeling a little embarrassed.

"I'm afraid I won't have anything to match these, if that is indeed what you were planning on doing. I do; however, have a set of *Royal Crown Derby* from England, and some early *Wedgewood* if you are interested."

"Can I see them?" Roland asked.

"Of course," she said, "they're back here."

She guided him through rows of closely packed tables stacked with various odds and ends that held little interest for Roland. To him, most of it looked like junk. *Why would anybody, in their right mind, want to clutter their home with shit like this?* He wondered to himself.

"This is the *Royal Crown Derby*," she explained. She was pointing to a stack of dishes that rested on a high shelf, on the back wall. There were six plates in all, with the sixth plate standing upright behind the rest, to show the pattern. "This is a superb pattern," she continued. "As you can see they are in excellent condition, and have never been used. "Over here," she pointed to another set of dishes on the same shelf, a few feet away, "is the *Wedgewood* set.' There were only four dishes in this set. "This is one of the earlier sets, and is also in excellent condition."

"What kind of money are we talking, here?" Roland asked.

"I could let you have the *Royal Crown Derby* set for five hundred dollars, and I would be willing to let the *Wedgewood* go for three hundred and fifty."

"OK, Roland said, "I'll take two of the *Wedgewood* and one of the *Royal Crown* whatever's."

"I'm sorry, sir. I'm afraid you don't understand. Plates come in sets. People collect them in sets. If you were to take two from one set and one from another, it would be very difficult to sell the remaining dishes."

"OK," Roland was desperate, "then I think I'll just take the Royal Crown thingies. Will you take a check?"

"I'm sorry, sir, I do not accept checks."

"But I assure you that my checks are good," Roland insisted.

"That is exactly what the last person said. I believe that check is still bouncing."

Roland reached into his billfold and produced a card. "I'm an attorney," he said, as he handed it to her.

She looked at the card, "Sir, please don't force me to relate how I feel about lawyers."

"OK, he said, "How about a credit card."

"Sir, this is a small business, I deal strictly in cash. Call me old-fashioned, but I trust cash."

"I don't usually carry a lot of cash." Roland had his wallet out and was rummaging through it. "The best I can do is three hundred and twenty dollars."

"For that," she informed him, after a brief pause, "I can let you have the *Wedgewood*. I'll even throw in the sales tax."

The woman took the plates down from the shelf, carefully wrapped them in newspaper and placed them in a small box. She held up the broken pieces Roland had placed on the counter. "Do you want to keep these?"

"I don't know why," Roland admitted.

She tossed the pieces into the trash and made out a hand-written receipt, calculating it three times in order to make it work out with the sales tax. Roland stopped off at the house before going to work. He removed the dishes from the box and spread them out, carefully, on top of the china cabinet. He scribbled a note and laid it on one of the dishes. It said, simply, "Sorry."

Paula usually had lunch with a long-time girlfriend, she had known from college. Although they no longer moved in the same circles, they had remained close friends despite the fact that Candace Wendell commonly referred to herself as *trailer trash*. Actually, Candace lived in a modest three-bedroom house in Anaheim. She was married, with two children, a boy, Kevin, who was fifteen, and a girl, Loraine, who had just turned fourteen. She was a housewife, a rare species by today's standards, and would often refer to herself as a *kept woman*.

Candace's trailer trash reference had more to do with her early upbringing. Her picturesque description of the family homestead in northern Virginia was a doublewide, brimming with children, clinging desperately to the side of a mountain. She spoke of her childhood with fond recollection, growing up in the sprawling mountains, playing and swimming in the cascading brooks, and on a clear day, it seemed that one could see to the edge of the earth.

She was the youngest of seven siblings. Her father, sickened by cancer, had died soon after she was born. Her mother struggled to raise the growing family. Although many material things were always out of their grasp, her mother gave them plenty of the things that were really important: love, courage, and respect. One by one the children fled the nest until, at eighteen, urged on by her mother, Candace came to California to attend college.

Candace's dream was to become an architect, and for nearly three years she struggled toward that goal. Then she met Brad and everything changed. They had gotten married and she became pregnant with Kevin. Not necessarily in that order. She realized that she wanted her children to have a full-time mother, a luxury she had always been denied.

Brad was a concrete contractor, who had a reputation for being honest, easy to work with, and for scheduling his work so that he would be there when he said he would. Everybody liked him, and even in the early years, he did rather well. Although they were far from rich, Brad did well enough so that Candace really didn't need to work. A dedicated mother and wife, Candace was indeed the model homemaker.

There was a *down-home* charm about Candace that you couldn't help but love. She often said, "You can take the girl out of the country, but you can't take the country out of the girl." She was honest to a fault, and never hesitated to tell it to you like it was.

"My God, honey, I could never wear anything like that." Candace was looking a Paula's pink top. "I wish I had your boobs." She placed her hands under her own breasts. "Look at these things," she said. "Even when they were full of milk, they were never that big."

Paula wasn't a person who was easily embarrassed, but she found herself looking around the restaurant to see if anyone was listening. To her relief, no one was.

"Of course," Candace continued, "if I had your body, Brad would screw me raw. Not that we don't do it, you know, regularly." She pulled up the front of her blouse, exposing her stomach. "With the stretch marks, and everything, havin' babies has sure made a mess out of my body. Y'know, though, sometimes I sure as hell wish I wasn't such a damn good cook. I have my mother to blame for that. Shit, here I am rattling on. OK, Honey, now y'all tell me what's wrong."

"What makes you think that something is wrong?" Paula said, innocently.

"I can read you like a book, Paula; besides, I can still see the mark on the side of your face."

Paula put her hand on her left cheek. "Is it still there?" she asked.

"I can see every finger mark. Roland's using you for a punching bag, isn't he?"

"We had a confrontation," Paula admitted.

"And he hit you?"

"Well, in all fairness, I did hit him first." Paula had pushed the rest of her salad aside, and was picking at her fried chicken fingers.

"Ain't no reason for a man to hit a woman."

"He's been under a lot of pressure lately."

"Jesus, Paula! Listen to yourself." Candace had been drinking her iced tea when she said that. She set her tea down and was now coughing into her napkin. "Sorry, but you've got to stop makin' excuses for the asshole. I've been married to Brad for over fifteen years, and he's never laid a hand on me."

"I don't blame him, Candace, Brad's probably afraid you would take a shotgun and blow his brains out while he was sleeping."

"Why would I do that, when I know someone who will do it for me."

"What are you talking about, Candace?"

"I just happen to know a hitman. For a few grand, he'll do the job, neat and clean, and make it look like an accident."

"Jesus, Candace!" Paula was again looking around. "Don't go saying things like that in public, even if you are kidding."

Candace leaned forward, and lowered her voice. "Who's kiddin'?"

Paula leaned forward so that her face was inches from Candace's. "You really mean that you know a *real* hitman?"

"Yes," Candace whispered, now looking around the restaurant herself. "His name is Fred; at least that's what he calls himself. We dated for a while before I met Brad."

"And you never turned him in?"

"Why? He's a nice guy. I still see him now and then, and he always says hello."

"But, Candace, he kills people!"

"To him it's just a job. He told me once that if he didn't do it, somebody else would have to."

"And he feels comfortable knowing that you know?"

Candace was mopping up the gravy on her plate with a folded, buttered slice of bread. "Oh, he told me once that if I ever told anybody he would have to kill me, or have me killed, if they put him in jail."

"Have you killed?"

"Yeah, it sort of a professional courtesy among hitmen. You shoot my snitch, and I'll shoot yours."

"Candace, you're crazy!"

"If I hadn't fallen head over heals in love with Brad, I might have married him." She held her hands apart over her plate, her index fingers extended. "He's like this. I'm not kidding."

Paula gaze swung back and forth between the two fingers. "My God!" she said, "how could you stand it?"

"Oh, but Paula, he is so gentle." Candace had her eyes closed, and was remembering. "Oh sweet Jesus," she sighed.

"Candace!" Paula's voice was now a loud whisper. "I can't believe we're having this conversation."

Candace snapped back to reality. "Actually, I doubt very much if Fred had ever considered marriage. I don't think he could ever make that kind of commitment. Y'know what I mean? In his line of work, he moves around a lot: New York, Chicago, Miami, places like that.

Nobody else knows this, but when he's in town, he'll give me a call. We'll meet someplace for dinner, and a quickie."

"My God, Candace! Are you telling me that you have been cheating on Brad?"

"Just once or twice a year. Fred still likes me: no tits, stretch marks, paunch, and all. Call me an addict, but it's hard to go cold turkey on something like that." Candace threw her hands out again, indicating, as Paula understood, something remarkable, at least for a human.

"But I thought that you and Brad . . ."

" . . . Had the perfect marriage?" Candace interjected, finishing Paula's sentence. "Well, in a way, we do. I love Brad dearly, but when it comes to lovemaking, well, he comes up a little short. When you've had béarnaise it's hard to settle for mustard."

"My God, Candace, I don't know what to say."

"Oh, come on, Paula, don't give me that condescending, holier-than-thou shit! You've been cheating on Roland for at least ten years that I know of. For Christ's sake, you've had more rubber in you than a retread factory."

"But that's different, Candace, Roland and I are . . ."

" . . . Not happily married," Candace interrupted, again. "Can't you see that maybe the thing that has kept my marriage on such an even keel is the fact that, at least once a year, I get a good, fuckin' lay?"

Paula sat back in her chair, and shook her head. "In all the years I've known you, Candace, this is one side of you I have never seen. I never even would have guessed."

"Brad has no idea, either, and that's the way I'd like to keep it."

"My God, Candace! You don't think that I'd tell anyone, do you?" Paula was definitely upset.

"Don't go ballistic on me, Paula. Of course I don't think that you would tell anyone. If I did, I wouldn't have confided in you in the first place. The reason I brought this whole think up is because I thought you might need Fred's services."

"What makes you think that I would want anything to happen to Roland?"

"He beat you, Paula."

"But, in fifteen years, this is the first time he has ever laid a hand on me."

"Yeah, well, my sister, Brenda, was married to a guy like that. Married for three years, they had lots of argument, but nothing physical. Then, one day, he came home drunk, and beat her up really bad. She ended up in the hospital with a broken nose and two badly bruised ribs. The next day he was at the hospital in tears. He brought her flowers and gifts, blamed the whole thing on his drinking, and said that he was giving up drinking, and that it would never happen again. Three months later she was in the emergency room at Community General. When she got out, she moved into my mother's house. He came to see her, once, but two of our brother's intervened. They convinced him that it would be better for his health if he left town and never came back. He did, end of story, she divorced the bastard, and she's lived happily ever after."

Paula thought for a moment. "Do you really think that Roland thinks that I would stand by and let this happen? Roland is always worried about scandals of any kind. How do you think it would look if I were to sue for divorce under grounds of physical abuse?

"Think about it, Paula. Roland is a lawyer with friends in high places. He could fuck you over and come out of it smelling like a rose; and you could end up with shit."

"A lot of Roland's friends are my friends, too."

"Get real, Honey. Roland is the man. All you are is eye candy for all the little soirées you throw. They look at your tits when you serve the hors d'oeuvres, and at your ass as you walk away. Other than that you could be an inflatable doll for all they care. They've seen better than you between the sticky pages of *Playboy*."

"Shit!" Paula grabbed her purse, removed a five and two twenties. She placed the two twenties on the restaurant bill and slid the five under her plate. "It's certainly good to know that my fifteen years with Roland haven't been wasted." She got to her feet.

"Sit down!" Candace said, authoritatively, "I haven't finished giving you a reality check, yet! It gets worse."

Paula sat down, obediently.

"What if Roland didn't want to go through a messy divorce?" Candace continued. "He could set it up to look like one of your admirers got jealous, did you in, and then turned the gun on himself."

"Come on, Candace, now you're being paranoid. Something like this is not going to happen."

"It happens all the time. Fred just loves to talk shop. He's done it a few times, himself. He claims it's easy. All you have to know is how to arrange the crime scene so that it appears to be a murder/suicide. He said that it takes a little skill to pull it off, but, if you're good at it, it's not all that hard. The main thing, he says, is to remember that cops aren't idiots; and that you need to have a strong alibi. Anyone who stands to profit from the decease's death is naturally a suspect. Husbands and wives are up front."

"Roland's not like that," Paula insisted. "He wouldn't have the heart to do something like this."

"He's a fuckin' lawyer, Paula. He has no heart."

"Now you're being cynical, Candace. Roland hasn't got a mean bone in his body."

"Reality check, Paula! That was not all love and sweetness that left those finger marks on the side of your face. Not only is he capable of it, sweetheart, he may be planning the whole thing while we talk."

"Now you're scaring me, Candace!"

"Well, you should be scared. You need to find out just what's up Roland's sleeve."

"And how am I supposed to do that?"

"Make him mad as hell, Paula."

"Are you crazy, Candace?"

"No, look. Say you get him really mad, and he tries to hit you again, what would this tell you?"

"That I'm an idiot, Candace."

"You're missing the point, Paula. If he hits you, or tries to hit you, it means that he's lost control, and that you had better get out of Dodge."

"And if he doesn't?"

"It could mean that he had realized his mistake, and won't do it again, or it could mean that he has already made arrangements."

"What do you mean by arrangements?"

"As Fred might say, "To have you snuffed.""

"So how am I supposed to differentiate between the two?"

"Well, for one thing, if he suddenly stops and smiles, your ass is in deep shit!"

Roland arrived home at seven-twenty pm. Paula's car was in the garage, but she was nowhere in sight. He could smell something cooking and wondered if Rosa was back. He crossed through the living room into the dining room. He noticed that the plates he had bought earlier were gone.

"Is that you, Darling," Paula's voice was coming from the kitchen. "Have a seat, Dear, supper is almost ready."

It had been so long since Paula had prepared a meal for the two of them, he had forgotten that she even knew how to cook. Paula was really a very good cook. At least she was when they had first gotten married. They both had to work during those first struggling years after graduation, and meals were usually hurried affairs. But as the business prospered, Paula quit her job, and meals became something to look forward to after a hard day.

Paula had many specialties, each as mouth-watering as the next. His favorite had always been something that she did with chicken and vegetables. It really had no name; something that she had dreamed up on her own that they always referred to simply as *Paula's dish*. It was an unusual mixture of wine in a seasoned sauce that now kindled memories so strong as to cause him to salivate as he removed his jacket and his tie, and took his place at the dining room table.

Roland smiled as he congratulated himself for so skillfully defusing an otherwise delicate situation. *Paula's dish*, indeed, was what permeated the living room air with scents from earlier times, and memories of more appreciative taste buds. How simple things were then. They were hard, struggling times, but he still looked back at them with a strange fondness and an unexplainable feeling of forlorn.

The evening began to play out in his mind's eye. A few "I'm sorrys", followed by handholding, and perhaps, after a few drinks, a roll in the proverbial hay. No quick jump, tonight. He would see to it that she was satisfied if he had to close his eyes and imagine that he was making love to Frankenstein. *Or Beatrice Culbart, the new court stenographer*, he thought to himself. He laughed. She had to be at least sixty, and as straight as a beanpole. If anything could turn him off, the thought of making love to her certainly would.

"Supper's ready." Paula came through the kitchen doorway, a plate in each hand. She placed a plate in front of Roland. "Bon appetit, darling," she said. She sat across from him, a Cheshire cat look on her face. She picked up her fork and toyed with the food. "Go ahead, darling, dig in. I made it especially for you."

Roland looked down. There was something odd about the food on his plate. It looked a lot more *colorful* than he had remembered. As he looked closer he realized why. For the vegetables, Paula had used the bouquet of flowers he had sent her earlier that day. There was also something familiar about the plate. As he moved the food aside he could see the pattern of one of the expensive, antique plates he had bought to replace the ones he had broken.

"Why?" he asked.

"Why do you think? Did you really think that if you bought me some flowers and a few pieces of cheap porcelain, everything would just smooth over?"

"Cheap? It may not be the same as the ones that got broken, but they certainly weren't cheap."

"Oh, now you're an expert on plates!"

"I know quality when I see it, yes."

"Horseshit, Roland! If it wasn't made yesterday, to you, it's junk."

"Horseshit? Is that some of the intellectual chitchat you picked up from your slut-friend, Candace?"

"How did you know I was with Candace? Oh, I see, you're still having me followed. Well then fuck you, Roland!"

"And fuck you back, sweetheart! See? Two can play at this stupid game."

"Why does Candace's name always creep into our conversations? What has she ever done to you?"

"You mean arguments, don't you, Darling. Yes, why is it that every time we have a little tit-for-tat I always think that Candace is behind it, somehow? It might be because I think that if I didn't watch her every minute she would shove a knife so deeply into my back I could pick my teeth with it."

"Jesus, Roland, I believe you are jealous."

"Not unless you're suddenly into the lickity-split scene, Paula."

"Candace and I are just good friends, Roland. Maybe if you had some real friends, instead of those social-climbing, gigolos, and bottom feeders that hang around waiting for the crumbs to drop, you would have some idea of what it's like to have a real friend."

"Does she help you pick out your lovers, too?"

"Oh, now we're back to that again."

"Well, it's not exactly a moot issue, Paula . . . Darling."

"OK, Roland, as long as we are on the issue of infidelity, why don't we talk about yours?"

"I don't know what the hell you're talking about, Paula."

"I'll tell you what I'm talking about. What about the lipstick I found on your clothes while I was checking the laundry?"

"You don't do the laundry. What were you doing, checking the clothes?"

"Let's just say that I had my suspicions."

"OK, so you found some lipstick on my collar. Sometimes clients get emotional. Maybe somebody at the office had an important event, or something. People hug."

"It wasn't on your collar, Roland. If I had found lipstick on your collar, I probably wouldn't have thought that much of it. I found this lipstick smudge on your underwear. Now you're going to tell me that you all go around on your knees, hugging in your underwear. I think that you and your secretary, Carol, have been having an affair."

"Caroline Pickard? Have you gone daft?"

"Why not? She's got all the qualities you like; big tits, nice ass, and she's over twelve."

"Caroline is married."

"So? What's your point? So are you."

"She's got a kid, for Christ's sake!" Roland was on his feet, pacing the room.

"Oh? Do a few stretch marks turn you off? Maybe it's a good thing we didn't have any children. We would be sleeping is separate beds, and you would be pounding off to your favorite porn flick."

"Denise."

"What?"

"It was Denise Fletcher."

"The little blonde in book keeping?" Paula was surprised.

"Yeah."

"My God, she couldn't be more than seventeen."

"Twenty-one."

"Now that's a revelation. And here I am thinking she was just a baby."

"Why do you think she left? I broke it off. I got her a job working for Phil Davidson."

"You broke it off?" Paula laughed.

"OK! She went back with her boyfriend." Roland went to the bar and poured a full glass of Scotch.

"Do you really need that, Roland? You know how you get when you drink."

"Believe me, Paula; my mood couldn't get any worse. What do you want from me? I'm sorry. I shouldn't have hit you back."

"Oh. Now I see. You think that because I hit you, that it gave you every right to hit me. Is that it?"

"No, Paula, that's not it. I had no right to hit you. Jesus, I see this all the time in court. It was stupid of me, I know that; can't we just let it go?"

"Maybe you can, Roland, but I have this feeling in the back of my mind, that it all could happen again. Only the next time it might be even worse."

"My God, Paula. Fifteen years and I've never laid a hand on you. Now, suddenly, I'm Ike Turner."

"It's happened before."

"Now, how would you know this?"

"Candace told me that . . ."

"OK! Now, we've come full circle." Roland threw his glass against the wall, his face flushed red with anger. "I knew that bitch had something to do with this!" he yelled. Suddenly Roland realized that it was all happening again. He took a deep breath and forced as smile. "Paula, I . . ."

Paula was on her feet and out the back door of the kitchen before Roland could finish.

"Where are you going?" Roland shouted from the kitchen door.

"I don't know. Out of here. Somewhere."

"What about your clothes?" he sounded concerned.

"I'll get them some other time, or maybe never. I don't know." Paula was crying. She backed out of the garage and was gone.

Roland went back to the dining room, found a fresh glass and the bottle of Scotch, and tried to understand what had just transpired.

Paula had been wrong about one thing; Roland did have one good friend. He and Bill Nolan went all the way back to grade school. Like Candace and Paula, they didn't move in the same circles. Bill was an over-the-road driver for a major trucking outfit. He took the long hauls: LA to Chicago, Cleveland, New York, Miami, maybe even Toronto. He would be gone a week, sometimes longer, home for a few days, then off again. Bill loved his job. He liked driving. He had confided in Roland, once, that if he hadn't been a truck driver, he would have probably had a military career. He said it was what kept his marriage together. Suzy, his wife of ten years, liked her independence, and Bill, if he spent too much time at home, began to feel claustrophobic. It was a marriage made in heaven, he explained. What were the odds of two people finding each other, loving each other dearly, but only being able to handle being together in small doses?

The only thing that disrupted this equation was Bill's nine-year-old son, Jason. If Bill had any driving reason to be at home, it was his son. Despite the fact that he was always teasing Jason about looking just like the mailman, it wasn't hard to see that he idolized the boy. It was impossible not to notice that Jason felt the same way about his father.

"Oh yeah," Jason would say. "Can a mailman's son double clutch a seven-speed, Road Ranger?" With this he would seat himself in a chair, and go through all the proper motions it would take to up shift and downshift a big rig.

"Well," Bill would admit, "you've got me there." He would hold his son's face in his hand and survey it carefully. "Y'know," he would say, "there might be some resemblance here, after all."

The truth was, Jason was nearly a clone of his father, when Bill was nine. Roland marveled at that fact. Many times he caught himself about to call Jason, Bill. More than once he, in fact, had.

Roland pulled into the driveway of the small, two-story house of his friend. It certainly wasn't anything you were likely to find in "House Beautiful". The lawn was nearly void of any grass, the house hadn't been painted in years, and Suzy's old VW Bug still occupied a place in front of the cluttered garage; its final resting place since Bill had promised to restore it eight years ago. The garage door, hanging precariously crooked, and lacking nearly three feet of being anywhere near closing, gave witness to a hodgepodge of family treasures most people would concede as being junk.

It was Suzy who answered his knock. She was a tall woman, nearly six foot, with the lean frame of an athlete. She looked much younger than her thirty-two years despite her lack of makeup and the fact that her thick, blond hair was cut in some kind of uneven pageboy. As Roland recalled, he had only seen Suzy dressed up and wearing makeup once. It was the only time she and Bill had ever come to one of Roland's fancy soirees. They couldn't have looked more out of place if they had been wearing blue genes, and Roland sensed they might have felt that way, too. They never came to another one, and after a while, Roland stopped inviting them.

"Well hello, counselor," Suzy said, smiling. She held open the squeaking, screen door. "What brings you to our humble abode? You're too late for supper, and too early for Christmas."

"I was just in the neighborhood," Roland said, jokingly.

"Yeah," Suzy laughed. "In a pig's ass. Well, get your ass in here, you're letting all the flies out."

Roland didn't have to duck as he slid under her arm and made his way into the kitchen. "So where's your other half?" he asked.

"The loser?" she joked. "He's out on the back patio. You might as well take a couple of these with you. Save us both a trip." She opened the refrigerator and handed Roland two cans of beer. "Hey Jason!" She shouted, "Uncle Ron's here!"

Jason met Roland in the living room and gave him a hug. Jason had to be the only person in the world that called him "Ron". When he was little, Uncle Roland was just a little too difficult to say, and there was no way he was going to let anyone call him "Rollie". "Ron" was a compromise that Roland could easily live with.

"Ask me something, Uncle Ron. Ask me anything."

Jason was a very bright boy for nine, or any age.

"Who was the sixteenth president of the United States?"

"Abraham Lincoln," Jason replied, without any hesitation. "That was too easy. Ok, now it's my turn. "How many terms did Lincoln serve?"

"Two," Roland said. Being a Civil War buff, he knew that Lincoln had been elected for a second term.

"Wrong!" Jason enounced. "He never got to finish his second term. He was assassinated."

"Why you little jerk." Roland grabbed Jason around the waist, and carried him out the back door. "Hey, Bill! Is it alright if I throw your son in the pool and drowned him?"

Bill rescued the two beers from Roland's free hand. "Yeah, go ahead," he said, pointing to a broken down, backyard pool, now half full of leaves, "but you might have a little trouble, seeing that the damn thing hasn't been able to hold water in over three years. But go ahead and throw him in there. I think I saw a coral snake crawl in there a little while ago."

"Was it an eastern coral, a western coral, or a South American coral?" Jason asked.

"I don't know," Bill admitted, "I forgot to ask him; smart ass. Why don't you find something to do while Uncle Ron and I get caught up?" After Jason left he turned to Roland. "The kid's as smart as a whip. I don't know where he gets it from, certainly not from me. Did you eat?"

"Well . . . not exactly," Roland admitted.

"Hey, Suzy!" Bill yelled, not bothering to get up from his chase lounge. "Heat up some of the spaghetti for Roland!"

"I don't want to be a bother, Bill. I don't like imposing on you like this. I can get something to eat, later."

"Bullshit! Lawyers have to eat, too. Or do you still think you guys eat manna and walk on water?"

"Some of that garlic bread, too!" Bill yelled out to the kitchen.

Suzy appeared shortly carrying a plate of spaghetti, a plate with bread on it and two more beers.

"I hate to impose on you, Suzy," Roland said, apologetically.

Bill took one of the beers from Suzy. "What do you think I keep her around for?" Bill said, smiling up at her. "The sex ain't all that good."

Suzy punched him in the shoulder, hard enough to move him on his chase lounge.

"Ouch!" he cried. "You hit me pretty hard!"

"That was a love tap, lover boy," she said. She was looking down at him, now, her hands on her hips. "If I wanted to, I could have knocked you right out of that chair."

"She's right, you know," Bill said to Roland. He was rubbing his shoulder and looking up at his wife. "Who do you think is the one who opens all the jars around here?"

She was hitting him, again, in the same shoulder. This time more femininely.

"I meant that as a compliment," Bill was trying to grab her wrists, "really."

Suzy grabbed the empty beer cans, and started back into the house. "If you want anything, just holler."

"Thanks, Honey," Bill shouted after her.

"I was talking to Roland," she yelled over her shoulder. "If you want anything, you have two legs."

"See why I love her?" Bill pointed after his wife. "Never a dull moment, but after three or four days of this married bliss, shit, I'm ready to hit the open road again. So what's up? You sounded a little upset when you called."

"It's Paula."

"Ah. Little miss sweetness and cream." Bill had little use for Paula. Once, while he was at Roland's place, Paula took him aside. She had been drinking pretty heavily, and was feeling no pain. She took him by the chin and looked him in the eye. "I don't know what your game is, Bill. I haven't figured it out as of yet, but lowlifes like you don't hang around my husband, unless they want something." It was all Bill could do to keep from decking her. "So, has she taken to bringing her lovers home, now?"

"No, Bill, nothing like that. We got into a little confrontation this morning and, well, I hit her."

"That's not like you, Roland, loosing control like that. She must have really pissed you off."

"Well, actually, she hit me first."

"OK. Now I see. So it was more like self-defense. No biggy, this shit happens all the time." Bill pulled himself up from the chase lounge and went into the house. He returned shortly with a six-pack of fresh beers. "Had to take a leak. Now, where were we? Oh yeah, Paula was beating on you and you defended yourself."

"Well, it wasn't exactly like that," Roland admitted. He popped the top from the beer Bill had handed him, and took a long drink. "In fact, it was a little scary for a moment. I just went ballistic. Like you said, that's not like me."

Bill laid back in the chase lounge, and took a sip of his beer. He spilled some on the front of his T-shirt. He was brushing at it with his free hand. "You have a very stressful job, Roland. It's hard not to bring some of that baggage home with you. She caught you at a bad time, that's all."

"Paula seems to think that I'm setting a pattern. She's left me."

"So, she went to stay with her mother for a few days."

"I don't think so. She just walked out of the house. She didn't make any calls. She didn't even bother to pack."

"When she comes back to get her clothes maybe you can smooth it over with her."

"She might not come back. You know what Paula's like. She might just go out and buy a whole new wardrobe. She's got a whole pocket full of credit cards."

"Hey, they're your credit cards, too, right? Put a stop payment on them. Tell the credit card companies that they were stolen. Then she'll have to come home."

"Paula has her own accounts." Roland was running his finger around the top of the beer can. "Last I knew she had over three hundred thousand in her personal checking. She's a partner in the law firm, secretary or something. She insisted on that. Since she helped me get through college, she felt she was owed something. I never argued with her. She only has a ten percent interest. I've always considered it like an allowance. I never thought that it would come back to haunt me."

"Whoa, three hundred grand! That sort of changes things; now she's a loose cannon."

"What do you mean; loose cannon?"

Bill was sitting up in the chase lounge. "Look at it this way, Roland. She's pissed at you, she's got plenty of bread, and she's a conniving bitch. Sorry, but that's the way I see her. There's no telling what she's got in store for you."

"Do you think she'll sue for divorce?"

"Hell no! You're a fuckin' lawyer, Roland, think about it. What would she have to gain, other that ten percent of the company and what few bobbles you might feel generous enough to let her have.

Fuck, most of the judges are personal friends of yours. Does she know that you've had her followed?"

"That's what started the whole thing."

"Then it's a done-deal, man. You don't have to be a lawyer to see that. Besides, with all your connections, what judge is going to give her anything?"

"So, what are you saying, Bill? You've painted a pretty bleak picture for her. What options are you leaving her?"

Now don't get all worked up until you've heard me out. The way I see it, her only option is to have you done in."

Roland emitted a nervous laugh. "Come on, Bill, that's completely absurd."

Bill took a long drink, and then laid back on the lounge, again. "Oh yeah, think about it Roland. She knows you've got her by her curly, little short hairs. I'm assuming they're curly. The absurd thing is that she would even think about dragging all that sorted shit to court. The papers would have a field day. They might even name her 'Slut of the Year'. Think of all the important people you have rubbed elbows with over the years; judges, governors, senators, cabbages, and kings. As power hungry as Paula is, do you think that she's going to want to lose all those contacts? How long do you think Paula could survive on a few hundred thousand and ten percent of the company?"

"A few months," Roland admitted.

"What are her options? Other than coming home and kissing your sweet ass. I can only think of one. Having been married to the woman for all these years, do you think she's capable of it?"

Roland was silent. He looked at the beer in his hand for a few minutes, then tipped his head back and downed it. He leaned forward and pulled another one loose from the holder. "No sense in letting them get cold," he said, almost mumbling.

"You're not answering me, Roland." Bill was setting upright, again, looking his friend in the face.

Roland's hands were trembling as he popped the top from the beer and took a long drink. "I know she is, Bill." His voice was breaking up; he was almost in tears.

Bill put his hand on Roland's shoulder. "I know how you feel, man, but you got to look at this in the proper light. You've got to protect yourself."

"You're right, Bill. I guess I need to hire some bodyguards."

Bill was shaking his head. "What, are you crazy? How would that look, a couple of bodyguards following you around all day. People will start to think you're paranoid. They'll think that you're some kind of gutless wonder. Who's going to vote for a senator with no balls? That's what you're shooting for, ain't it pal? You want to be our next senator."

"I thought that I had a good chance. I had some pretty good backers, but now . . ."

"Jesus, Roland; when have you ever been a quitter? You still have a good chance. You just need to get her before she gets you."

"What?"

"This is crazy, Candace," Paula was saying, "I can't go through with anything like this."

"Think about it, Paula, what are your options? Do you really want your whole life drudged up in court? Roland will have you looking like a two-bit whore. You'll be lucky to get away with cab fair."

Paula was pacing the room of the third-rate hotel in which she was staying. She had called Candace from her cell phone the minute she pulled out of the drive. Candace made all the arrangements for Paula at the Hillman. Paula had signed in as Mrs. James Jones. At the better hotels they would have wanted to see ID and possible a plate number, but here they never even asked. In fact, most of the time she was checking in, the desk clerk just stared at her breasts. She knew that he was looking at her ass as she made her way to the elevator; she made it worth his while. Funny, looking around the dingy room, she suddenly felt like a two-bit whore.

"I know you're right, Candace, but murder?"

"Think of it as a life adjustment. We all have to go sometime; Roland's time will just come a little earlier."

"That's not even funny, Candace!" Paula was crying, again, as she had been the minute she left the house.

"OK, Paula, I know you still have feelings for Roland, but do you still think that he gives a shit about you?"

"I don't know, Candace." Paula sat on the edge of the bed, the springs squeaked as they yielded to her weight. She took in the musty ambiance, and wondered if she could actually sleep in this room. "I don't think so, but what if, you know, after it's over, I realize that I really did love him?"

"*I don't know, maybe, what if?* Listen to yourself, Paula. Fifteen years of conditioning has turned you into a powder puff. You were always so sure of yourself in college. You, more than anyone, knew what you wanted. When you met Roland, you latched on to him like a hungry tapeworm. I don't think you really loved him then. He had potential, ambition, his family had a little money; I think you saw him as a meal ticket, and you were hungry. It didn't hurt that he was cute."

"How can you make me out as so hard, Candace? I have some very tender memories of my first years with Roland."

"Was all this warmth and tenderness there when you were fuckin' Ted Crofton?"

"He was just a momentary diversion."

"How about Christian Hollaway?"

Paula sighed, "He had a nice ass."

"And Coach Piel?"

"Jesus! You knew about Piel?"

"I sure did, honey, and I was jealous as hell."

"That was during my 'older man' phase."

Paula couldn't see the smirk on Candace's face. "Now, tell me again how much you were in love with Roland."

"Well, the sex was good for a while, but you know me. Why be satisfied with vanilla pecan, when there are so many other assorted flavors."

"Now there's the Paula we all know and love."

"OK. So if I decide to go through with this, not saying I will, what will it cost me?"

"Paula, Honey, if y'all are talkin' money, you've already decided. Fred says that a straight hit, you know, where they put a bullet through their head from a long way off . . ."

"Jesus Candace! I don't want to hear this shit!"

"Well, anyway, that cost about fifty thousand."

"Christ! I had no idea it would be that expensive. In the movies they used to do it for a couple of grand."

"When Humphrey Bogart was doing it, maybe. You've been watching too many of the old classics. Today, things cost a bit more. Beside, it's a lot harder to get away with shit like this today. Brace yourself for this, Paula, to make it look like an accident, it will cost you double."

"One hundred thousand?"

"I recommend that you go that way. It's a whole lot safer."

Paula looked as if she were in shock. "That's a lot of money."

"How much does Roland have in the bank right now?"

"Oh, I don't know." Paula thought for a minute, "two or three million, maybe."

"Stocks, investments, what do you think they're worth?"

"Eight, ten million, maybe."

"And the business?"

"I couldn't even begin to guess."

"Shit, Paula! And you're fussin' over a hundred and twenty grand?"

Paula picked up on that, quickly. "What do you mean, 'a hundred and twenty grand'?" she said. "I thought you said one hundred."

"Well, there is a finance charge."

"Why would I have to finance anything? I've got enough money in the bank to cover one hundred thousand."

"What are you going to do, write him a check?"

"No, I can draw it out of my savings."

"How is that gonna look? Your husband gets killed, and the cops find out that you drew one hundred smackers out of your savings the week before. Think about it, Paula."

"So what am I going to do?" Paula threw her arms back. "Do I let him take it out in trade?"

"Over my dead body, Honey girl! But that's why there's a finance charge. After everything is over, and you've had a proper length of time to play the grieving widow, you can start paying him back a few thousand at a time, maybe over a six-month period. Fred's setting this up, mostly as a favor to me."

"And Fred is going to trust me for the money?"

"Honey, it's not a good idea to cheat a hitman."

Paula thought about it. "I see your point."

"Make up your mind, Paula, are you going to do this or not?"

"Yes." Paula's face suddenly flushed. "When would it happen?"

"Fred will get back with me on that. You'll have to go on with your regular routine, but at the time it is to happen you have to be somewhere where you'll be recognized. Do you understand?"

"Yes. I'll need an alibi. I hope this is over with soon. It's going to tear my up, knowing."

Roland was in his office, when the call came in. "Jesus, Bill, should you be calling me here?"

"Calm down, Roland. You're not on a speaker phone, are you?"

"No."

"Is this a secure line?"

"Of course, this is a law office."

"Then listen. All the arrangements have been made. Do you have any way that you can come up with a large amount of money without anyone knowing about it?"

"I have a few bonds I could cash in. What kind of money are we talking about?"

"Fifty thousand up front, and fifty thousand after." There was a pause. "Roland? You still there?"

"I had no idea. I was thinking eight, ten thousand, maybe."

"Where have you been the last ten years? You can't even buy a halfway decent used car for that. We're talking, you-know-what, here. Now, do you know where Paula is staying?"

"Yes, she's staying at the Hillman Hotel, under the name, Mrs. James Jones. My private detective followed her there."

"Private detective! Jesus, Roland, you're not still having her followed, are you?"

Roland was wiping his forehead with a tissue. "It's been an ongoing thing. I've had her followed for years. Should I dismiss him?" There was a long pause, which made Roland even more nervous. "Bill, are you still there."

"Yeah, yeah, I was just thinking. No. This might be a good thing. I'll just have to let, you-know-who, know about it. With a private eye watching her, he could testify that it was not you."

"No, I don't know."

"Know what?"

"You-know-who."

"Yeah, Roland, it's best that you don't know. I don't even know myself."

"Then how do we know he's going to, you-know, when he says that he's going to, you-know-what?"

"This shit has to go through channels, Roland. You don't think you just dial up, you-knows-are-us, and say I want a you-know-what, do you?"

"Well, no, Bill. Are you on a cell phone?"

"Do I look crazy to you? Don't answer. I must be crazy, or I wouldn't be involved in this whole, crazy thing."

"It was your idea, Bill."

"Maybe, but I don't see you backing out."

"Should I?"

"It's a little too late, now, Roland. The die is cast, so to speak. At this moment plans are in the works."

"Couldn't we just tell them that we changed our minds?"

"Roland. Who do you think we're dealing with? These are the kind of people you just don't want to jerk around! When you're dealing with people who crack walnuts for a living, you don't want to come up looking like a filbert!"

"What the hell is that supposed to mean?"

"I don't know. This whole thing has got me rambling on like an idiot. We both need to take a deep breath and go on as if nothing has changed."

Roland tried to compose himself. "OK, but until this is over, it's going to be hard putting up a 'business as usual' front, knowing that at such-and-such a time, you-know-who is going to you-know-what to you-know-whom."

"You're a lawyer, Roland, don't you people deal with shit like this all the time?"

"Those are cases, Bill. It's a whole lot different when you put a face on it. For Christ sake, I've slept with this woman for fifteen years. I can close my eyes and see her face. My God. When I was twelve, I grieved for a month when a car hit my dog. I wanted to kill the guy who did it."

"You've got a bar. Pour yourself a stiff drink. That's what I'm doing."

"Where are you? You're not calling from home, are you?"

"No. I'm at Casey's."

"You're at a bar?" Roland went to the small bar behind his desk and poured a large drink. He downed it without stopping and poured another."

"Don't worry, I'm at a pay phone. There's hardly anyone here, it's too early."

"Are pay phones safe?"

"You tell me, councilor."

Roland thought for a moment. The Scotch was beginning to have an effect on him. He sat back in his chair and leaned back. "About as safe as anything else, I guess. Hell, these lines could be bugged, even my phone at home. Who's to know?"

"Now you're talking crazy, Roland. Even if I was talking on cell phone, and somebody was listening in, they would probably just hang up. No on wants to get involved anymore. Besides, in this town, who even fuckin' cares? Now, try to chill out, Roland. I'll call you at home when I hear something."

Roland had just finished his second drink and was pouring another. "Hear about what, Bill?"

"That's it Roland, you sound better already."

Fred pounded the side of the pay phone as the number rang for the third time. He was a big man; about six foot three inches, with broad shoulders that challenged the limits of the confining phone booth. He tossed his long, blond hair with his free hand, as the phone rang three more times

"Your dime," the voice on the other end was that of an older man.

"What the hell'r you doin' to me, Sharkey! Y'booked me a double, one right after the other, on the same day. Are you, fuckin' crazy?"

"Nice ta hear from you, too, Fred. I see y'got the packets all right, then. This should be a snap for you. Bam, bam, y'knock these off, you're off to Chicago, and y'pocket a hundred grand. Not bad fer a day's work."

"One hour apart! I know I'm good, but I don't know if I'm that good."

"Hey, did y'look at the sheets I sent. These two keep a tight schedule. They will be in the same area at the same time. Jesus, they'll practically be in each other's lap."

"Do you know who these people are? Are they important, or somethin'?"

"You know I don't ask those kinds of questions. I don't want to know what they are. Just in case they torture me, or somethin'. All I ever ask for is their names, daily routine and some recent photos. Hey, did y'look at the pictures of the broad? Not bad, huh? Kind of a waste, I think, but what the shit, I ain't never gonna get any of it." He was laughing.

"Sharkey, you have a very sick mind. You really need to get some help."

"This coming from a guy who makes a living blowin' people's brains out."

"It's a living, Sharkey. I don't have ta like it. Not everybody likes their job."

"Yer so full of shit, Fred, there's no room fer earwax. You like what y'do. You don't fool me one minute. Now, if you think you can't handle it, I could give one of the marks to someone else."

"No, it just might work out good. I could arrange it so I could hit them one after the other, and use the same method. The way I see it . . ."

"Whoa! Don't give me no details. I want to know nothin'. I've got my fingers in my ears, and I'm hummin'. Y'hear me, hummmmmm."

"OK, Sharkey. Payment in the usual place?"

"When I read about it in the paper, you get your cash."

"Fine." Fred hung up the phone and pushed open the door of the phone booth. He wondered if it had been a good idea to give Candace the number of his contact. It wasn't Fred's way to do business with anyone, directly. The payment thing was his idea. He knew he wouldn't see any of that money until Sharkey got all of his. Maybe the double thing was a blessing in disguise. After all, he had planed on retiring shortly, and having a hundred grand coming in a few months down the road, would be a little like having a pension."

He walked back to his car and put the key in the lock. He looked the back seat over carefully. After all, in this kind of a neighborhood, one can't be too careful. As he slid into the seat he picked up the dossier for the first mark, a Mrs. James Jones. It sounded a bit phony, but then he reasoned that there are a lot of people named Jones, so why not. Sharkey had his own standard form that he had made up himself.

Everything was right there in plain sight: name, sex, height, weight, hair color, complexion, eye color, measurements, and even shoe size. There were always several photos, as well as a description of any moles, warts, birthmarks, bumps, bruises, or tattoos. Sharkey even went as far as describing typical clothing, sunglasses, jewelry, hairpieces or wigs that the mark might normally wear. It was quite detailed. No one wanted to pay for the wrong mark.

Sharkey had been right about this one; she was rather pretty. Five-four, it said, thirty-seven-years-old, light brown hair, measurements—thirty-eight, twenty-six, thirty-six, approximately one hundred and ten pounds, blue eyes, straight posture, good teeth, nice legs, and no visible blemishes, or abnormalities. She likes to wear form-fitting clothes to show off her figure; brown leather purse; gold necklace, with diamonds; matching bracelet; one diamond ring, eight carat; one plain gold band; usually wears earrings and high heals; but never wigs. Presently staying, downtown, at the Hillman Hotel.

Fred knew the Hillman. He wondered why a woman of this apparent quality would want to stay in a fleabag like that. Oh well, he was a hitman, not a detective; although, if you wanted to stay alive, in this business, you had to think like one. Still, he couldn't help but wonder. The only reason that crossed his mind was that she didn't want to be found. Apparently, it hadn't worked. This only brought up another question. Why didn't she want to be found? And the third inevitable question: did she know that she was a mark, or think that she possibly could be?

He swung around and headed downtown to the older section of town. He found a parking garage near the Hillman. He studied the woman's photos for a moment, and committed the times and places of her usual, daily activities to memory. He exited the car, locking the files in the trunk. He found a small café across the street from the Hillman, and settling into a booth near the window, he ordered a cup of coffee.

One of these, Fred knew, had to do with Candace. If this was some bitch that was having an affair with her husband, he might have done it for nothing. But, in keeping with his policy of never getting himself personally involved, he had referred her to Sharkey to make all the arrangements. Hell, if Candace wanted him to, he'd pop the husband, too.

Candace was the only woman he had ever really loved. It was too bad that it never worked out between them, but what he did was his life, and he sure as hell wasn't going to bring anyone he really loved into it. Still in all, there were times when he thought of taking her husband out of the picture. He wouldn't though; she had a kid, and she seemed genuinely happy.

He was grateful that he hadn't lost her, altogether. Once or twice a year was a whole lot better then never seeing her at all; although, it was getting harder and harder to say goodbye. Her husband was a lucky fucker. Fred wondered if the poor bastard knew just how lucky he really was. Not likely.

Fred looked at his watch. The mark should be going to her exercise center shortly. He figured the Hillman didn't have valet service, so she must have parked at one of the local parking garages. Maybe even in the one where he had parked. The place was across town, and any prudent person would give himself or herself an hour to get there; therefore, she should be leaving any minute.

A woman emerged from the hotel entrance. She was wearing shorts, a T-shirt, and quite obviously, no bra. She was even more striking in person. Fred whistled under his breath. He paid for his coffee and exited the café quickly. By now, she was a block ahead of him walking like a woman with a purpose. This was fine. Fred never liked to follow too closely. She crossed the street, and even from a distance he could hear the click of her high heals on the pavement. He watched as she entered the same parking garage he had parked in. Shortly, he noticed a blue Triumph emerge and head west. He compared the plate number with the one he had gleaned from Sharkey's forms. It was the car.

He didn't bother to follow. He knew where she was going. Later, he would check to make sure that she was there. He looked at his watch. In twenty minutes, his second mark would be arriving at work. If he left now, he would have plenty of time to get there before he arrived.

The law office of Bradshaw, Carter, and Wheeler was in an office complex with its own parking garage. Spaces were reserved for the law firm, with extra parking for clientele. Fred eased into one of these spots and slid down behind the wheel. While he waited he went over the dossier of the second mark.

Roland Bradshaw was forty-years-old, five—eleven, one hundred sixty pounds, brown hair, brown eyes, forty-two inch chest, thirty-two inch waist, about average build and wore a size nine shoe. He had a small scar on his left cheek, hardly visible; a birthmark on his left shoulder; a mole on the back of his neck, left side; caps on his two, upper, middle teeth, not noticeable; he was slightly balding; and walked with a slight limp, an old high school, football injury. He drove a red Porsche, with personalized plates (ROLAND).

Fred flipped to the page with the man's timetable. He looked at his watch and started a countdown. "Five-four-three-two-one." A red Porsche pulled into the 'Roland Bradshaw' designated parking slot. "Right on time." Fred made a mental note. He watched as Roland grabbed his briefcase from the passenger's side, pulled himself out of the car, and pressed the button on his key chain that locked the door and initiated the security system. He then walked to the elevator and punched the button for the fifth floor.

Fred started out of the parking garage. On the way he summarized what he already knew. The Jones woman was a no-brainer. If, in deed, she was a slave to routine as indicated on her dossier which he observed himself, her fate was doomed. She would have to cross the street at approximately the same time and place as she did today. She would wait for a break in traffic, and when she stepped onto the street, he would be there. All he needed was a stolen car, something with a little ass. He would pick one up the night before and stash it in a garage he kept for just such a purpose.

The Bradshaw guy wouldn't be quite that easy. For this, he would need to acquire a second vehicle, something close by, maybe right there in the same garage. Yes, he decided, that would be the easiest way; although, it wouldn't be all that easy. Stealing a car at night from a dark street is hard enough, but in broad daylight, and having to stay in the area, is an entirely different thing.

Fred's idea was simple enough. He would steal one car earlier that day, and park it in Bradshaw's parking space. Then, driving another car, he had stolen the night before; he would go to where the Jones woman would be leaving the hotel for her morning appointments. While she was crossing the street he would pull out from the curb, where he would be waiting, run her down, then head back to the parking garage and wait for Bradshaw. Bradshaw would pull in, see that someone was parked in his space, and inevitably would go to the back of the car to get the plate number. Fred would be waiting. Bradshaw would be dead before he knew what happened. After, Fred would ditch the car a short distance away, maybe right there in the parking garage, and leave the area at a leisurely pace.

It would be a little complicated, because of the second car, but Fred had the iron nerve to pull it off. There would have to be a contingency plan, in case something went wrong. The Jones woman would be, more than likely, cut and dry. Things could, perceivably go awry at the parking garage: other cars to close, Bradshaw not true to form, or maybe not being able to get a parking space close enough to get a clean hit. He wouldn't want to spook a mark. The whole thing could always be set up for another time, and place. Maybe after he got back from Chicago.

Of course, the biggest fear of anyone who plans anything is Murphy's Law. Fred was fully aware of that. His old man had always told him that a man couldn't do better than his best. What a jerk! How would he know? The jerk spent most of his life in jail. Fred was grateful he wasn't there most of the time. He and his mother sure as hell didn't need the beatings he used to give them. His own father had been his first mark, at sixteen. It was pure irony that someone was willing to pay him for the hit. He would have done it for nothing.

He found an empty pay phone and called Sharkey. "Let's plan on this for Tuesday. Figure about eight am for the broad, and a little after nine for the lawyer."

"OK, Fred, I'll pass it on. You see any problems?"

"Nothin' I can't handle."

"That's what I figured. You're a good man. Give me a call when y'get back from Chicago. There's a lot of new money in town. Business is pickin' up."

Roland picked up the phone on the second ring; his fingers were trembling. "Hello."

"Hey, Roland." Bill's voice sounded a little shaky. "How you doing?"

"Not worth a shit, Bill! OK. What have you got?"

"Eight a.m., tomorrow morning."

"Jesus! This guy doesn't waste much time, does he." Roland looked at his watch. Twelve hours and ten minutes.

Bill cleared his throat. "Why prolong it? It's best to do it and get it over with."

"Yeah." Roland carried the phone over to the bar and poured a tall drink. "You're probably right. I don't know if I could stand dragging this out for a couple more days. Did they tell you how they were going to do it?"

"Get serious, Roland. Would you really want to know something like that?"

Roland took a long drink. "No. Not really. You don't think she'll suffer, do you?"

"Hey, man, of course not." Bill's voice was sympathetic. "Remember, these guys are professionals. A lot of them, I'm sure, have wives and kids. If you met the guy at a bar and had a couple of drinks with him, he would probably come off just a regular guy."

"You just described Ted Bundy and half of the serial killers." Roland could hear Bill let out a deep breath.

"Jesus, Roland, I'm beginning to feel really shitty about this whole thing. I wish we could just stop the damn thing, right now."

"Can we, Bill?" Roland asked, anxiously.

"No," Bill admitted. "I already asked the contact that. He said that he has no way of contacting the hit man. He won't hear from him until he calls about the next job. Once the whole thing is put in motion there is no way of stopping it. The whole thing sucks, man! It was my fucking bright idea. I feel like I've got Paula's blood on my hands, already. I really don't know how the hell I'm going to live with that."

"Don't beat yourself up, Bill. I went along with it. I could have just said that I thought it was a crazy idea, and that would have been the end of it, but no, I had to get caught up in the fucking moment!"

"Well, I'm sorry, anyway, Roland. I guess that's what I get for starting in on the booze early. I've got to go. Call me in a couple of days. Try not to take it so bad."

Roland went to the bar and refilled his glass. After that, he retreated to the living room, grabbed the remote from the coffee table, and clicked on the television. However, he couldn't get interested in the news, or even the ball scores. Sliding into his favorite recliner, he placed the remote and glass on the table next to it. He put his head between his hands and began to sob softly to himself. He was glad that he had sent Rosa home early. She thought that he was upset just because Paula had left, if she only knew.

Suddenly he sat bolt upright in his chair. *Wait a minute!* he thought. *There is still time. I can put a stop to the whole thing, right now. All I need to do is find Paula, and tell her.* He jumped up from his chair, grabbed his car keys and headed for the garage. As he backed from the garage, he saw Paula's car pulling into the drive. He jumped out and ran to her.

"Paula!"

"Roland!"

"He's going to kill you!" they said in unison. **"What do you mean?"** also together. **"Did you hire a hit man? Yes."**

Roland grabbed Paula in his arms, "I'm sorry, Paula. I don't know what I was thinking."

"I'm sorry, too, Roland. The whole thing is so stupid, it's almost funny."

Roland held Paula at arms length. "I can't believe that you actually hired someone to kill me."

"I wouldn't have thought of it on my own. It was that damn, Candace!"

"Yes," Roland said, now clutching his wife close, "Bill talked me into it. I was drunk."

"Well, Candace made it sound like it was my only choice. She said that, if we got a divorce, you would leave me with nothing."

"My God, Paula! What kind of monster do you think I am?"

"Well, Roland, you did hire a hit man."

"Ok," Roland said, "you've made your point." He looked around nervously, "We need to get your car in the garage, and get out of sight. You never know who might be watching. It could be . . ."

"Them?" Paula was looking back, over her shoulder. "I think you're right."

They pulled the cars into the garage, and closed the door. They retreated to the living room where Roland poured them a couple of drinks, Scotch for him, Brandy for her. They sat across from each other, next to the fireplace.

"What do we do now," Roland asked, half to himself.

"To coin a phrase from Candace, 'get the hell out of Dodge'."

"How long before I'm supposed to you-know-what?" Roland asked.

"Nine am tomorrow morning." Paula was crying softly.

"My God, within an hour of one another. That doesn't give us a whole lot of time. In a little over twelve hours we are going to have a couple of hit men really pissed at us. How much did you have to come up with?"

"I had to give up my necklace and my rings."

"Jesus, Paula, you're talking about thirty thousand."

"What was I supposed to do, Roland, they don't take checks? Besides, this little fiasco must have cost you something."

"Fifty down and fifty when the job was done."

"Yeah, well actually, the jewelry was only the down payment. I had six months to pay off the rest."

"They let you finance it? Holy shit! What the hell is this world coming to?"

"Roland! I think you're missing the point. These guys are going to want the rest of their money, whether they earned it or not. They might even put two and two together, and figured out that we snitched. I understand that these people don't much like snitches. They might just want to kill us just for the principle of the thing. How much money do you have, Roland?"

"Well, with the savings, the stocks, the bonds, I could probably put my hands on about six million."

"No, Roland, I'm talking about right now, in your pocket."

Roland opened his wallet. "I've got about two hundred and fifty dollars."

Paula was picking through her pocketbook. "I've got three hundred and thirty-six dollars, not counting my change. We could stop at the ATMs and draw the max on our credit cards. How much would that be?"

"We could draw one thousand from each bank. Between you and me, that's four grand."

"That gives us over forty-five hundred, in cash. That's not a lot of money, but it will get us out of here." Paula paused for a moment. "We need to grab anything of value; anything that we can convert, later, into cash, my plates, and your coin collection."

"Jesus, Paula, I've been collecting those coins ever since I was a kid."

"They won't be much use to you if you're dead."

"Good point. Your other plates are in the kitchen. Rosa washed them, very carefully."

"I'm sorry about that, Roland. Another one of Candace's ideas, I'm afraid."

"Promise me, Paula," Roland was holding her by the shoulders, "that if we live through this, you will never mention that cunts name again."

"Whose name, Roland?"

They kissed briefly, softly, much like the first time they had ever kissed, so many long forgotten years ago.

"I love you, Roland.

"I love you, too, Paula.

Fred looked at his watch, again. Eight twenty-five, where the fuck was she? This was the bitch that was supposed to be so punctual. He leaned out the window and took a deep breath. With the engine running, the exhaust fumes were beginning to give him a headache. It was just his luck to swipe a car with a bad muffler. He maybe should have taken it back and found another one, but when it was moving, it wasn't a problem. He didn't know that he was going to be parked here for so long. What the hell, did she oversleep?

He had already moved a car into Bradshaw's parking space, and if the broad didn't show in a few more minutes, he would have to go on to his next hit to be there in time to catch him as he arrived. No sense in blowing both of the jobs. He looked at his watch, again.

Fred was upset, but he had never been the kind of guy that looses his composure. Keeping a cool head, rolling with the punches, being able to think on your feet, where the hallmark of a good professional. Fred was a professional. Only once, had he let his emotions get the better of him.

Twenty years ago a man named Bernie Palezetti had approached him. He was a smalltime bookie who liked to hire the local punks to do little jobs for him. Mostly, it was collecting from some deadbeat who owed him a few bucks. But this time it was different. Palezetti wanted someone to make an example of a smalltime crook that had taken him for a couple of grand. The guy's name was Frances Ekes, Fred's father. Fred was actually Frances's namesake, for his real name was Frances Ekes Jr., a name he thoroughly detested.

Palezetti knew that there was no love lost between the two Ekes men. Palezetti was a scuzz-bag, and normally Fred avoided him like the plague, but this particular job held a kind of challenge for him. Palezetti knew that with the pent-up anger inside of Fred, he would be sure to get his money's worth. His only concern was whether or not Fred had the guts to stand up to his old man.

Fred had waited for Frank outside a dingy bar on the lower, east side. It was a place Frank was known to hang out, and Fred was pretty sure that he'd find him there. There was a twelve-inch piece of iron pipe slid up the left sleeve of his shirt. The end had been plugged and filled halfway with lead. Fred had used it a couple of times; once in a neighborhood rumble, and once on a couple of punks that had it in for him. This time he had it because he knew that once he started anything with his old man, he had to finish it.

His father stopped short of him, the usual cockeyed sneer on his face. "What do you want, shit ass? Did your mother send you to try to get some money from me, again? Well, go home and tell her to go fuck herself. I'll be home when I fucking well feel like it." He pushed Fred away with his arm. "Now fuck off, you little punk!"

Fred pulled the pipe from his sleeve and swung it hard at the side of his father's head. Frank instinctively blocked the blow with his hand. The force of the blow; however, was so strong it drove his father's hand into the side of his head with such force as to knock him to the ground.

"You little fuck!" he screamed, "wait till I get my hands on you!" He reached out with both hands to try to grab Fred by the legs.

Fred brought the pipe down again, this time on his father's hands, trapping them between the pipe and the pavement. Frank cried out in pain as both his hands were shattered, spreading blood and bone across the pavement and up Fred's pant's legs. Fred swung again, this time he caught his father on the back of the neck, the force driving him into the pavement with such force it dislodge five of his teeth.

"That was for Mom!" Fred shouted. "This is for me!" Fred's next blow hit his father on the side of his head with so much force it seemed to explode. It sent Frank tumbling into the side of the building.

"Hey!" Someone was standing in the doorway of the bar. "Someone call the cops! Someone's beating the shit out of Frank. Jesus! He's covered with blood!"

Fred started to run. He ran down alleys, jumped fences he never could have jumped, and crossed through back yards. He was three blocks away before he realized that he was still holding the pipe. He removed his shirt, wiped the blood from the pipe, and slid it into the side of a trashcan. He waited until he was a couple of blocks away before he did the same with the shirt. He looked at his pants; the legs were covered in blood. He took a knife from his pocket and cut them off at the knee.

He was home and in bed when the cops arrived. He was surprised to see his mother crying. After all the bastard had done to her, he would have thought she would have been happy. The cops had no reason to suspect him. They asked all the usual questions and went through the motions, but they figured that it was a gangland thing. They even said that they thought he had been worked over by a professional.

The witness was of little help. He hadn't seen the man's face, only his back as he was running away. He described him as tall, husky, maybe two fifty, two eighty, and dark; Puerto Rican, maybe or even black. Well, one out of four ain't bad. Fred was tall for his age.

They had taken his clothes, that night. They found bloodstains on his shoes, and a couple of spots on his pants. Not much, just a few drops he had missed. While he had been swinging the pipe with all of his strength, the pipe had dug into the palm of his hand. He showed the cops the cut and told them he had tripped and fallen on the way home from school. The blood type matched his, so they had no reason not to believe him.

A couple of days later he confronted Palezetti and demanded his money. "Hey, how do I know it was you, kid? The cops seem to think it was the work of a professional. Why should I pay you for what someone else done?"

Fred grabbed Palezetti by the front of his shirt and slammed him up against the side of a building. "Because I said I did it, and if I could do that to my old man, what do you think I would do to you?"

"OK, OK, kid, I get your point. But I only wanted you to teach the jerk a lesson, not waste him. Now, how the hell am I supposed to get my money?" Palezetti placed a hundred dollar bill into Fred's open hand.

"You wouldn't have gotten that money, anyway, and you know it. Just think of it as, well, you're helping rid this city of some of its vermin."

"You know, Fred," Palezetti said, "you're one cold fish. I sure as hell wouldn't want to be on the wrong side of you."

Looking back, there were only two things he regretted about that time. One was how sad it had made his mother, even though he still thought he had done her a favor. The other was the fact that he had been so sloppy. If he hadn't had cut his hand on the pipe, it would have been a lot harder to explain the blood on his shoes. What if the blood types had been different? Even blood relatives don't always have the same blood type. Just the fact that he had never gotten the shoes back, still made him nervous whenever he thought of it.

"Damn!" The bitch was a no-show now, for sure. He had run out of time. He slammed the car into gear and pulled away from the curb, right into the path of a patrol car. "Shit!" The police officer turned on his siren and motioned him to pull over. Fred took a deep breath and regained his composure. "I'm sorry, Officer," he said in his most polite voice as the cop came up to the driver's side door, "I'm afraid I didn't look. I was in too much of a hurry."

The officer showed no signs of emotion. "Turn the engine off, please. May I see your license and registration?"

Fred opened his wallet and handed the officer his license. "I'm afraid I don't have the registration. This is a friend's car. I'm new in town and he let me borrow it. Of course, it might be in the glove compartment. Do you want me to look?"

"That won't be necessary, sir. Will you please step out of the car?"

"Why? I haven't done anything?"

"Sir, I will ask you again. Will you please step out of the car?"

Fred looked up into the rearview mirror and noticed another patrol car turning onto the block. He knew then that the cop had checked the stolen car list, found the plate number, and had called for backup.

"Yes, of course," Fred said, politely. He reached for his seatbelt and the officer drew his piece.

"Slowly," he said, stepping back and holding his gun on Fred. "Now step out of the vehicle."

Fred slowly unfastened his seatbelt, opened the car door, and raised himself slowly out of the seat. He held his hands in front of him, palm side down, and waist high. He watched as the other patrol car pulled in front of his car. As the other officer began to emerge from his car, the first officer turned his head slightly to get a better look.

It might have been the last mistake he would ever make, if Fred hadn't taken that very second to think it over. "*They've got me for grand theft auto,*" he thought. "*Ok, so I get a good lawyer, what will I get? I have no record; maybe a couple of years. If I pull this gun and shoot this bozo, I'm looking at life or worse.* I've got a gun," he shouted, placing his hands behind his head.

The first cop patted him down and found the gun in his shoulder holster. "Do you have a permit for this?" he asked.

"Yeah," Fred informed him. "In Chicago."

"Fat lot of good that's going to do you, here," the other officer informed him, as he placed him in handcuff. "You're not in Kansas anymore, Dorothy. Here we're fussy about who carries guns."

Paula turned onto I-15 North. Roland was studying the map.

"I still think we should have headed to Mexico," he said.

"Are you nuts? That's the first place they will look for us. I think Canada is much safer."

"Maybe we're being a little premature. Maybe if you got in touch with your hit man and I got in touch with mine, we could just straighten this whole thing out."

"Roland, do you really think that it's all as simple as that? I was supposed to give them another seventy-five thousand after you were dead. Then there is the fifty you were supposed to pay. Do you think they are going to say, "OK, let's just forget the rest of the money?""

"No," Roland admitted. "We'll probably have to make good on the rest of the money."

"Don't you think they are going to be a little pissed when they find out that even if they had succeeded, they wouldn't have gotten their money, because we would have both been dead?

"They wouldn't have to know that."

"What the hell are you talking about, Roland?"

"My hit man thought your name was Mrs. James Jones."

"Do you mean to tell me that, even after you hired a hit man to kill me, you still had your private investigator following me around?"

"Yes. It was Bill's idea, actually. He thought that if I broke routine, it would look suspicious, later."

"Roland, you're an idiot! You're a big shot corporate lawyer, and you're letting some lowlife, construction worker run your life for you?"

"Truck driver, actually, but Bill is very intelligent. He's just an underachiever. Damn! I just happen to think, Paula."

"Well, It's about time, Roland."

"What if these two hit men, poking around in the same places, happen to run into one another, and start comparing notes? What if they already know each other?"

"Jesus, Roland! We're fucking dead! Also, I didn't deal directly with the hit man. Did you?"

"No, I don't thinks so," Roland admitted. "I believe there was some kind of broker."

"You don't think that they are going to be a bit upset when they find out we botched up the whole deal. They might even get the idea that we were working for the Feds or something. Maybe that's not such a bad idea. What if we went to the police and told them everything?"

"Are you kidding, Paula?" Roland was shaking his head. "Plotting to kill your spouse can land you in prison for a long time."

"What if we tell them that we forgive each other?"

"The intent was there, Paula. We went through the motions. Getting cold feet might be the difference between twenty years and forty years. I would just as soon not be looking through bars, even for twenty years."

Roland looked back at the map. "So, where are we going, Paula?"

"I don't know, Roland. I'll know when we get there."

"I do love a take-charge woman."

"It's your dime. Hey Fred, why are you calling me? I thought you were on your way to Chicago."

"There's been a change in plans, Sharkey. I need you to get me a good lawyer."

"Shit, what happened? Did something go wrong?"

"Yeah, Sharkey, you might say that. They got me for grand theft auto."

"How did the job go, Fred?"

"It didn't happen, Sharkey. I want you to look into that, too. The bitch was a no-show, there was a cop right there; the whole thing stinks. It's got Fed written all over it. Can't talk now. You know what to do."

"Yeah, Fred, I know what to do with snitches." Sharkey hung up the phone and picked up his little notebook. "William Nolan." He picked up the phonebook and thumbed through the pages. There were five William Nolans. He compared the numbers with the one he had scratched into his notebook. "There you are, Mr. Nolan. I know this area, ticky-tack and trailers. So, you want to play games with us, do you?"

He flipped a couple of more pages. "Candace Wendell. Well, what do you know? This bitch was stupid enough to give me her right address. She's either the stupidest bitch I know, or she's got a death wish." He reached into the drawer of his desk and pulled out a 44 magnum. "Your wish is my command."

Sharkey picked up the phone and dialed a number.

"Hello," came a sleepy voice on the other end.

"Duncan, you fuckin' shyster, you still got a license?"

"This you, Sharkey? Yeah, the shit doesn't rub off. I'm as clean as a nun's habit."

"Where the hell have you been, Duncan, nuns don't wear habits anymore. They've all been liberated. Next year, they'll all be posing for Hustler. Now kick out your snuggy, slip into something that don't smell too bad, and get your ass downtown. I got a boy who needs your help. His name's Fred Ekes. At least that's what he was calling himself, last I knew."

"What is it, murder?" Duncan asked.

"Nah. Grand theft auto."

"Poof. Piece of cake." Duncan said, into the phone. Then, as he turned away, "Scoot over, honey, I need to get a clean shirt out from under the mattress." Returning to the phone, "Give me twenty minutes. Make that thirty. I already paid up front for this session, and besides I hate to waste a perfectly good condom."

"Well don't fuck around too long," Sharkey warned, "Fred don't like being in a cage, he starts to get a little wacky. If some puff pats him on the ass, he's going to be up for murder."

Sharkey slipped on a well-worn suit jacket, slipped his piece into a shoulder holster and stepped out into the hallway. The apartment house he lived in was old and weathered, the neighborhood somewhat run down. There were three other tenants in the building . . . families. He liked living in a neighborhood; it gave him a feeling of legitimacy; just another working stiff.

A small boy was riding his tricycle in the hallway. "Hi, Johnny, how y'doing?"

"Horsy ride?" he asked, holding his arms out.

"Not now, sweetheart," Sharkey replied. "Maybe when I get back."

The boy's mother appeared in the doorway of the next-door apartment. "Johnny, you leave mister Sharkey alone. You stop bothering him."

"Hey, no problem, Mrs. Rodriquez, he doesn't bother me." He patted little Johnny on the head. "I got a job to do, right now, but maybe when I get back." Seeing the disappointed look on the little boy's face, he got down on one knee and took the boy by the shoulders. "I'll tell you what, kiddo, how about if I pick you up something, something real nice?" Sharkey kissed the boy softly on the forehead, "Y'better watch out. I might just steal him from you, Mrs. Rodriquez."

"You are such a good man, Mr. Sharkey." She pointed to the other apartments. "They only complain, he makes too much noise."

"I love the sound of children," he said, smiling down at the young boy. "You just tell the rest of them to go to hell."

"I could not say such a thing, Mr. Sharkey."

He took the young mother's hand and kissed it. "I'll bet you couldn't, Mrs. Rodriquez. You leave that stuff to people like me."

Duncan was waiting in the interrogation room, when they brought in Fred Ekes. He was impressed with the man's size. *This guy works out*, he thought. *Shit, what I wouldn't do for a body like that. Obviously, I wouldn't work out.* Duncan," he said, offering his hand."

"Fred Ekes," the big man said. "How soon can you get me the fuck out of here?"

"Patients, Fred. May I call you Fred? These things take time."

"Time, I don't have, Duncan. Is that your first name or your last name?"

"My full name is Finley J. Duncan. I have to put that on my business cards, my driver's license, and my passport, but I can call myself whatever I like. I prefer Duncan. In school they called me 'Finny Fish-face'."

"I've been called worse."

Duncan looked surprised. "And they lived?"

"I wasn't always this big. I was a late bloomer."

"Interesting." Duncan stood up and adjusted his three-piece suit. "I'm forty-eight, do you think there is any hope for me?"

"Y'might try steroids."

"With my luck I'd just grow a twenty-inch dick, and die from blood loss the first time it got hard. I got you on the docket for tomorrow morning. Is this your first offence?"

"Yeah."

"Nothing else?"

"Not nothin'."

"Then we shouldn't have any problem getting bail. You'll be good for it, I hope."

"No problem."

"Maybe I can talk to the owner, and get him to drop charges."

"The piece of shit wasn't worth $500, but if he wants to sell, I'll give him whatever it takes. I'm good for it."

"On the police report, the owner claimed that it was a fully restored classic."

"If the shit-for-brains had put a muffler on that piece of shit, the cops probably wouldn't have pulled me over, in the first place."

"OK, then." Duncan got up to leave. "I'll see you in court tomorrow."

"Wait! Sit down. I need you to do somethin' for me. You got paper and pen?"

"Of course," Duncan said. Sliding back into the same chair, he opened his brief case and handed Fred a piece of paper and a pen.

Fred knew that he was being watched. He knew that the cops couldn't hear what they were saying, but he knew they were monitoring all that was transpiring in the interrogation room. He shifted his body to shield the paper as he wrote.

"I want you to get a hold of Candace and tell her to get the hell out of Dodge. I know how Sharkey thinks, and he is going to hold her responsible for what happened. There's no telling what he might do. Also, I want you to hand deliver this note to the guy whose name is on the front. I don't want you reading it. You understand? If anything goes wrong, I swear, I'll hang your sorry ass out to dry!"

"Hey! Don't worry about me. The less I know, the better I feel." He took the paper Fred handed him. It was folded so he could read the name 'Candace' and a phone number, and the address of a man called, simply 'Cheeko'. "Is that all?"

"That's all. Just get me out of here as soon as you can."

The phone rang five times before anyone answered, it sounded like a young boy. "May I speak to Candace, please?" Duncan asked, politely.

"Mom!" the boy screamed, so loudly that Duncan had to hold the phone away from his ear. "Mom! It's for you."

"Yes," a woman's voice answered. "Even this one word conveyed the essence of a Southern drawl."

"I'm a friend of Fred Hanley. He asked me to call you and convey this message. He said, and I quote, 'Get the hell out of Dodge'."

"My God! What the hell does that mean?"

"I believe it means that something has gone awry, and he wishes you out of harm's way."

"Oh my God! Oh my God! What am I supposed to do?"

"I would suggest that you do what Fred has suggested. He seems to me like a man that needs to be taken seriously." He hung up the phone. "Now to deliver the note."

Sharkey had never been one to jump into anything without first checking things out. He always made, what he called, a reconnaissance run. He would make a mental image of the terrain, the best points of entry, the best line of departure, natural and manmade obstacles, as well as some idea as to the layout of the house. At each house, he discovered something that was very disturbing. At the Nolan house he could see a swing set, a bicycle, as well a various game balls, and bats strewn about the premises. At the Wendell home he watched as two children, a boy and a girl got off two different school busses.

Sharkey's one weakness was children. There was no way he could ever hurt a child. He thought of his own tortured childhood, when at the age of twelve, he was deprived of his mother and father. They had been killed coming back from a rock concert, when they were hit head on by a drunken driver. It had been his anniversary present to them. Money he had earned delivering papers. How could he inflict that kind of pain on another child? He had to think this over.

He headed back to his apartment, thinking that maybe he had been a little hasty. Perhaps what happened to Fred was simply bad luck. One thing for sure, the thought of leaving little kids orphaned left a bad taste in his mouth. He stopped on the way and picked up a toy car for Johnny.

He stopped to check his mail before he went to his apartment. There were two bills and a small package. He set them on the kitchen table while he removed his jacket and hung it in the closet. One bill was his car loan and the other was the electric bill. He examined the package carefully. There were no stamps, no cancellations, and no return address, only "Sharkey" scribbled on the outside of the envelope.

Carefully, he removed the contents of the envelope. There was a videotape accompanied by a short note. It said, "Thought you might get a big bang out of this," and it was signed, "Chico." Sharkey breathed a sigh of relief. Chico was the local "mail man". If you wanted something delivered, and you didn't want to go through the normal channels, Chico was your man. He could open any lock whether it was on a door, a car, or a mailbox.

Sharkey looked at the enclosed videotape. "*Unforgiving*", with Clint Eastwood. Anyone who knew Sharkey well knew that he was a diehard, Clint Eastwood fan. He boasted a large collection of Clint Eastwood movies, but this was one of the few he didn't possess.

1992. Twenty-five years after his famous 'Spaghetti Westerns', and ole Clint proved that he still has it, he thought. He retrieved a beer from the refrigerator, slipped the tape into the VCR, and pushed PLAY. The resulting explosion cleared the room, blew out the windows, and the wall to the apartment next door. Fortunately, little Johnny had gone to play with a neighbor kid. Mrs. Rodriquez was not so lucky.

The D. A. was in the interview room when Frank was brought in. There were two men standing behind him. He introduced himself as Thomas Hanley.

"What's this all about?" he asked. "My lawyer already sorted it out. The owner is going to drop the charges. It was all just a big misunderstanding. As for the gun charge, I'm pleading guilty to not having an appropriate permit. What's the biggy? I shouldn't even be here."

The D.A. looked down that the papers before him. "You're Frances Ekes Junior, right?"

"Yeah, so?"

"Have you ever heard of DNA, Mr. Ekes?"

"Yeah, I think I've heard of it before, but what's that got to do with me?"

"About twenty-one years ago your father was murdered in Chicago."

"Yeah, they thought it was a hit. My old man wasn't too well liked." Frank was feeling a bit uneasy; unusual for him.

Hanley looked down at his papers. "Do you recall a pair of bloody shoes that you were wearing?"

Frank was pulling at the collar of his shirt. "Yeah, it was my blood. I fell down and cut my hand. They tested it and said that it was mine."

"Not exactly, Mr. Ekes. They only proved that it was the same blood-type. There was no DNA testing back in those days. Today things are different. If they can get a good blood sample, they can get the DNA. That's exactly what happened. When we did an inquiry on you, the Chicago P.D. tested the shoes. We sent them your DNA sample. It didn't match. The DNA on the shoes; however, is a match to Frances Ekes Sr's. blood. It turns out, you're not even related. You just happen to have the same blood-type.

Frank jumped to his feet. "What! You mean the son-of-a-bitch wasn't even my father." Frank broke into a hardy laugh. "Oh, Mama, you little slut. It was the butcher, Palazio. Mama and him were always giving each other goo-goo eyes whenever she went in to get some cold cuts, or some chicken. He was always throwing in a couple of steaks or pork chops. He always said that it was due to expire, and he would rather give it to her than feed it to some stray dog. The asshole really had a way for words, didn't he? He was a married man. Yeah, his wife was as big as a horse, and beat the shit out of him on a regular basis, but was that reason enough to cheat? Well, at least they had that much in common." He settled back down in the seat.

"Since the man who owned the car has dropped all charges. Apparently, you have acquired a taste for classic cars, and have offered him four times what the car is worth. The men behind me are U.S. Marshals. Romano and McNally are here to escort you back to Chicago. I have released you into their custody. With the grand theft auto charge off the board, we only have the pistol permit charge. We have decided to retain the pistol permit violation charge so we might be able to check further into your background. I think there is more to you than meets the eye, Mr. Ekes.